M000284045

STILL WATERS

BOOKS BY MATT GOLDMAN

Still Waters

A Good Family

Carolina Moonset

NILS SHAPIRO NOVELS

Gone to Dust

Broken Ice

The Shallows

Dead West

STILL WATERS

MATT GOLDMAN

TOR PUBLISHING GROUP

NEW YORK

This is a work of fiction. All of the characters, organizations, and events portrayed in this novel are either products of the author's imagination or are used fictitiously.

STILL WATERS

Copyright © 2024 by Matt Goldman

All rights reserved.

A Forge Book
Published by Tom Doherty Associates / Tor Publishing Group
120 Broadway
New York, NY 10271

www.torpublishinggroup.com

Forge® is a registered trademark of Macmillan Publishing Group, LLC.

The Library of Congress Cataloging-in-Publication Data is available upon request.

ISBN 978-1-250-32569-3 (trade paperback)
ISBN 978-1-250-32567-9 (hardcover)
ISBN 978-1-250-32568-6 (ebook)

Our books may be purchased in bulk for promotional, educational, or business use. Please contact your local bookseller or the Macmillan Corporate and Premium Sales Department at 1-800-221-7945, extension 5442, or by email at MacmillanSpecialMarkets@macmillan.com.

First Edition: 2024

Printed in the United States of America

0 9 8 7 6 5 4 3 2 1

In Loving Memory of:
Helen Goldman
and
N. Walter Graff

STILL
WATERS

· CHAPTER 1 ·

The Ahlstrom twins were not really twins. They were Irish twins, though they weren't Irish either. But they were siblings and estranged ones at that. Odd because they seemed to get along with everyone else. Friends and coworkers had accused each sibling of being Minnesota Nice. So nice they might as well have been Canadian.

Liv and Gabe Ahlstrom had not spoken to each other in over a year when Liv picked up her phone and called her brother, who was not even a favorite in her contacts. Her florist was. The wine store down the street was. Even her dentist was. If your dentist is a favorite but your brother isn't, well, that's saying something. Months had passed since Liv had last thought of Gabe. Years had passed since she'd last seen him. For Liv, growing up with Gabe in northern Minnesota felt like something that had happened in a previous life, a life Liv had no desire to revisit.

"Hello?" said Gabe.

"Hi," said Liv. "Listen, I have some bad news. Mack is dead." She said the words out loud for the first time. They left her mouth in a rapid-fire, matter-of-fact tone. Liv felt empty and expected grief to fill the void, but grief did not come. She had hardly known her older brother. She did, however, know her slightly younger brother, Gabe, all too well.

"What?" said Gabe. "What do you mean Mack is dead? What are you talking about?"

Liv stood in the bay window of her townhouse looking down on

Bedford Street. Spring splashed color on the West Village. Tulips bloomed in sidewalk planters. Green buds tipped tree branches. The dark overcoats and boots of winter had been closeted in favor of pastel jackets, athletic wear, and sneakers. Liv kept her eyes on the street. She needed a distraction when talking to Gabe: her laptop, the TV, gazing down on passersby in lower Manhattan. Something. Anything. Talking to Gabe made her anxious, and a diversion softened the edge.

"I just got off the phone with Diana," said Liv. "Mack had a seizure at the office yesterday. They rushed him to the hospital but he never regained consciousness. They took him off life support and he died this morning." Liv caught her reflection in the window. She was thirty-eight years old and finally looked like the grown-up she'd always pretended to be. Organized. Driven. Focused. Responsible. There was a girl in there somewhere who Liv didn't allow to have any fun. The pressure she put on herself had crinkled the corners around her eyes and lined her forehead.

"My God," said Gabe. "Mack was only fifty. Damnit. A seizure? How did that happen? He'd never had a seizure before, had he?" The sad truth was that neither Liv nor Gabe knew whether or not their older brother had ever had a seizure. They were as distant from him as they were from each other.

Liv listened for emotion in Gabe's voice but heard none. At least they had that in common. Maybe they were both in shock. Maybe they both had hearts as cold as a northern Minnesota winter. Or maybe they were both healthy, well-adjusted, compassionate human beings except when it came to family. No shame in that. It's why we have self-help books and moving boxes. Liv turned away from the window and sat on the couch next to her laptop. She scrolled through Facebook and said, "Diana told me Mack had been acting strange lately."

"What does that mean?" said Gabe. "Strange how?"

"She said Mack seemed anxious. Nervous. Couldn't sleep. Weird, right? And that he talked about us a lot."

"That is strange," said Gabe. "Mack wanted nothing to do with us. How did Diana sound?"

"Destroyed," said Liv. "Totally destroyed. Her husband died."

So much distance lay between Liv and Gabe: three thousand miles, three time zones, and three decades of disharmony. They had never liked one another, at least that's how Liv remembered it. But that couldn't have been completely true. Their brother Mack was half a generation older and rarely around. Their parents were busy running the family resort, leaving Liv and Gabe to fend for themselves—Liv and Gabe must have found a way to get along at least some of the time. And yet, after graduating high school in consecutive years, they each moved away from northern Minnesota. Liv went east. Gabe went west. They'd seen each other only a handful of times since. A handful of times in the past twenty years.

Gabe said, "When's the funeral?"

"Thursday," said Liv.

A short pause, then, "I wonder why Diana called you."

Here we go, thought Liv. Gabe just learned his brother died and a minute later he's wondering why Gabe's widow had called Liv first and not him. This was where Liv had to be careful. She'd never put Gabe down for not going to college. She'd never pooh-poohed his dream of being a rock star. She'd never denigrated his parade of odd jobs while he chased that dream. Liv had never boasted about her accomplishments. And yet Gabe had a hair-trigger inferiority complex. "I don't know," Liv said. "She had to call one of us first."

"I should give Diana a ring," said Gabe.

"Yeah," said Liv. "You should. She'd appreciate it."

"Are you going to the funeral?"

"Of course," said Liv. "I mean, we have to, right? Doesn't matter if we hardly ever saw Mack. He's our brother. We're the closest blood relatives he has."

Gabe hesitated then said, "Do airlines still have discounts for a death in the family?"

Money. Another topic where Liv had to be careful. Liv and Gabe weren't friends in real life but they were on Facebook, which allowed her to peek into his world, if only voyeuristically. In the photos he'd posted, he never wore anything nicer than jeans and a T-shirt. His apartment appeared small and modest. His travels seemed limited to day trips in Southern California—Mount Baldy, Malibu, San Diego. Liv was obviously doing a lot better than Gabe when it came to finances.

"Gabe, don't sweat it," said Liv. "I have tons of miles. They're going to expire soon. I can get your ticket."

"Really?"

No, not really. Last year Liv cashed in 300,000 miles to fly Cooper and herself to Paris first class. "Yeah," lied Liv. "Use 'em or lose 'em. I can get your hotel, too."

"Thanks," said Gabe. "Appreciate it."

"Yeah-yeah, of course." Liv heard her husband's footsteps on the narrow wooden staircase leading up to the third floor. Their townhouse was thirty feet deep and twenty feet wide and two hundred years old and, Liv often thought, the foundation of their relationship. They'd lucked into Bedford Street in their mid-twenties. They'd pooled every resource they had and then some to buy it. Liv couldn't imagine living anywhere else.

She was about to call out to her husband when her laptop dinged. She looked at her screen and saw the notification. It was an email from Mack Ahlstrom. Mack Ahlstrom, her and Gabe's older brother. Their older brother who had died hours ago. Liv's throat went dry. She manipulated the pointer on her screen to hover over the email. Her fingers trembled. She took a deep breath . . . and clicked on it.

· CHAPTER 2 ·

Gabe hadn't taken Liv's call the first time he saw her name on his phone's screen. She had called a second time. And a third. He finally answered, figuring it must be important. And sadly, it was.

He sat on the balcony of his Santa Monica apartment next to his bike, a paddleboard, and a wet suit drying in the California sun. He had mounted an urban garden on the balcony's guardrail. Wooden boxes planted with herbs, cherry tomatoes, arugula, kale, and mini cucumbers. He'd moved to California from Minnesota nineteen years ago but was still amazed to live in a place where plants grew year-round.

Gabe was eleven months younger than Liv. When they were children, people said, *Those Ahlstroms are peas in a pod!* Same gray eyes, blond hair, and fair skin. Gabe lived a less stressful life than Liv—his face had remained smooth despite his twenty years in the land of relentless sun and his thirty-seven years of having Liv as an older sister.

He heard a "Ca-kaw!" and despite the macabre news his sister had just delivered, he smiled. He couldn't help himself. *Ca-kaw* was Carly's signature call from the street below, and her not-even-close impersonation of a crow felt like aloe on a bad sunburn. He peeked over the balcony rail and there she was, walking her Cavalier King Charles, Ms. Ramirez, and waving up at him. Long dark hair on brown shoulders. Eyes of liquid amber. And that smile showing teeth a little too big for her mouth—that according to Carly. Gabe thought they were perfect.

Carly lived in the apartment building next door and, like Gabe, tended bar at night. They were both home during the day and often ran into each other in front of their buildings, Santa Monica's sidewalks being one of the few places in Southern California where being a pedestrian didn't make you a second-class citizen. Gabe motioned that he was on the phone but waved for Carly and her dog to come up.

"Oh my God," said Liv. Gabe had forgotten for a moment his sister was on the phone. "I can't believe this. I just can't . . ." She sighed. "Gabe, this is so creepy . . ."

Gabe heard a knock at his door. "Hold on a second," he said to Liv. "I'll call you right back."

"Gabe, don't hang—" said Liv.

He ended the call, left the balcony, and walked across his small living room, which contained a loveseat, its sad upholstery covered by an equally sad fleece blanket, an old recliner he'd found on the curb, a TV, and a media center made of bricks and boards that held a 1980s Marantz amp, a Technics turntable, old Klipsch speakers, and a few hundred vinyl record albums. The stereo and records had belonged to Gabe's parents when he was a kid except for the vinyl he'd purchased since then. Gabe's apartment looked like it belonged to someone fifteen years younger than himself. It was as if he'd stopped aging at twenty-two years old. He didn't feel that way in his heart and mind, but he knew it looked that way. It didn't help matters that three guitars rested in stands. Three symbols of his dream unrealized.

It was just so damn presentational. *Three guitars is who I am.* But in reality, the shelves made of bricks and boards equally defined Gabe. It was fine when he was twenty-two. It made perfect sense when he drove by that construction site in Van Nuys, popped the hatch on his Toyota Yaris, and helped himself to the wood and cinder blocks. He wouldn't have makeshift shelving long, he reasoned.

Soon he'd buy some real furniture. But then time did what time does. It moved forward without a care in the world for Gabe Ahlstrom, his plans, or his self-esteem.

He answered the door. Carly stood holding Ms. Ramirez. "My last name is Ramirez, too," said Carly the day she met Gabe. "I named her Ms. Ramirez so people know she's family." Carly wore a white gauze top, ripped jeans, and a pair of vintage Nike waffle trainers, yellow with blue swooshes, and no socks, exposing sun-browned ankles. She was a native Angelino, which scored points in Gabe's mind. People say Los Angeles is full of weirdos and it is, but those who are born there aren't the problem. It's those who move there running away from something or chasing dreams of fame and fortune. *Like me*, thought Gabe.

Carly stepped into Gabe's apartment, scanned his face, and said, "Hey, man. What's going on?"

Gabe took Ms. Ramirez from Carly and carried the dog to the loveseat. Ms. Ramirez snorted her affection through her truncated snout. Gabe sat on the fleece blanket and said, "Remember I told you I have a much older brother I never see? Mack, who lives in Chicago?"

"Right on," said Carly, sitting next to Gabe and Ms. Ramirez. "Mack with a K. That's what you call him."

"Correct. And my sister, Liv—"

"Who you also don't talk to."

"Yeah, well, I just talked to her because Mack died."

"Oh God, dude. That's terrible. I'm so sorry."

"Thank you," said Gabe. "I hardly remember Mack from when I was little. He was thirteen when I was born and he moved away when I was only four. When my mom was diagnosed with cancer, Mack never came back to visit. He was there for the funeral but barely. But when my dad died eight years later, Mack came back to be my legal guardian so I could live at home until I graduated. Liv was there for a few months before she left for college, but then it was just me and Mack. I looked up to him. He was my cool older brother. But we weren't close."

Carly's eyes were so big and brown and warm—they were beacons of empathy aimed right at Gabe. Had anyone ever looked at him like that? Carly's eyes rattled him more than the news of Mack's death. He felt he was about to cry when she said, "Why didn't Mack visit when your mom was sick?"

Gabe took a moment to calm himself and said, "I don't know. I should have asked him when he came to live with me but I was seventeen and all I could think about was girls and guitar. And it was cool to have my older brother around. He let me stay out late. Bought me beer. Didn't care if I brought friends home. I guess I didn't want to scare him away by asking a lot of questions. After I graduated, he sold the family resort to pay for Liv's college tuition and give me some cash to move out here. Then Mack went back to Chicago and disappeared from my life again."

Carly squeezed Gabe's hand and said, "Ugh. Brutal. I'm so sorry, man."

Gabe nodded. "I should call Mack's wife now. Her name's Diana." He forced a smile. "Not Mack's wife. Mack's widow."

Carly stood. "I'll give you some space."

"No." Gabe held on to Carly's hand. "Please stay. I'm glad you're here."

"Will there be a funeral?" said Carly.

"On Thursday."

"Let me know when you're flying out. I'll drive you to the airport."

"Oh no," said Gabe. "If you want to keep your friends, you don't ask them for a ride to LAX or for help moving. "

Carly's forehead wrinkled. "You're not moving, are you?"

"God no. Got it too good here."

Carly smiled. "Yeah, man, you do because I'm your neighbor and I'm driving you to the airport."

He had promised himself he wouldn't screw up his friendship with Carly. By thirty-seven years of age, Gabe understood he had a habit of falling in love too quickly and too often. He'd had over a dozen loves of his life. It was as if Gabe had some kind of bottomless love pit that couldn't be filled. Carly did not escape Gabe's vacuous pull. He was in love with her just as he was with the others before her. Except with Carly, Gabe was trying to right past wrongs by establishing the foundation of a friendship before advancing to anything romantic and/or physical. Part of the reason was practical. She was his next-door neighbor. If things went bad—no, *when* things went bad, seeing her every day would be unbearably awkward. One of them would feel compelled to move. But they couldn't move—they had coveted rent-controlled apartments in Santa Monica, California. Moving away would be residential and financial suicide.

Gabe's phone rang. He looked at the caller ID and said, "Oh, crap."

"What?"

"It's Liv. I told her I'd call her back." Gabe took a deep breath as if he were inhaling courage and answered the call. "Hi. Sorry."

"Have you checked your email?" Her voice was sharp. Strained.

"No, a friend came over and—"

"Read your damn email, Gabe. We just received one. *From Mack.*"

"What?" said Gabe. "How is that possible?"

"He explains it in the email," said Liv. "Just read it."

Gabe lowered his phone and flipped over to his email.

· CHAPTER 3 ·

Liv had heard of people receiving snail mail a day or two after the sender died. And who hadn't seen a birthday reminder on Facebook for someone who had passed, their family not ready to face the finality of removing their loved one's Facebook page? But getting an email from a dead person? Liv had never heard of that.

She looked up and saw her husband, Cooper, leaning against the doorjamb. He wore a navy suit and a pale yellow tie over a pressed and starched white shirt. He had short-cropped hair and round gold wire rims that shined warmly against his olive skin. Liv saw concern in his eyes and said, "What's wrong?"

"You're crying," said Cooper. "You tell me what's wrong."

Liv hadn't realized she was crying. The news of Mack's death hadn't caused it—it was his email. "I just got a call," said Liv. "Mack died this morning."

"Oh hon," said Cooper. "I'm so sorry. How are you?"

"My brother is dead. I'm a bit in shock. And . . . I just got an email from him."

"That he sent before he died?"

Liv nodded. Cooper walked into their bedroom and put an arm around her. She could smell his sandalwood soap and rosemary mint shampoo. His touch was well-intentioned, but it gave her no comfort. It was as if electrical wires touched her but the wires were connected to no power source.

"Thank you," said Liv from a faraway place. "Mack sent the email to Gabe, too. I'm waiting for him to read it."

· CHAPTER 4 ·

Mack Ahlstrom

Subject: A word from beyond . . .

To: Liv Ahlstrom, Gabe Ahlstrom

Dear Liv and Gabe,

If you're reading this email, I am dead.

I know this will sound strange, but someone has been trying to kill me. I have no idea who or why. First, a car sped out of nowhere and tried to run me over. I jumped over a concrete barrier, which saved my life. A few weeks later, a mugger pulled a gun on me and demanded my wallet. I handed it over but the mugger didn't lower his gun. He was about to shoot when a Good Samaritan knocked him over. The mugger ran off, dropping my wallet in the process. A few weeks after that, I was sitting in a park, and a bullet grazed my jacket. I told the police, but Detective Ryan Fitzpatrick said there was nothing they could do. I have not told Diana any of this because she's a worrier and the attempts on my life might push her over the edge. And I haven't previously told you two because I don't deserve your concern. I have been an awful older brother and the last thing you needed was for me to waltz back into your life only because I was concerned about my safety.

But I have to tell someone about the attempts on my life. So I will put this email in my outbox and schedule it to be sent tomorrow. Every morning I wake up, I will reschedule it to be sent the following day. And I will continue to do so until I don't live to postpone its sending. So like I said, if you get this email, I am dead.

Sorry to dump this on you now—I don't want to burden Diana now that I'm gone—but someone needs to know that regardless of appearance, my death was not an accident. It was not natural. I was murdered. Please accept my apology for unloading this information. And if it's worth anything at all, please accept my love.

—Mack

· CHAPTER 5 ·

The minute Liv hung up with Gabe she did what Liv did best. Get stuff done. She got right back on the phone and booked flights and accommodations for herself and Gabe, shared their itineraries with Diana, phoned her office to tell her number two that she'd be gone for a few days, and called Detective Ryan Fitzpatrick of Chicago PD and, although it took some cajoling, scheduled a meeting with him. She and Gabe were Mack's only living immediate family members—if they didn't check out Mack's claim, who would?

Liv landed at O'Hare at ten A.M. the following morning. She Ubered into downtown Chicago weaving around and under the L, which reminded her of the elevated trains in Brooklyn. She checked her carry-on with the bellhop and sat in the lobby of the Peninsula Hotel wearing a black and white houndstooth skirt, black sweater, and black leggings. She read Margaret Atwood between glances toward the main entrance and considered ordering a martini. Liv had never been much of a drinker and never a day drinker, but thinking of the hours ahead turned up the volume on her anxiety. One brother dead. One brother alive. If Gabe and Mack had somehow switched places, if Mack had lived and Gabe had died, she would feel more sadness but also less anxious. Why was that? she wondered. Why did Gabe make her feel like an unstable, explosive compound that shouldn't be jiggled or transported over bumpy ground?

The three Ahlstrom siblings had lived in relative peace for the last twenty years aided by geography and a lack of communication, which was no easy feat in the age of communication. Like soldiers after a war, they didn't want to talk about it. But unlike soldiers after a war, they didn't know they'd been in a war, at least Gabe and Liv didn't. They only knew they'd felt compelled to get the hell out of Birchwood, Minnesota, as soon as they could. Neither Liv nor Gabe had returned to their hometown. Ever. No high school reunions. No childhood friends' weddings. No Fourth of July celebrations. Nothing. Nil. Zippo. Liv turned her head to look for a waiter when she heard:

"Hey."

Gabe had landed at Midway and took the L into the Loop. Liv said she'd reimburse him for a cab or Uber so Gabe chose the train, which was one-tenth the cost. Some younger siblings feel like they walk in their older sibling's shadow. Gabe felt like he crawled in Liv's toxic chemtrail. It took him seventeen years to break free of the expectations she'd created for him. Expectations held by their parents, their teachers, and worst of all, Gabe himself. He still compared himself to Liv and still felt like a failure. Liv had been valedictorian of her high school class. A National Merit Scholar. Recipient of a full scholarship to the University of Michigan. She earned a master's at Parsons. After two years of learning on the job, she started her own agency representing wardrobe stylists to the stars. And although Liv still ran that agency, she had sold it to CAA for more money than Gabe would make in his lifetime, even if he lived to a biblical age.

Liv looked up. Gabe stood wearing jeans, Blundstone boots, a butterscotch leather jacket, and an insecure smile. Liv felt her chest tighten and her eyes sting. Why? she thought. Why do I feel this way around him? She inhaled and exhaled her trepidation before forcing a smile of her own. "Gabe," said Liv. She stood and hugged her brother.

To Gabe, the embrace felt like wrapping his arms around the

North Pole. Cold and distant. He had never known Liv as anything but.

They parted after a few seconds and Liv said, "How come I've aged and you haven't?"

"The L.A. smog has preservatives in it," said Gabe. "And what are you talking about? You look great."

"Yeah, well, thanks," said Liv.

Gabe looked around and said, "Nice digs." Liv had booked Gabe into a place called Staypineapple, a lovely hotel but four stars, not five. Gabe didn't know if his sister had chosen the Staypineapple Hotel for him because it was cheaper than the Peninsula or because it was a mile away. He guessed it was the latter. Money didn't seem to be Liv's problem.

"Is something wrong with your hotel?" said Liv.

"No. Not at all. I stopped there and dropped my bag. It's very nice. I really appreciate it. Thank you."

They spoke to each other like strangers, which, in a way, they'd become. They no longer knew the day-to-day of each other's lives. The ups and downs. The comings and goings. Liv had no idea if Gabe was in a relationship. Gabe had no idea Liv had lost a midterm pregnancy two years ago.

Liv dropped her eyes for a moment, knowing they were in the polite, considerate preamble of reacquaintance. She wasn't sure if she loved this temporary truce for its peace or hated it for its dishonesty. Probably both. And yet she held out hope that things would be better this time, maybe for no other reason than they were older now. They had each learned to, if not manage life's expectations and disappointments, then endure them.

"So where are we meeting the cop?" said Gabe.

"Prime and Provisions," said Liv. "It's a steakhouse."

"Steak for lunch?"

"Detective Fitzpatrick picked it."

"Sounds expensive," said Gabe. "I wish I would have known . . ."

It wasn't what Gabe said, thought Liv, it's how he said it. Like if he'd known they were taking the cop to an expensive lunch, he would have brought a big sack of cash. "Don't worry about it," said Liv, "I've got it."

"You sure?" said Gabe.

"Yeah-yeah. Absolutely."

"Thanks."

"No problem," said Liv. But it was a problem because even though she knew Gabe had neither said nor done anything wrong, his indirect way of asking her to pay bugged her to infinity.

"Am I okay wearing jeans?" said Gabe. "I'm so used to L.A. where you can pretty much wear jeans anywhere. Should I go back to the hotel and change?"

"We don't have time for that now. If you had come straight here instead of going to your hotel first . . ." Liv stopped herself. She didn't want to start their reunion by criticizing Gabe. ". . . It doesn't matter what you wear. It's not like New York. It's lunchtime in Chicago."

There she goes again with *it's not like New York*, thought Gabe, who, when attending her wedding six years ago in the Big Apple, was warned repeatedly *it's New York. You'll need to wear a jacket at every event,* implying that it's New York, which is not L.A. It's way better. Everything Liv did was better. At least that's what she seemed to tell Gabe. Liv was wealthy. He was not. She had an important job. He was a bartender. She was married to a man she'd been seeing for fifteen years. He'd never had a relationship last longer than one year. Gabe hated how he felt around his Irish twin sister.

"I'm sure there will be plenty of people wearing jeans," added Liv. "You'll be fine . . ."

Gabe forced a smile and sat across from his sister. "I talked to Diana," he said. "She used some big word for Mack's seizure."

"Status epilepticus," said Liv.

"Yeah. That. I think she made the right choice taking him off life support."

"I do, too," said Liv. "But it would have been nice if she'd waited so we could have said goodbye."

Gabe nodded then said, "But he wouldn't have been able to hear us."

"I know. Still it would have—" Liv heard the shrillness in her voice and stopped herself. She took a breath and closed her eyes and pictured the tranquility app on her phone. Calmer, quieter, she added, "I just think it would have been nice for us to have that moment. You know, for some closure. It doesn't matter. It's not like we were close."

Gabe and Liv had a simultaneous thought. Is this how it'll be when one of them dies? In forty, fifty, or sixty years? No goodbye? No last chance at reconciliation? Just a phone call in the middle of the night confirming what they already knew—there was no hope for the Ahlstrom siblings. Gabe and Liv caught each other's eyes for a moment then quickly looked away.

Gabe said, "Shouldn't we go see Diana before talking to the cop?"

"Now is the only time the cop is available. It's his day off so we're lucky we get to talk to him at all." Liv looked at her watch. "We should probably get going," said Liv, hoping the distractions of a city sidewalk would provide some relief from Gabe.

"Yeah," said Gabe, standing. "Time to find out if Mack was delusional about someone trying to kill him or just crazy in general."

· CHAPTER 6 ·

"I probably shouldn't be meeting with you two, but hey, a guy's got to eat." Detective Ryan Fitzpatrick had the day off but looked like a cop on duty. He wore a seen-it-all look on his face expressed by the contrast between his dull skin and sharp eyes. His shirt matched his skin, a once-white button-down that had been washed to a lifeless gray. He was a fifty-year-old man with bangs—his dishwater-brown hair crept down his forehead and stopped two inches above his eyes. His tie looked like a clip-on. Liv guessed that he wore it not so much to present an air of authority but to hide a stain on his sad shirt.

Liv and Gabe sat on either side of Detective Fitzpatrick at a four-top covered in white linen and white china. They stole glances at each other when the cop's eyes drifted down toward his lunch. He'd ordered the soup *and* the salad to precede his twelve-ounce filet mignon, the first of several upcharges. The best thing about Detective Fitzpatrick, thought Gabe, was that he was a visual atrocity. No one would look at Gabe and think, *How dare that other guy wear jeans?*

"Thank you for meeting with us, Detective Fitzpatrick," said Liv. "We know you're going out on a limb talking to us."

Detective Fitzpatrick crushed a handful of oyster crackers into his lobster bisque, brushed the crumbs off his hands, and said, "Happy to answer anything I can for you. I know how hard it is to lose a sibling. Hey, do you think it's possible to get some of that cheesy garlic bread?"

"Of course," said Gabe. "Wouldn't mind some myself."

Liv stared at her brother through the tops of her eyes. She was happy to pay for his meal but she didn't need him fueling Detective Fitzpatrick's gluttony. It was obvious that the cop was making a power play, and that was the best-case scenario. It was also possible he had no information and was just bilking Liv for an extravagant lunch. Now Gabe was encouraging him.

Gabe caught Liv's eyes but not her drift. He said, "Did you check out any of Mack's claims about someone trying to kill him?"

"No, I did not," said Detective Fitzpatrick. "The near miss with the car happened on Michigan Avenue during a construction project. Trucks were parked all over the place. Concrete barriers divided the construction zone from the regular street. If you were crossing, it was hard to know where to look. Situations like that, accidents happen. People get struck by moving vehicles. Sometimes they get killed. Construction workers and civilians." Detective Fitzpatrick shrugged with a spoonful of bisque hovering in front of his mouth. He blew on it and added, "The price of progress, you know." He inhaled the soup off his spoon.

"And the bullet that grazed Mack's jacket?" said Liv.

"Mack was in Washington Park. Bullets are not uncommon in that area. They often miss their targets then go a ways. Wrong place, wrong time. He's lucky it only grazed his jacket."

"Did he show you the jacket?" said Liv.

Detective Fitzpatrick nodded. "Looked like something caught the fabric. Could have been a bullet. Could have been a piece of fence wire. Nothing conclusive."

"And the mugger?" said Liv, unconsciously folding her arms and dropping her chin in response to the feeling that this cop was ripping her off.

"Listen," said Detective Fitzpatrick with a mouthful of salad. "Like the alleged hit-and-run attempt and the near miss with the bullet, there's no way to verify that your brother had a gun pulled on him. He said someone tackled the mugger and scared him off, but Mack couldn't give me a description of that witness. Or the mugger for that matter. Just some white guy who hadn't seen a dentist in a while. He couldn't even give me height or hair color. Got to be honest. Not sure any of what your brother said was true. I mean, you tell me. You knew him better than I did."

"Actually," said Gabe. "Not really. Neither of us had spoken to Mack in years."

Detective Fitzpatrick nodded as if that information confirmed Mack had the profile of a serial liar. "Did your brother have a history of emotional instability?"

"Not that we know of," said Liv. "He sold business insurance at the same company for decades. He'd been married for a long time. He lived in the same condo for years."

"Sounds like he might have been nutso though," said Gabe.

Liv glared at Gabe. "We're here for Detective Fitzpatrick's opinion."

"I'm just repeating what Detective Fitzpatrick said," said Gabe, justifying his comment. And his existence.

The server dropped off the plate of cheesy garlic bread. Detective Fitzpatrick took a piece and said, "And another beer, hon. Thanks." He winked and turned back toward Gabe and Liv. "And how again did your brother die?"

"Apparently, he had a seizure," said Gabe. "He had a condition called diabetes insipidus. It has nothing to do with sugar diabetes. His wife said he had to take these pills. If he didn't, he became thirsty and had to pee all the time. Even if he didn't drink anything. I guess his body didn't know how to hold on to water. He just peed it out. The doctors think he missed several doses of his medication and got too dehydrated, which messed up his potassium and sodium levels, creating an electrical imbalance, and that's what caused the seizure."

"So you think someone messed with his meds to kill him?"

"That doesn't seem likely," said Liv. "He took one pill four times a day and if he missed one he could tell. That's what his wife told us. He'd have to miss several doses for it to cause a seizure."

"Well," said Detective Fitzpatrick, "I've seen this before. A person has a few close calls and they think someone's trying to kill them. Were there witnesses to your brother's death?"

"Yes," said Gabe. "He collapsed at the office. Just dropped to the floor and started convulsing. They called 9–1–1, but he never regained consciousness. They put him on life support but he was essentially brain dead so his wife decided to pull the plug."

"Sounds like a natural death to me," said Detective Fitzpatrick.

Liv said, "Did you ask Mack if he knew of any reason someone might be trying to kill him?"

"That was my first question," said the cop with a mouthful of cheesy bread. "He said he had no idea why anyone would want to kill him. So I got specific. Asked if he was cheating on his wife. If his wife might be cheating on him. If he owed anyone money. If he'd broken anyone's heart. If he'd been blackmailing anyone. If he'd told some gangbanger or Russian mobster to go fuck themselves. The usual kind of stuff that might get you offed. Mack said he did none of that."

"Do you think Mack was lying?" said Gabe.

The server appeared and set a steak in front of Detective Fitzpatrick, a steak salad in front of Gabe, and a French dip sandwich in front of Liv. All that with a massive bowl of fries and an assortment of sauces and condiments and enough side dishes to bury the table.

"Not lying exactly," said Detective Fitzpatrick. "But sometimes peoples' imaginations get the best of them. For example, if ten people all witness the same crime, and we interview those ten people individually, we'll get ten different stories of what happened. Everyone thinks they know what they saw, but the truth is, people can't be trusted as witnesses unless they're trained properly.

See, everyone's got a story going on in their head, and the brain interprets events to fit that story. So if your brother Mack was walking around thinking someone was trying to kill him, then he'd see everything through that filter. A car comes close to him on Michigan Avenue, an attempted hit-and-run fits the narrative."

"So what you're saying," said Liv, "is there's no way Mack was murdered."

"Not necessarily," said Detective Fitzpatrick. "I know you two coastal dwellers think I'm some dumb Chicago cop. And yeah, I'm a little rough around the edges. I admit that. But I will tell you this, being a cop, you learn a thing or two about people. We ain't always right—we make mistakes like anyone else. But sometimes, you got to play the odds. Like when it's the hottest day of the year and you see a guy walk into a liquor store wearing a long trench coat, chances are he's up to no good."

"I'm not sure I'm following what you're saying in regard to Mack," said Liv.

"Let me put it this way," said Detective Fitzpatrick, digging mayo out of a ramekin with a crinkle-cut fry. "Most accidents are just that—accidents. But on the rare occasion when a murder is made to look like an accident, more often than not, the killer identifies themselves to police long before they commit the murder."

"And how do they do that?" said Gabe.

"They marry the victim."

· CHAPTER 7 ·

"Why did you suggest dessert?" said Liv. "What in the hell were you thinking?" They walked uptown on Wabash Avenue toward Mack and Diana's condo, hoping the journey would make a dent in their midday caloric intake. The streets seemed empty to Liv, who lived in a city of pedestrians, and busy to Gabe, who lived in a city of automobiles.

"Detective Fitzpatrick was helpful," said Gabe. "I thought he might appreciate dessert."

"Helpful? He was useless," said Liv. "According to him, Mack was either out of his mind or his five-foot-tall wife murdered him."

"Well, maybe she did."

"Are you kidding? Diana? The woman who sends us birthday cards and Christmas cards every year? The only person in this broken family who has tried to put us back together? The woman who works sixty hours a week as a pharmacist? That Diana? Yeah, she's got murderer written all over her."

"Hey, if I had to work under fluorescent lights and deal with sick people sixty hours a week, I'd think of killing someone. Plus," said Gabe, "it's obvious she could have messed with his medication. She's a *pharmacist*. She'd know exactly what to do. And what the hell are you mad at me for? Detective Fitzpatrick doesn't know Diana. He just said when murders are made to look like accidents, the spouse is often—"

"Yeah-yeah-yeah," said Liv. "I know what he said. I also know he ordered the Chocolate Cake Roll for himself, the Brown Butter Apple Tart for you, and the Caramel Banana Pie for me without even asking us because we were going to all share and then the vacuum cleaner with a badge inhaled all three not to mention two cappuccinos after his three pints of beer. He's like a python—he won't have to eat again for a month."

"Okay, okay," said Gabe. "Sorry I had a thought. Sorry I said anything. I'll sit in my hotel room next time."

"There won't be a next time," said Liv. "We'll spend the afternoon with Diana and go to the funeral tomorrow then head home."

"And just forget about Mack's email? Don't we have a responsibility to look into that? He said someone was trying to kill him."

"Apparently he said a lot of things. Our brother's dead. We're never going to see him again. Isn't that bad enough? Let's just leave it at that."

"Fine," said Gabe. "I'll drop it."

"Good," said Liv.

"Great. I don't need you bossing me around anymore."

They walked the remaining ten blocks without saying another word. Gabe felt Liv was pushing the pace a bit hard but maybe that was the New Yorker in her. It's not that he had a hard time keeping up, but her strident strides felt like a nonverbal way of expressing anger. Anger at him. She was punishing him by power walking, and in a skirt and heeled shoes, no less. Gabe always felt that way around Liv. It's why he made no effort to see her. It's why he almost hadn't attended her wedding. And it's why he probably would not have seen her for another decade if Mack hadn't died. Gabe didn't know what he'd done to deserve Liv's ire. Or maybe that was just Liv and she was like that to everyone. She was a successful talent agent after all. Agents have a reputation for a reason.

Liv wished she hadn't offered to pay Gabe's way to Chicago. It wasn't about the money. It was about Gabe. If she hadn't covered his airfare and hotel, he might not have come. He'd always felt like an anchor dragging her down, messing things up, just plain being a nuisance. Mack had told only one other person about the suspected attempts on his life. Detective Ryan Fitzpatrick. They had one chance to glean some information from the greedy cop, and Gabe acted as if it were a casual social lunch. It was a complete waste of time. The sooner she got away from Gabe, thought Liv, the better.

Diana buzzed them into the building. In the elevator, Liv said, "Let's just try to be here for Diana, okay? Can we do that?"

"What does that mean?"

"It means this is about her. Not about us. Right? She needs support right now."

Liv is the Law, thought Gabe. That's what he dubbed her when he was eight years old. Why hadn't his parents stood up for him? Why hadn't they told her to mind her own business and leave him alone? Why did he have to fight that battle by himself, a battle in which he was outgunned, outwitted, outmaneuvered at every turn? But all Gabe said was, "Of course Diana needs our support. What'd you think I was going to do?"

"I don't know," said Liv. "But after that lunch, I thought it was worth mentioning."

"Do you want to write me a script so I say everything exactly the way you think is right? Should I pretend I have laryngitis? Or that I'm a Buddhist now and Mack died while I'm in the middle of a ten-day silent retreat?"

"Now you're just being an ass. Why do you have to be an ass?"

"Just trying to be like my big sister."

The elevator door opened, and Liv stepped out without responding to Gabe's comment.

Diana Chien opened her apartment door and burst into tears. "Liv," she said. "Gabe." Diana was short and, even at fifty years old, girlish in appearance. She wore her hair long—the gray strands shined like silver veins in black marble. She spoke with a slight Chicago accent of hard A's and O's.

Liv embraced her and said, "I'm so, so sorry, Diana."

"I'm sorry for you," said Diana. "For both of you." She went to Gabe, pulled him tight, and cried against his chest.

"Oh, Diana," was all Gabe could manage to say as he held her.

Diana stepped back, wiped away her tears, and said, "I'm so glad you two are here. Please come in."

They stepped into Diana's living room. A beige couch, two red armchairs, a Persian rug of reds and blues over tan wall-to-wall carpeting. A large bookcase held sculptures of jade and glass, most purchased on Diana and Mack's trips to China. A framed photo of Mack sat propped on a console table behind the couch. It was taken at Mack and Diana's wedding. Unlike his siblings, Mack had dark hair like their mother. The photo was surrounded by arrangements of flowers, all white. Liv knew from her Chinese friends and associates that white flowers symbolized death and mourning. The same white flowers people in Western cultures purchased to celebrate weddings.

"Thank you for coming," said Diana. "It is important Mack has his family here."

"What can we do for you?" said Liv.

Diana exhaled and shook her head. "You're doing it. Just being here. I am lucky I have my family." She gestured to the display of white flowers surrounding Mack's photograph. "But it is difficult." They sat on the couch, Liv and Gabe on either side of Diana, a woman they hadn't seen since Liv's wedding six years ago. But the three of them together like that on one piece of furniture felt more like family than anything Liv or Gabe had experienced in a long time. "I just can't help but think that Mack's behavior had something to do with triggering the seizure," said Diana. "He'd been acting so strangely. I asked what was wrong and he said nothing other than work stress. But it sure didn't seem like work stress."

Gabe glanced at Liv. She felt his gaze but didn't return it. "Why didn't it seem like work stress?" he said.

"Because I had seen Mack stressed. I was used to it. I don't know if you know this about your brother, but he was one of those people who always had to be on time. No matter if it was important or not. He would get to the airport three hours early. He'd get angry if he thought I was making us late for a dinner reservation. He'd be on edge at work if he thought his sales numbers were not up to par. But lately, it wasn't anxiety I saw in Mack—it was fear. I had never known him to be a fearful person. Not in seventeen years of marriage."

"I don't remember him being fearful at all," said Gabe, as if he hadn't received Mack's posthumous email, as if he hadn't just heard a firsthand account of Mack's fear from Detective Ryan Fitzpatrick. He and Liv had agreed not to mention the email to Diana. Not yet anyway. There seemed to be no point. She'd just lost her husband. Introducing the possibility that he'd been murdered didn't seem helpful or kind.

"Did he give you any clue as to what he might be afraid of?" said Liv.

"No," said Diana. "He wouldn't even acknowledge that he felt afraid. But there was another odd thing. For the first time since I met Mack, he talked about growing up on Leech Lake. At first, I was excited. I wanted to know more about his childhood. More about your parents, who I never had the pleasure of meeting, and of course, more about the both of you."

"What do you mean at first you were excited?" said Gabe.

"Well," said Diana, "I always imagined growing up at a lake resort would have been idyllic. Fishing and swimming and snowshoeing in the winter . . ."

"It was," said Gabe.

"Especially when we were young," said Liv. "We had the run of the place. It was heaven."

"That's what I assumed," said Diana. "But Mack said there was something broken about your family. I pressed him on what exactly was broken, but he wouldn't say. The only thing he said was he regretted not spending more time with both of you."

Gabe's eyes stung. Just hearing that Mack regretted the Ahlstrom siblings' estrangement felt like a step toward reconciliation. But a step that came too late.

Liv responded in a businesslike tone. "That surprises me," she said, "because Mack didn't seem interested in spending time with us when we were kids or when we were grown up."

"I know. I would always say to him: Visit your brother and sister. They are your family. And he would say he couldn't. It was too painful. Then one night about a month ago, he'd had too much to drink. Your brother was not a drinker but that night we went to dinner and he had two martinis and you came up again. I said you two were his closest living blood relatives. It was his responsibility to maintain a relationship with you because he was the oldest. And then he . . . he . . ." Diana dropped her eyes and shook her head.

Liv put her hand on her sister-in-law's back, hoping it would give Diana the courage to continue.

"He what?" said Gabe.

Diana looked up with a pained expression. "He said you three siblings weren't the blood relatives everyone thought you were."

"What does that mean?" said Liv.

"Mack said he had a different father than you and Gabe."

· CHAPTER 8 ·

Liv's spine felt like it might push out of her skin. She looked at Gabe, but his head was down and shaking from side to side. It's how he reacted when he was a child, eyes to the floor, head moving back and forth, not to convey denial but to rock himself in search of comfort. It's how he'd dealt with thunderstorms, bad report cards, and fights with his sister. Liv had assumed he'd grown out of it, but apparently not. Liv looked from Gabe to Diana and said, "Why did Mack say that? He didn't have a different father than us."

"No," said Gabe, eyes still on the floor. "He didn't."

Diana folded her hands in her lap, sighed, and allowed her tears to flow. "I'm sorry," said Diana. "That's what Mack said. I'm sorry. It must be shocking to hear."

Liv took Diana's hand in hers. "But it doesn't make sense, Diana. Mack was conceived when our parents were still in high school. They were madly in love, right? Everyone has always said so. That's all we heard growing up. It's why they got married when they were eighteen years old. How could Mack have a different father if our parents were inseparable?"

Diana shrugged. "He wouldn't say. He refused to discuss it anymore that night, and when I brought it up a few days later, he looked at me like he didn't know what I was talking about."

Gabe lifted his head to face Liv and Diana. He ran his fingers through the blond mess atop his head and grimaced as if what he was about to say pained him. "Was Mack having issues?"

"What do you mean, issues?" said Diana.

"How was Mack's mental health?" Gabe shrugged as if to apologize. "Is it possible he was delusional or paranoid?"

"I don't think so," said Diana. "Mack was his usual self other than seeming anxious and afraid and saying he had a different father than you two. Other than that—"

The phone on the wall rang. Gabe looked at the landline as if it were an alien device. Diana said, "Excuse me," walked to the phone, and answered it.

Gabe whispered, "I can't believe Mack had a different father."

"Maybe because it isn't true," said Liv. "Maybe it was part of his psychosis."

"Or it's a smoke screen."

"What do you mean?"

"If . . ." Gabe pointed his chin at Diana. ". . . she killed Mack. Maybe she's trying to create a diversion."

"Are you serious?"

"I'm just saying."

"Maybe you should think before you just say." Liv's words spilled out. She could see the hurt on Gabe's face, the pain in his eyes as if he were five years old. She was about to apologize when Diana hung up the landline and turned toward them.

"People from Birchwood are here," said Diana. "The Otsbys. Do you know them?"

"Yeah-yeah," said Liv. "Otsby's resort is just across the bay from our family's resort. Andy Otsby was in Mack's class at school."

"Yes. I know him as Andrew. I've also met his parents. Mack has had them over for dinner a few times."

Liv said, "Are many people from the Leech Lake area coming to the funeral?"

"I'm not sure," said Diana. "I called the local paper to put in a notice about Mack. I thought people would want to know."

There was a knock at the door. Diana opened it and in walked three Otsbys: Andy and his parents, John and Judith. Andy was fifty now, and both Liv and Gabe were surprised by his appearance. Gone was the small-town teenager they remembered, gangly and awkward and unsure of himself. Now Andy Otsby seemed the portrait of style and sophistication. He wore a charcoal suit, white shirt, and blue necktie with pink diagonal stripes. His shoes looked expensive and so did his haircut. His hands appeared soft and delicate—his fingernails glowed in the aftermath of a manicure. And a perfectly trimmed crop of stubble darkened his jaw.

Andy took both of Diana's hands in his and said, "We are so very sorry for your loss, Diana. Mack was a dear, dear soul." Andy began to cry. He searched for more words but gave up and pulled Diana into an embrace.

"Too young," said Judith. "Too goddamn young. A real loss. We saw Mack last week and he seemed fine. Tragic."

"It is a real shame," said John. "Just terrible."

Diana thanked them for their condolences and excused herself to make tea and coffee.

Liv wondered if the Otsbys knew anything about Mack having a different father than their father, Bobby Ahlstrom. Judith and John were just a few years older than their parents would have been had they lived. But this seemed neither the time nor the place to ask them.

"Is that Liv and Gabe Ahlstrom?" said Judith Otsby. Seventy years old and tethered to her husband by an oxygen tube that ran from each nostril to a tank John wheeled next to her. Judith carried a pink, aluminum cane, the kind with three little feet that can stand on its own. She wore a floral print dress that fell to below her knees, exposing swollen ankles that spilled over her shoes, swollen wrists that may or may not have hidden bracelets in their folds, and swollen jowls that encroached on the lace collar of her dress. Her eyes looked like peas behind a pair of thick lenses in blue plastic frames. "I haven't seen you two in decades. How come you never visit Leech Lake? Too good to come back to where you grew up?" Her tone was even harsher than her words, and spittle sprayed from her mouth as she pronounced the *p* in *up*. "I'm surprised you showed up for your own brother's funeral."

"Nice to see you, Mrs. Otsby," said Liv, who hadn't forgotten Judith Otsby's rancorous demeanor.

"You look . . . well," said Gabe.

"What are you, blind?" said Judith Otsby. "I'm falling apart. I can't go anywhere without an oxygen tank. I'm like a deep sea diver but on land."

"Now, Judith, you are not," said John. "You've just had some bad luck." John wore Wrangler jeans and nondescript white tennis shoes that looked like they were designed to go with a nurse's uniform. He'd lost weight in the last twenty years—his jeans were cinched over his hips with a weathered, leather belt. A chamois shirt of forest green was tucked in tight, a pair of reading glasses pushed up the flap of one breast pocket, and his once fair hair had given way to gray. He had a full beard, presumably to hide the gaunt hollows on his face. Standing near Judith, it looked like she'd consumed him over the years, as if their aggregate weight had remained a constant but the balance had shifted—she was getting heavier and he was getting lighter. John wheeled Judith's oxygen tank with one hand, and in the other carried a vase of flowers with carnations dyed pink, yellow, and blue. He turned toward the Ahlstroms and smiled. "Please forgive Judith. She has a leaky valve and it makes her ornery."

Judith Otsby harrumphed and headed toward one of the wingback chairs. John followed, wheeling her oxygen tank and setting the supermarket-purchased floral arrangement on the console table next to the other flowers.

"Why are you in Chicago?" said Liv.

"Well, we're sure as hell not here for the grimy streets and homeless panhandlers assaulting us every time we walk by. If those people put that kind of effort into finding a job, they wouldn't be living on the street. I tell you, walking around here, it almost convinces me to get the vaccine. But what do you expect in a city? There's enough corruption in the Chicago government to fill ten jails."

"Mother," said Andy with an edge in his voice. He then shut his eyes as if he were counting to calm himself, opened them, and turned toward Liv and Gabe. "What a surprise this is. It's terrible, what happened, but I was hoping I'd see you two."

"We wouldn't be anywhere else," said Liv. "And it's so nice to see you, Andy."

"It's Andrew now," said Judith Otsby with the same scorn she'd unleashed on the city of Chicago. "Can you believe that? It's not even his legal name. Says Andy Otsby right on his birth certificate. Or it used to anyway. He went and had it legally changed to Andrew." Judith Otsby coughed without covering her mouth. Just blasted it out there once, twice, three times. "It's a code is what it is. A man using a full name like that."

"I don't believe that's true," said Liv while giving Andrew an *I'm sorry* look.

"They're taking over," said Judith. "You raise 'em right and decent and God-fearing and your son goes over to their side anyway."

Andrew exhaled. Gabe wondered why Andrew put up with this from his mother and guessed it must have been her money. Judith's great-grandfather founded Otsby's on Gull Lake in 1916. The original resort had hosted presidents, famous industrialists, and film stars, not to mention loads of vacationers from all over the Midwest. Judith's grandfather expanded the original resort and also founded more resorts—Otsby's on Rainy Lake, Otsby's on Lake of the Woods, Otsby's on Leech Lake, and eight others. In total, there were a dozen Otsby's resorts, all built on land purchased before 1940, land paid for long ago, and Judith Otsby was the sole heir to the empire. Gabe vaguely remembered something about Mack almost selling their family resort to the Otsbys, but then decided to keep it in the family when their Uncle Denny made an offer.

Andrew Otsby dismissed his mother with a subtle eye roll and turned his attention toward Liv and Gabe. "I can't remember the last time I saw you two. It must be thirty years. That's how long ago I left Minnesota to live in Chicago."

"You've lived in Chicago thirty years?" said Gabe. "How come I remember you?"

"Birchwood is a small town. Everybody knows everybody." He then stage-whispered, "It's why I left."

"I heard that," said Judith.

"What brought you to Chicago?" said Liv.

"Northwestern University," said Andrew. "And I went to medical school at the University of Chicago. I interned and did my residency here and stayed."

"We're very proud of his career," said Judith. "But it wouldn't kill him to give us some grandchildren. They have kids now, the gays. I've seen it on television. Kids with two moms. Kids with two dads. They make it seem very normal. All my friends have grandkids. Every damn one of them. You should hear the way they talk about Christmas. They actually make it sound fun."

Everyone in the room seemed to ignore Judith. She was either oblivious or was ignoring them ignoring her.

Liv said, "Are you a GP or—"

"Internal medicine," said Andrew.

"You weren't Mack's doctor, were you?"

"I was," said Andrew.

"Isn't that something?" said John Otsby. "Two small-town boys living in the big city. It's nice they remained friends. You can take the boys out of Minnesota . . ." He chuckled.

"We didn't so much remain friends as rekindle our friendship," said Andrew. "Mack and I were best friends before you two were born. But we kind of went our separate ways as teenagers. Hung out with different cliques. So it was really nice to become friends again here in Chicago. That was just a little over a year ago. I saw Mack a couple of times as his doctor, and we socialized four or five times. I'll always be grateful we reconnected."

Diana returned to the room and set down a tray covered in mugs, one pot of coffee, one teapot, and two small ceramic canisters. "I have tea and coffee for those who want it."

"Thank you," said John Otsby. "Judith, would you like tea or coffee?"

"Coffee," said Judith. "The usual way."

Diana poured a cup of coffee. John approached and said, "Which of these canisters is the sugar?"

"Neither," said Diana. "I have individual packets of sugar and artificial sweeteners in this caddy."

"Oh." John smiled. "Then what's in the canisters?"

"Mack. I mean his ashes. I had the crematorium distribute Mack's ashes in three urns. One for me, one for Liv, and one for Gabe." She looked at the siblings and managed a smile. "Maybe you could spread them up at Leech Lake. Mack would love that. I'm sure of it."

· CHAPTER 9 ·

Liv and Gabe sat in the lobby of the Peninsula Hotel with their canisters of Mack and two well-earned cocktails. A martini for Liv, Hendrick's with blue cheese–stuffed olives, and tequila for Gabe, Don Julio 1942, neat with a slice of orange. Bartenders know the good stuff.

"Oh. My. Goddess," said Liv. "How awful is Judith Otsby? I'm surprised she didn't refer to Andrew as *a gay*."

"Can you imagine being married to her?" said Gabe. "Poor John, wheeling around Judith's oxygen tank. He should get a medal for not twisting the valve shut."

"Or offering her a cigarette."

The siblings shared a laugh, their first since Gabe's arrival in Chicago. It sparked a memory in Liv of them laughing together when they were children. Laughing while catching fish off the pontoon boat. Laughing while sharing a bag of microwave popcorn and watching *Friends* and *Everybody Loves Raymond*. They had laughed together, Liv was sure of it. So why didn't they get along and why did their animosity persist into adulthood, even when they lived three thousand miles apart?

"I'll pay you back for all this one day," said Gabe, raising his fifty-dollar drink. "I promise."

"I appreciate that," said Liv, "but don't worry about it. Seriously. My business is killing it. I just added two more agents and I trust my number two completely, which is why I can take some time to be here. And Cooper . . . Wall Street is another world."

Wall Street was another world, at least to Gabe. He wasn't even sure what to ask about it so instead he said, "How is Cooper?"

"Fine," said Liv. "The same."

"And how is married life?"

Liv shrugged and managed a twisted smile. "Fine. Also the same. We've been together since college. Nothing changed when we got the piece of paper. Same shit, different day, yeah?" She sipped her martini and said, "What about you? Anyone special?"

Gabe was surprised by the question. Not that it was unusual for someone to inquire about his love life, but it was unusual for that someone to be Liv. He couldn't remember that ever happening before. "There might be someone special," he said. "But she has no idea."

"No idea she's special or no idea you think she's special?"

"Both. Her name is Carly. She's my neighbor. We're friends. Just friends."

"Because she friend-zoned you?" said Liv.

"No," said Gabe. And then added almost like an apology, "I just haven't made a move."

"Why not?"

Gabe stared into his amber tequila. How many tequilas had he shared with Carly? It was their beverage of choice when sitting out on one of their balconies, when playing cribbage in one of their kitchens, when walking Ms. Ramirez around the neighborhood during the thick of the pandemic. Walking in public, they sipped tequila from reusable Starbucks cups, fooling the world. They spent so much time together in each other's bubble—Gabe felt like he'd taken a crash course in Carly Ramirez. A crash course in which he was earning straight A's but was afraid to take the final exam. Gabe winced at his sister and said, "I like her too much. I don't want to screw it up."

Liv watched her brother hide in his drink. He was still shy after all these years. Was *shy* the right word? Or was it *insecure, unsure, afraid*? He lacked confidence, thought Liv, because he wasn't aware of how others saw him. Liv was quite aware of how she appeared. She worked in the image business. Style, taste, beauty—it's what she dealt with every day. Being tuned in to those things allowed Liv to recruit the best wardrobe stylists, makeup artists, hair stylists, photographers, and set designers. If you see the cover of *Vanity Fair* or *Elle* or *Vogue*—there's a good chance one of Liv's artists had something to do with it. Liv understood image. But her own brother had no idea how handsome he was. How appealing he was. He was like a seventh grader embarrassed over liking a girl who might not like him back. Gabe might not be the best marriage candidate only because he still dreamed of being a musician and supported that dream by tending bar, but Carly was also a bartender. She wouldn't think less of Gabe because of that.

"Gabe Ahlstrom," said Liv, "you're thirty-seven years old. I think you should take a swing."

Gabe smiled. "Maybe I will when I get back."

"You do that," said Liv. She removed a stuffed olive from its tiny metal skewer, popped it into her mouth, and said, "Do you think Mack was gay and he and Andrew had something going on?"

"I don't know," said Gabe. "I've been wondering the same thing. But who keeps that secret in the 2020s? I mean, Andrew's not even hiding it from his hateful mother. I'd understand if he remained in the closet just to guarantee his inheritance, which by the looks of it, should be any day now."

Liv smiled. *"You look . . . well."*

Gabe laughed. "Not my best moment."

Their laughter died down then Liv seemed to drift off to somewhere else. She looked out at all the people gathered in the lobby of the Peninsula Hotel then said, "I can't stand not knowing."

"Not knowing if Mack was gay?"

"No, I don't care about that." Liv turned back toward Gabe. "I can't stand not knowing if Mack was delusional. Did Mack imagine those attempts on his life? Maybe something happened and he just snapped. I mean, Diana said he'd been acting oddly. He'd been talking about us and Leech Lake, which he never talked about. And that email he sent seems so out of character. At least for the Mack I knew."

Gabe downed the last of his tequila and said, "Maybe not delusional but confused. Early onset Alzheimer's?"

"I don't think so," said Liv. "But only because he emailed us. I know we've all grown apart. We've all gone our separate ways and live our separate lives but we've always come together for the big things. Weddings and funerals. So the simple act of emailing us was a coming together, in a way. Which meant to Mack that whatever was going on with him was a big thing, yeah?" Liv ate her second olive and shook her head. "I mean, he went to the police. Just because Detective Fitzpatrick didn't believe him doesn't mean Mack's fears weren't grounded in reality, right?"

Gabe considered Liv's question. The din of the lobby had grown loud with the happy hour crowd. The activity seemed to be pushing Liv and Gabe together. "Maybe we should ask Andrew what he thought," he said. "He was Mack's doctor and they'd become friends again. Maybe he knew if Mack was having mental health issues."

"Not yet," said Liv. She saw Gabe's inferiority complex flash in his eyes so she added, "It's a good idea, but as far as we know, we're the only people Mack reached out to other than Detective Fitzpatrick. Right now I think the chance that Andrew or Diana had anything to do with Mack's death is slim, but I want to keep them in the dark about Mack's email for a while because . . . well, I don't know why. It's just a feeling."

"So you've changed your mind. You don't want to leave right after the funeral. You want to stay here for a few more days?"

Liv shook her head. "I think after the funeral we should have a memorial service for Mack up at Leech Lake. Something simple. I'll plan it. Make a few calls and spread the word. I have time. There are no crises at work so I can just check in and make a few calls when I need to. And we can scatter Mack's ashes up there and—" Gabe looked at her dubiously. "Oh, come on, Gabe. We're Mack's only family other than Diana. And we're the only ones who know about his supposed near misses. If we don't look into it, who will?"

Gabe softened his voice. He didn't want this to be a confrontation. "Didn't I say that earlier today?" he said. "Like about two hours ago?"

"Yeah-yeah, you did. I didn't agree with you then but I've changed my mind. Besides, I'm curious if Mack really did have a different father than us. Someone up in the Leech Lake area has to know."

"I would think so," said Gabe. "No one can keep a secret in a small town."

"Excuse me," said the server who'd appeared out of nowhere. "Would either of you like another drink?"

"Better bring us two drinks each," said Gabe. "We're headed home."

· CHAPTER 10 ·

Liv planned Mack's Birchwood memorial service. It was to be Sunday afternoon at Ahlstrom's, the family-owned resort where Liv, Gabe, and Mack had grown up. She'd called their Uncle Denny, who now owned and ran Ahlstrom's Resort. He was happy to provide food and drink and spread the word, especially because he couldn't attend Mack's funeral in Chicago. She invited Diana, but Diana declined, saying she needed some time to herself after the funeral.

Gabe and Liv decided to drive all six hundred miles from Chicago rather than flying to Minneapolis or Duluth and driving from there. It was as if they needed a slow approach in order to acclimate to their childhood home. If they flew and arrived too quickly, they could fall victim to the emotional bends. Liv rented a Chevy Tahoe for the drive north. She wanted a big SUV. It was late April so a Minnesota blizzard couldn't be ruled out. The drive took twelve hours, including stops for lunch in Wisconsin Dells and dinner in Duluth. The siblings spoke little, using the drive to take a break from each other despite being separated by nothing more than a center console. Liv insisted on doing all of the driving.

"It helps the time go more quickly," said Liv.

And you always have to be in charge, thought Gabe but he said, "No problem. I can nap and play games on my phone."

Games on your phone? What are you, twelve? thought Liv but said, "Want to listen to an Anthony Horowitz book? There's a series of his I haven't read yet."

"Who's he?"

"British author. Mysteries. Good pace. Funny. He also writes TV. I think you'll like him."

"Sure," said Gabe.

They listened to *The Word Is Murder* with a few breaks so Liv could deal with work calls, but finished the book before pulling into town.

"My God," said Liv. "So much has changed."

Birchwood, Minnesota, sat on Highway 371, north of Leech Lake Township and south of Wilkinson. It had grown since Liv and Gabe had last seen it. It now had *two* stoplights and *two* gas stations, one on each end of town, a Caribou Coffee with a drive-thru, a pastry shop, and a small modern-looking brewery called Mad Musky that was made of concrete and glass—you could see large steel fermentation tanks inside along with plenty of people. A full-sized supermarket from the chain Super One Foods occupied half a block that once contained some of the town's oldest homes. All that along with what was there twenty years ago, including a hardware store, a bakery, a sporting goods store, a few family-owned restaurants and souvenir shops, and the three-story, brown brick K-12 school Liv and Gabe had attended, although now it was a community center. The small cinema still had a marquee, but the building now functioned as an antiques store.

"Look," said Gabe. "The Dairy Queen is still here." It was a tiny building with a walk-up window, and Gabe could picture his ten-year-old self waiting in line to order a Dilly Bar, most often after a Little League game or sometimes for no reason at all. Ahlstrom's Resort was less than two miles from town, and he'd often pedal his bike just for a frozen treat.

"And the library is still here," said Liv. "And look, Millie's Pies. God, I loved that place."

"Ugh," said Gabe. "A dollar store. There goes the neighborhood."

"But at least there's a supermarket now," said Liv. "People don't have to drive all the way down to Walker. We'll have to check it out tomorrow." Liv watched a group of teenagers leaving Caribou Coffee, backpacks slung over their shoulders while getting into cars. She imagined they were the planning committee for prom or graduation or they'd been studying together for an upcoming test the way she and her friends had done. "It's like everything's changed," she said. "Everything and nothing."

"I know what you mean," said Gabe. "My whole childhood is rushing at me. Hard to pretend it didn't happen when you're looking at where it did happen."

Liv stopped at the second stoplight and looked over at her brother. She knew exactly what he meant.

One windy road and five minutes later, Liv pulled onto the drive of Ahlstrom's on Leech Lake. It was eight P.M. and even though it was dark, they could see how much had changed. The once gravel drive was now paved. The handmade sign that had read WELCOME TO AHLSTROM'S—YOUR FAMILY'S FIRST RESORT had been replaced with a professionally made sign that read AHLSTROM'S ON LEECH LAKE—A RED PINES PROPERTY.

"Man," said Gabe. "I check out the resort every few years online to see what's changed, but it's another thing to see it in person."

A crop of new buildings was connected by paved paths lit by low-voltage garden lamps. The building that had doubled as the family home and office had been remodeled and was now just an office. Uncle Denny and his family lived in a new house near the office. The original lodge was still intact, but there were two new enormous buildings: a rec center that included an indoor pool, and a banquet center.

"I barely recognize this place," said Liv. She found a parking spot marked FOR CHECK-IN AND CHECK-OUT ONLY and said, "Kind of bossy with the parking rules, aren't they? The old lot wasn't even paved much less painted with lines and posted with signs."

"Grab that spot," said Gabe. "It looks crowded. How can that be before the fishing opener?"

"I don't know. It doesn't make sense. Should we have made reservations?" said Liv.

"Uncle Denny knows we're coming. This is where we grew up. Our name is the same as the resort. Aren't reservations assumed?"

They exited the Tahoe and followed a new concrete walk to the office. The old clapboard siding had been replaced by faux wood logs. The windows and roof were also new. Ahlstrom's bucolic Northwoods feel had been replaced by a sterile facsimile as if it were a Northwoods–themed hotel in Las Vegas.

"Looks like Disneyland," said Gabe.

"Yeah, it does," said Liv. "But I suppose change is normal. It has been twenty years."

They entered the office. The old sheet paneling had been replaced with real wood paneling. The linoleum floor was now low-pile carpet. The hanging flypaper was gone and a chandelier made of deer antlers hung in its place. A series of plaques on the counter bragged about the awards Ahlstrom's had received, all mentioning they were a Red Pines Property, and an attractive young woman stood behind the reception desk. She wore a white shirt and gray vest with a name tag that read: ANNABEL JOHNSON—BRAINERD, MINNESOTA.

"Good evening," she said with a hospitality-degree smile. "How may I help you?"

"Hi," said Liv. "We're looking for Denny Ahlstrom."

"May I tell him your name, please?"

"Gabe and Liv Ahlstrom," said Gabe. "His niece and nephew. We grew up here."

"One moment, please," said Annabel Johnson from Brainerd with no change in expression before she disappeared behind the counter, as if Gabe and Liv Ahlstrom were just a couple of strangers who'd wandered into Ahlstrom's by mistake.

"Whoa," said Liv. "The place has gone corporate."

"Be prepared to show two forms of ID and submit a urine sample," said Gabe.

"I did not care for that woman's plastic smile."

"What happened to the help-yourself jar of buttermints?" said Gabe. "Those were everyone's favorite."

"I don't know," said Liv. "Covid? Insurance liability?"

The front door opened. A man in his late sixties entered walking two golden retrievers. He was tall and handsome and had long sideburns. He wore jeans, mud boots, and a canvas field jacket. He looked down at the dogs as he said, "Good girls. Come on, let's go get your treats."

"Ed?" said Liv.

The man looked up as if he'd walked into a different dimension and was just realizing it.

"It's me, Ed. Liv." She had more light in her eyes than Gabe had seen in years.

The recognition registered first in Ed's eyes, blue diamonds set deep in his smooth face. Then he smiled and said, "Little Liv?"

"Yes. And this is Gabe," she said, looking at her brother.

"Gabe?" Then another wave of recognition. "You came home. You both came home."

"And you still work here?" said Liv.

"Oh, sure," said Ed. "Every day. I mow the lawn and clean the guests' fish. I plow the snow and walk the dogs. I don't fix the plumbing anymore. A man in a truck comes to do that. Denny says it's because the Red Pines people won't let me fix plumbing anymore. And I don't put the docks in or take 'em out anymore. Raymond does that."

"Who's Raymond?"

"Oh, he's Renee's brother. He has long dark hair and scars on his face. He looks scary but he's nice. He lives in a pink house right by Dairy Queen—talk about a lucky guy—and he does a lot of jobs I used to do because he's younger and stronger. The docks don't have posts anymore. They float on the water and Raymond pulls them up on the land with a truck before the water turns to ice and he pushes them back when the ice turns to water. It's still out there, you know, the ice. The car's still on the lake. I picked April 23rd at 11:04 A.M. on my raffle ticket, so if it falls through in two days I might win."

Both Liv and Gabe smiled the most genuine smiles. They'd known Ed Lindimier their entire childhoods. He was Ahlstrom's groundskeeper and all-around maintenance man. Their parents had grown up with him and, when Ed dropped out of school in junior high, back when people used the R-word as part of their everyday speech, the Ahlstroms hired Ed to work at the resort. When Ed turned eighteen, Liv and Gabe's grandparents gave Ed a small cabin on the back edge of the resort by the woods.

"Maybe I'll buy a raffle ticket for April 24th," said Gabe.

"Oh, no," said Ed. "You can't. They stop selling them April 1st."

Gabe smiled. "That's right they do. I forgot. Well, I'll keep my fingers crossed for you."

The ice-out raffle had been a tradition in Birchwood since 1952 when a stubborn old fisherman named Ollie Odegaard towed his broken-down Ford out onto frozen Steamboat Bay. He'd removed the passenger seat and cut a hole in the floorboard to use the old car as an ice-fishing shelter. By March 1st, when anglers had removed their ice-fishing shacks and had stopped driving cars on the ice, Ollie Odegaard kept his out there. "It's been a cold winter," he said. "Ice out won't be until May. I got plenty of time."

That was the quote in the local paper, and Ollie's old Ford became the talk of the town. Wagers were made on whether or not the car would fall through the ice. When it became clear that Ollie really did believe he could tow it back in on May 1st, a death pool was formed. Not for Ollie but for the Ford. The car fell through the ice on April 28th. Ollie wasn't in it at the time, but for all the guff he took, he probably wished he had been.

Ollie's car falling through the ice was all anyone talked about for three days, and the mayor of Birchwood, astute politician that he was, noticed two things: first, Ollie Odegaard's Ford and its perilous predicament injected excitement into Minnesota's least exciting time of year. The dreary month of March is neither winter nor spring—it torments with fifty-degree days followed by thirty-inch snowfalls. The ice is dangerously thin. The grass is still buried. The snowmelt of daytime freezes at night, coating the roads and sidewalks with ice and making morning commutes for vehicles and pedestrians a neck-risking experience.

The second thing the mayor noticed was that speculation about if and when Ollie Odegaard's old Ford would fall through the ice led to a lot of money exchanging hands.

The following year the mayor monetized Ollie Odegaard's folly by creating a raffle called the Great Leech Lake Ice-Out. He convinced Hank of Hank's Fill 'er Up to donate a '22 Packard and tow it out onto the same spot where Ollie's Ford had rested the year before. A one-dollar ticket gave the purchaser one guess at the date and time the car would fall through the ice. A battery-powered clock was lightly affixed to the car's roof and attached to a rope so they could pull it free and reel it in to ascertain the exact time the clock hit the water. Half the money raised went to the winning raffle ticket holder. Half went into the city's coffers.

Even in the 1950s, people raised environmental objections to sinking an oily car into the lake, so the following winter they used a gutted Chevy. No engine, no radiator, no seats. Just a frame and body. After the car fell through the ice, they reeled the whole thing in with a winch so they could do it all over again the next year.

In the 1980s a welder created a fake car. The vehicle was open.

Just a frame on a chassis with a metal steering wheel and plastic seats under a roll cage. There was no engine, no body panels, no doors. The tires were solid rubber, and they rolled on axles so the thing could be towed out onto the ice, but that was the extent of its function. It looked like a big go-cart. A non-toxic, reusable go-cart.

In the beginning, the raffle raised hundreds of dollars. Word spread to nearby towns, vacationers bought tickets in the summer, and soon the raffle raised thousands. After the internet and webcams came along, the raffle raised tens of thousands from all over the country. A few years ago, they'd replaced the old alarm clock with a solar-powered clock and solar-powered Christmas lights. Now the Great Leech Lake Ice-Out raffle ranked right up there with the fishing opener and Birchwood's famed Fourth of July celebration.

"I can't believe you're still here, Ed," said Gabe. "It's so good to see you."

"I live here," said Ed. "I'm always here."

"Are you in the same cabin?" said Liv.

"Oh, sure," said Ed. "I don't want to live anywhere else. I like my cabin. Feels real homey."

"Do you still have that girlfriend?" said Gabe. "What's her name?"

"Marjorie," said Ed. "She's not my girlfriend anymore. Her parents sent her to a special school in Minneapolis and that's where she lives. She visits me when she comes to town. She's still real nice and pretty."

"And no other girlfriends?" said Liv.

"There was one. Her name was Alice. She wanted me to live in a house and get a different job, but I wouldn't do it." Ed smiled. "How come you two got older and I didn't?"

Gabe laughed. "Oh man, Ed. Is it okay if I give you a hug?"

"Sure," said Ed. "I like hugs."

Gabe stepped toward Ed and wrapped the older man in his arms. He held him for a moment and then Gabe began to cry.

"What's wrong," said Ed. "Did I squeeze you too hard?"

"No. I'm just sorry I didn't come back to visit you. I'm really sorry, Ed. I'm so sorry."

"You should be happy, not sad, because you're visiting me now."

"I am happy, Ed. Happy to see you."

Liv felt her phone buzz in her hand and looked down expecting to see a text from her husband, Cooper. She hadn't spoken to him since yesterday. She glanced at the screen to see the notification but it wasn't a text from Cooper. It was another email from Mack. She felt a shudder throughout her body.

"Do you want a hug, too?" said Ed.

Liv couldn't take her eyes off her phone. She was about to open Mack's email when she heard . . .

"Liv," said Gabe. "Ed wants to know if you also want a hug."

"Oh," said Liv. She looked up and manufactured a smile. "Of course. I'd love a hug, Ed."

Liv dropped her phone into her purse, stepped toward the tall man, and wrapped her arms around him, pressing the side of her face into his chest. She thought she was making a courtesy gesture, but hugging Ed actually made her feel better.

"You smell the same," said Liv.

"It's Irish Spring soap. The only kind I use because it's as fresh and clean as a whistle." Ed whistled.

Liv burst out laughing.

"I'll be damned. Look who came back to Leech Lake."

Liv looked up and saw her Uncle Denny standing behind the reception desk.

· CHAPTER 11 ·

Denny stepped around the reception desk and into the lobby wearing designer jeans, pressed and creased, and a plaid Pendleton shirt tucked in over his paunch. Red suspenders arched over his slight shoulders to hold the entire package together. He looked like he'd either just shaved or didn't need to shave and wore his chestnut-brown hair parted on the side and just over his ears. When Denny bent over to greet the golden retrievers, his gray roots shined like a thousand points of light. When he stood upright, he held out his arms toward Liv and said, "Welcome home, Liv."

Liv and Gabe hadn't seen their Uncle Denny in seventeen years but used to know him well. He was close with his older brother, Bobby, their father, and visited the resort often. Uncle Denny had moved away after high school just like they had. He went to Minneapolis to attend the University of Minnesota and didn't return until he was in his mid-forties with his wife and young daughter when Mack sold him the resort after Gabe had graduated high school.

"Uncle Denny," said Liv. She wanted to read Mack's most recent posthumous email but hadn't seen her uncle since Mack and Diana's wedding. Mack and his email weren't going anywhere, so she opted for her uncle's embrace.

"Hey, Uncle Denny," said Gabe, who hadn't looked at his phone. Gabe shook his uncle's hand. Denny was not of a man-hugging generation.

"So sorry about Mack," said Denny. "He was a good kid and good man."

"Mack with a K died," said Ed. "Just like Bette and Bobby did. We won't see him ever again."

"No, we won't, Ed," said Liv. "It's very sad."

"I've spread the word about the memorial service," said Denny. "Should get quite a crowd on Sunday. Annabel, where are we putting Liv and Gabe for the next few days?"

"I'm so sorry," said Annabel Johnson. "We have no vacancies this evening. We're all booked up with the Outboard Motor Association's annual meeting. You might want to try Anderson's Cove up the road."

"Hold on," said Denny. "Liv and Gabe are family. I put family first. Always have. Guess I'm just wired that way."

Liv had forgotten that Uncle Denny was one of those people who would use any excuse to tell you their personal code of ethics, their priorities, and whatever traits and habits made them most enamored with themselves.

"We must have space somewhere," added Denny.

"We really don't," said Annabel Johnson from Brainerd. "I'm sorry." She aimed her official smile at Denny then Liv then Gabe.

"Cabin 14," said Ed.

"Excuse me?" said Annabel.

"Cabin 14. It's full of old furniture, but everything works. Gabe and Liv could stay there."

"Well, that's an idea," said Denny. "It's not too dusty?"

"I keep tarps over everything," said Ed. "Wash 'em once a month and have housekeeping dust and vacuum. And I run the water every week to keep the pipes from turning the water brown."

"I'm sorry to be Debbie Downer here," said Annabel, putting on her hospitality-degree serious face, "but Cabin 14 has not been permitted for occupancy because the bathroom and kitchen aren't up to code."

Gabe felt his phone buzz, glanced at the screen, and saw that he'd received an email from Mack. Gabe's mouth went dry. He looked at Liv and gathered from her expression that she'd also seen dead Mack's most recent email. He was about to excuse himself to read it when . . .

Denny waved away Annabel's objection. "The kitchen and bathroom are fine. People stayed in that cabin for decades and I never heard a complaint. I'm the kind of guy who puts common sense above rules and regulations. Why make life more stressful than it needs to be?" He placed his hands on his paunch as if it were something to be proud of. "Number 14 is yours, Liv and Gabe, if you want it."

Liv tried to remember Cabin 14. She pictured the resort twenty years ago, mentally going from building to building. *Ugh*, she thought. *Cabin 14 is one big room.* Liv turned toward Annabel Johnson. "Did you say Anderson's Cove has vacancies?"

"They might," said Annabel. "I can call for you. The only issue is they're hosting the Upper Midwest Toastmasters convention. They held their convention here at Ahlstrom's last year. Nice people but they try to corner other guests and practice their speeches on them."

The front door opened and an attractive, Indigenous American woman in her mid-sixties walked in dressed head-to-toe in Lululemon. Her dark hair was pulled back into a tight ponytail, and she stood ramrod straight, her head held high over her long neck. The dogs ran to greet her as she said, "Hello, Liv and Gabe." She stopped and stared and smiled. "It's been way too long."

"Liv and Gabe," said Denny, "you remember my better half, Renee."

They exchanged hellos. Renee had grown up in Minneapolis and had met Denny ten years before he moved back to Leech Lake. She taught yoga classes to the resort guests and invited Liv and Gabe to attend anytime they wanted.

"Well, I'm going to get back to my baseball game," said Denny. "It's early but Minnesota doesn't look half bad this year. And I'll see you two later," he said to Gabe and Liv. "I always take the late-night patrol at eleven P.M. Just to make sure no one's breaking the no noise after ten P.M. rule."

"We'll keep it down," said Liv.

Renee smiled and said, "You'd better, or you're likely to get a knock on your door and a friendly warning."

"We don't want that," said Gabe.

"Ah," said Denny, "you're a bunch of wisenheimers."

After a bit more small talk, they said goodnight, and Ed went ahead to meet Liv and Gabe at Cabin 14.

The siblings stepped outside. Liv took out her phone and said, "We got another email from Mack."

"I saw," said Gabe, taking out his phone.

They each turned their faces toward rectangles of blue light and read:

Mack Ahlstrom
Subject: One last thought . . .
To: Liv Ahlstrom, Gabe Ahlstrom

Dear Liv and Gabe,

If you're reading this I have been dead for five days.

I wanted to let you sit with my last email before sending this. By now you've returned home to your respective cities. You may have made some inquiries in an attempt to discern if anything I'd written in my last email was true. You may think I had lost my mind before getting killed. And you very well may have differing opinions. I know you two are not close and I fear my first email or maybe simply my death has pushed you beyond reconciliation.

But please don't give up on each other. I've long regretted the way our family disintegrated after our parents died. I often wished I'd initiated our getting back together to heal old wounds and forgive each other for a past that was not our fault. We were just kids. And I would have done just that if I didn't fear drawing you into the danger that had befallen me. Hopefully, the danger to our family has died with me. But if it hasn't, know that I tried everything to learn who was trying to kill me. I failed, or you would be reading a far different email.

The one thing I did not do in the past year is return to Leech Lake. Something kept me from doing so. Call it intuition or fear or self-preservation or some combination of the three. It's almost impossible to murder someone in a major city without a witness or a security camera or cell phone revealing the murderer's location. But in a rural setting, where few people are spread out over a big area, where technology is not as prevalent, it's much easier. And for that reason, I suggest you not return to the Leech Lake area.

This is my last email.

Love,
Mack

· CHAPTER 12 ·

"Forget Cabin 14," said Gabe. "Let's get the hell out of here."

Geese honked their way north high in the darkening sky, a sure sign that spring was on the way and a better weather predictor than any computer model. Both Liv and Gabe felt comforted by the sound, even without consciously making the connection, because the migrating geese had taught them that the world was bigger than the town in which they lived. Those geese came from somewhere else and they were going to somewhere else. The world offered other places, other people, and wondrous possibilities.

"You can leave if you want," said Liv. She missed the familiar crunch of gravel as she walked the now-paved path toward the Tahoe. "I'm staying. I want to spread Mack's ashes. I want him to have a memorial here. And I want to ask around to see if there's any validity to Mack's claim that he had a different father than us."

"Okay," said Gabe, "but aren't you worried for our safety after reading Mack's latest email? He told us not to come here."

Liv looked up at the night sky. The geese had started to circle, looking for a place to bed down for the night, and stars had begun to show themselves. She couldn't remember the last time she'd been outside of a major metropolitan area, the last time she'd seen twinkling lights in a field of black. So many stars that they created their own smear of radiance. That alone seemed worth staying for. She said, "Mack told Diana there was something broken about our family. Do you remember feeling that way?"

Gabe remembered his parents as kind, pleasant people. He had few memories of Mack, but what memories he did possess were happy. The only thing he remembered as broken was his relationship with Liv. But that was normal, wasn't it? Isn't sibling rivalry just a way of training kids to navigate the interpersonal relationships they'd have as adults? When he and Liv weren't fighting, he remembered running through woods and across expansive green lawns. Fishing and sledding and playing capture the flag. Not that they got along but at least they'd had fun. Gabe remembered his father shoveling snow off the ice where they played broomball and hockey and pom-pom-pull-away until well after dark, a single floodlight illuminating the ice and snow. There always seemed to be other kids around. Some local. Some staying at the resort. He couldn't deny that despite the heartache and loss he'd experienced at this resort, he still loved the place.

"I don't remember our family being broken," Gabe said. "I have mostly happy memories of this place."

"So do I. But why haven't we come back to visit? Not even once. I mean, explain that."

Gabe sighed. He had wanted to visit since leaving but every time he'd thought of doing so, he'd found an excuse not to. "I don't know, Liv. I don't know why we haven't come back."

"Me either. But it's weird, right?"

"Yes," said Gabe. "It's weird."

"There must be a reason, yeah? Not a logical reason but a psychological one. Emotions are more powerful than rational thought. I have to remind my artists of that all the time. Photographers, wardrobe stylists, set designers . . . Talented as hell but their emotions get the best of them if they don't stop and reason things out. Or if I don't do it for them." Liv still looked up at the night sky. When she was a little girl, she'd stay out long after sunset trying to memorize the constellations. That was her rational aim. Emotionally, she loved feeling small in the vastness. Her smallness gave her permission to fail. "Maybe something happened when we were little," she said to the Big Dipper. "Something we don't remember. Or we were too young to realize. And us being here is the only chance we have of finding out what that was."

"Even if it gets us killed?" said Gabe.

Liv took her eyes off the sky and looked at her brother. "Have you ever felt something's wrong in your life? I mean, like something's fundamentally wrong? Like it's in your bones? Like you're bad at life?"

"Well, yeah," said Gabe. "I'm thirty-seven years old, have never been in a long-term relationship, live paycheck to paycheck, and see no chance of things getting better. Is that what you mean?"

Liv was surprised to hear Gabe describe himself in the same light in which she saw him. She had assumed he didn't possess that kind of self-awareness, that kind of self-criticism, and it broke her heart a little to hear those words come out of his mouth.

"Not really, no. I'm sure those things are hard, but that's not what I'm talking about because I have a good job, a husband, a lovely home, and money in the bank, but I still feel something isn't right. I wish I could explain it better than that but I can't."

Gabe glanced down at his phone and reread the end of Mack's email and said, "Mack's warning us not to be here. I'm taking that warning seriously."

"Then go," said Liv. "Don't stay if you don't want to. I mean it." Liv opened the Tahoe's driver-side door and added, "But damnit, Gabe. You need to learn to deal with shit when it gets hard."

"What does that mean?"

"It means running away solves nothing. Facing this might be good for you. It'll help you face the next challenge and the challenge after that. You'd be doing yourself a huge favor. Maybe it will even give you the courage to tell your neighbor how you feel about her." Liv sat behind the wheel and started the engine.

"Oh, I get it. This is all just an opportunity for one big life lesson for me because my life is crap. A teachable moment, if you will."

"Everything's a teachable moment, right? For everyone. You don't have to take everything so personally."

Gabe sat in the passenger seat and said, "I knew things would go to hell between us."

Liv put the Tahoe in reverse and watched the backup camera. "Maybe the reason things keep going to hell between us is also what I'm looking for."

"Or maybe you should stop criticizing me all the time. Maybe it's that simple."

"There's nothing wrong with criticism. I criticize myself constantly. Because here's the thing about being an adult, Gabe—"

Gabe held up his phone. "Hold on. Let me record the wise words of Liv Ahlstrom so that future generations can—"

"The key to being an adult, Gabe, is knowing no one else gives a damn. No one cares. If you don't make your own way in the world, you're screwed because no one is going to do it for you." Liv started down the curved road toward Cabin 14.

"Sounds like a sad and lonely outlook on life."

"It is." Liv drove in silence for a minute and then parked the car in front of Cabin 14. Ed stood in the open door, warm light leaking out from behind him. Liv and Gabe got out of the car without finishing their conversation.

"Welcome home," said Ed as they stepped inside Cabin 14. He had already lit a fire in the fireplace. The big room smelled clean with a hint of burning oak.

"I can't believe this place," said Liv. "Cabin 14 must be the only building at the entire resort that hasn't changed."

"Cabin 14 and my cabin are the same as they used to be," said Ed. "That's why I like 'em best."

Cabin 14 was the original building at Ahlstrom's, a log cabin

with a stone fireplace so large that Liv and Gabe could walk into
it without ducking when they were almost teenagers. The kitchen,
sitting area, and beds were all in one big room. A bathroom had
been added in one corner before they were born and separated by
sheetrock walls. The windows were original but clean. The kitchen
had Formica countertops and pine cabinets. The cabin had pine
board floors. Braided, oval rugs defined the living and dining areas. The furniture was original, mid-century Scandinavian, and
both Liv and Gabe wondered if Uncle Denny realized its value.
The back wall was lined with freestanding shelves made of two-
by-four boards. The shelves were filled with cardboard boxes, each
sealed and free of dust.

"Is this all of our stuff?" said Gabe, pointing to the filled
shelves.

"Oh, sure," said Ed. "I would never throw out your things. All
of that belonged to your mother and father. And to Mack with a
K and Little Liv and Little Gabe."

"Is it okay if we go through it while we're here?"

"Oh, sure. It's yours. Maybe you want to take some of it when
you leave. I'll pack up whatever you don't want and keep it right
here."

"Thank you, Ed," said Liv. "It's so nice you've stored all of this.
Did someone ask you to do that?"

"No, I wanted to. Because Bobby and Bette were so nice to me.
And there's one more thing I keep at my cabin. I'll go get it." Ed
started toward the door.

"You don't have to do that now," said Gabe. "We'll be here a
few days."

"Oh, I think I should. It's not mine, and I don't keep belongings that are not mine. I don't do bad things."

"No, you don't, Ed," said Gabe. "You're good. You do good
things."

Ed smiled, continued to the door, and exited.

Liv sat on the couch and said, "This furniture must be worth a fortune."

"It is in New York or L.A. Maybe Uncle Denny will let us take it. I can't believe Ed put all this in here and has kept it clean." Gabe walked over to the shelves. "I have no idea what could be in these boxes."

Liv took a deep breath and said, "It smells the same. Wood and wood soap and the northern Minnesota air and . . . I don't know what else, but it makes me feel like I'm ten years old."

"Yeah," said Gabe. "Me, too."

"Open one of the boxes," said Liv. "Let's see our old stuff."

Gabe picked up a box and carried it over to Liv. He took a credit card from his wallet and drew its edge down the packing tape. The box opened, and Gabe smelled the last millennium. He removed a soccer ball, sad and deflated, a Sony CD Walkman wrapped in its headphone wire, and a cordless telephone with a broken antenna.

"Ooh," said Liv. "We're rich."

Gabe pulled out a pink Gameboy. "I believe this is yours." He pulled out a blue Gameboy. "And this is mine. Here's your Barbie. My G.I. Joe. No gender fluidity when we were kids."

"Didn't we ever have a garage sale? Why does this stuff still exist?"

Gabe pulled out a jewelry box covered in maroon velvet. "I don't remember this."

"I do," said Liv. "Mom let me borrow necklaces and bracelets when I played dress-up."

Gabe flipped open the lid. "It's full." He turned the open clamshell toward Liv and they heard a knock on the door. "Come in."

Ed opened the door and entered carrying a framed 5x7 photograph. He walked into the large room and handed it to Liv. "This belongs to you and Gabe."

"Oh, Ed," said Liv. She turned the photograph toward Gabe. The colors had faded but they could clearly see that, in the photo, their mother, Bette, stood on the dock next to Ed, arms around each other and facing the camera. "You were so handsome, Ed. How old were you in this picture?"

"Sixteen," said Ed. "So that would have been . . ." He looked upward as if into his brain and counted on his fingers. "I think 1972. Isn't Bette beautiful?"

"Very," said Gabe.

"That is my first day working here at Ahlstrom's. It was Bette's idea. She made him hire me."

"Made who hire you?"

"Bobby's dad, Mr. Ahlstrom."

"I didn't know that," said Gabe. "That was very kind of Mom to do that."

"Yes. That's why I loved her. And she loved me."

"I'm sure she did," said Liv. Ed blushed and looked away. Liv smiled. "What is it, Ed?"

He lowered his voice and said, "She told me."

"She told you what?"

Ed smiled and said, "She told me she loved me. Bette's the only person who ever said it."

"No," said Liv. "You're not being serious."

"Yes. Bette's the only one."

"That's not right," said Liv.

"Oh, I think it's good," said Ed. "Bette made me feel good. She was always nice to me."

Liv opened her mouth then hesitated. She didn't want to ask the question that had popped into her head but she couldn't help herself. "Ed, your parents never told you they loved you?"

Ed shook his head.

Ed was sixty-eight years old, thought Gabe. The world might be falling apart, but some things had changed for the better. It must have been far more difficult for a child to grow up with Ed's challenges when he was a boy than it was now. "Lots of people love you," said Gabe. "Especially us."

"You do?"

"Absolutely."

Liv looked over at Gabe. He drove her crazy most of the time, but right now, she wanted to hug him for what he'd just said. "Yeah-yeah, Gabe's right," said Liv. "We've loved you since we were Little Liv and Little Gabe."

Ed smiled, walked toward the door, looked back at them, and left.

· CHAPTER 13 ·

Liv stared into her mother's open jewelry box and said, "It couldn't be Ed, could it? I mean . . ."

"What *do you mean*?" said Gabe. "Are you talking about Ed being Mack's father?"

"I'm just thinking out loud. Mom was so kind to Ed, and the timing is right."

"Mom wouldn't have done that," said Gabe. He set down the box and headed to the shelving to get more stuff. "When Ed was sixteen he must have had the emotional and intellectual capacity of what, a ten-year-old? And Mom always said she thought of Ed as a brother." Gabe returned with another cardboard box. "When Mom got sick, she told us to take care of him after she died."

"And we did. For a while anyway." Liv's expression grew sour, as if she were looking in a mirror and saw a person she didn't like. "Then we abandoned Ed. Totally forgot about him. Like he'd died or something."

"I know . . ." Gabe shook his head and sliced open the new box. "It was horrific of us. So awful . . ."

Liv pulled something out of the jewelry box and said, "Hold on a minute." Liv picked up the picture Ed brought from his cabin. Gabe looked over her shoulder and took another look at his mother when she was sixteen years old. She still lived in his heart and mind, but he never thought of her as any other age than when she was his mother. But she also deserved to be thought of as a child, thought Gabe, and she especially deserved to be thought of as the old woman she would have become if cancer hadn't taken her away. "What's going on?" said Gabe. "What are you looking for? "

"I'll show you." Liv took out her phone, switched the camera to the macro lens, and took a close-up of her mother. She enlarged the photo and said, "Look. Look at Mom's necklace."

Gabe looked at the enlargement and said, "It's an old skeleton key. I don't remember ever seeing it before."

"Well," said Liv, "you're going to see it now." She opened her fist and dropped a skeleton key from a silver chain. The key looked functional, not ornamental, made of silver-colored metal, dull and oxidized.

"Is that the same one as in the picture?"

"It's impossible to tell," said Liv. "But it sure looks the same."

"Maybe that was the key to the house she grew up in," said Gabe. "She was only sixteen in that photograph."

"If it was the key to her childhood home, why did she keep it?" said Liv.

"Sentimental reasons?" said Gabe. "Or maybe she just never cleaned out her jewelry box. There're a million reasons. Lots of people have old keys lying around. Keys that don't go to anything or they can't remember what they go to. Or maybe Dad gave it to her. It's the key to her heart. Or his heart. I don't really know how that works."

"If it was the key to her heart or his heart or anyone else's heart, why did she stop wearing it?"

Gabe set the box aside, sat down and stared into the fire. He inhaled the sweet smell of woodsmoke, and said, "Well, the obvious answer is Mack's biological father gave it to her and she stopped wearing it when she married Dad."

"I agree," said Liv. "That is the obvious answer."

He jabbed the fire with a metal poker. "So if we find the door that the key opens, we open it, and boom—Mack's father will be sitting there and he can tell us why someone might have wanted to kill Mack."

Liv stared at her brother for five silent seconds then said, "Are you being a jerk right now?"

"Yeah, a little," said Gabe. "I don't understand what we're doing. If Mack had a different father than us, he'd be at least sixty-eight years old. Right? And he could be older. A lot older. Maybe he's dead. And what does Mack having a different father, if he did, have to do with Mack's death? I mean, why would it?"

"I don't know," said Liv. "It just seems important, yeah? I've told you something doesn't feel right. Something hasn't been right for a long time. Maybe this key will help us figure out what that something is."

"You think that key is literally the key to our childhood? That would be convenient."

"Stop it!" said Liv. "Stop shitting on this. If you don't want to participate then don't. But don't stomp all over the one little kernel of something we have that might lead to more information. Seriously, Gabe. You can drape a wet blanket over your life but keep it the hell off of mine."

The fire popped and hissed, saving them from dead silence. Gabe poked at it some more though it didn't need poking. The fire didn't need anything, but *he* did. "What does that mean?"

Liv bit her lower lip, shook her head, and said, "Forget it."

"No." Gabe turned away from the fire and looked at Liv. "What does it mean that I've draped a wet blanket over my life?"

"It means," said Liv, "that no one has stopped you from achieving but yourself. You can't get out of your own way. You hold on to lofty ambitions of being an artist, which you keep alive by working low-skilled jobs. It's all just an excuse to not make anything of yourself. And it's that kind of thinking, that kind of 'but what does it all mean?' bullshit that ruins everything. How do you get out of bed in the morning with an attitude like that?"

Headlights swept the room from a distant car. Gabe turned back toward the big fireplace and stirred the logs again. "Or," he said, "maybe I haven't achieved much because I've never recovered from being mentally squashed by my older sister."

"Oh, bullshit. That's just another excuse, Gabe. I didn't mentally squash you."

"Really, Liv? You were a nightmare." Gabe set the poker against the hearth but kept his back toward his sister. "I couldn't do anything right or say anything right. You laughed at me in front of your friends. You left town the second you could and never looked back. Never checked in to see how I was doing. Never gave me another thought. I was like some kind of punching bag you used to hone your skills then you threw me out and moved on. At least Mack was gone from the beginning. You know, you and I were best friends at one time. You've probably forgotten that. We did everything together, running around this resort as if it was our private playground. Fishing and frog catching and tree climbing and skating on the frozen lake. Remember we flew a kite from the rowboat and it pulled us all the way to Oak Point? We had to borrow change to call Dad from a pay phone to pick us up."

He turned back toward Liv and added, "And other days you wouldn't even talk to me. Wouldn't look at me. If you needed a friend, I was there. If you didn't, you pretended I didn't exist. When you were in sixth grade and I was in fifth, Mom dropped us in town to see a movie. You ran into your friends there and ditched me, just left me by myself. Took off with them after the movie and didn't even tell me where you were going. You were like two people: a friend and an enemy. You could be so mean. So damn cruel. Maybe it's true that I'm my own worst enemy . . ." Gabe put another log on the fire. Its bark crackled in the big fireplace. ". . . but I learned it from you."

Liv watched sparks rise up and disappear into the chimney. Her chest tightened, and her eyes stung. "I'm sorry," she said. "I don't know why I was like that. I was a kid, right? I didn't know what I was doing. I wish I'd acted differently. I wish . . . I'm sorry."

Gabe added another log to the fire and said, "I'll take the bed in the far corner."

· CHAPTER 14 ·

Liv and Gabe hardly spoke to one another walking to breakfast. It was their first time seeing the resort in daylight. Snow surrounded splotches of brown, dormant grass. Leafless tree branches appeared black against the bright blue sky. The lake was still frozen, and the ice-out raffle car sat a hundred yards offshore, tethered by a steel cable.

The path passed a once-sacred spot for the Ahlstrom family. Now the family's pet cemetery was a tourist attraction, the old handmade wooden crosses replaced by small, granite tombstones. A group of kids stood and pointed, laughing.

PENNY THE PORTUGUESE WATER DOG 1986–2000
THUMBS THE CAT 1978–1997
ISAAC THE GERBIL BORN 1995–MIA 1996
TIM THE LIGHTNING BUG 10:14 P.M.–7:32 A.M.

Liv stopped well short of the kids and said, "I cried every time we buried a pet. Now our pain is a tourist attraction."

"You want me to say something to them?" said Gabe.

"Like what?"

"Like the pets come alive at night and kill the people who laugh at their tombstones. Even kids. *Especially* kids. That's how our brother, Mack, died. Then we show the kids his urn of ashes and spread a little on the pet cemetery to appease the pet zombies in the hope that they don't come for us. Which they probably won't. Because the pet zombies prefer kids. Kids are easier. Kids are more delicious."

Liv shook her head and laughed. "I don't think Uncle Denny would appreciate you scaring off his clientele. And when did you get so dark?"

"I watch a lot of TV."

"Maybe you should watch less."

The new dining hall overlooked the lake. It looked like a big log cabin on the outside but appeared Vegas-esque on the inside. Round tables surrounded a long buffet. The carpet was a kaleidoscope of color designed to hide spilled coffee and flipped trays of fried walleye. Uniformed servers carried à la carte orders and beverages. A barista stood behind a coffee bar, grinding beans and steaming metal cups of milk. The Outboard Motor Association members buzzed with excitement over scrambled eggs and cinnamon rolls while wearing corporate logo shirts that read *Yamaha*, *Honda*, and *Mercury*.

The siblings scanned the room for an open table. Gabe said, "There's Uncle Denny and Aunt Renee."

They walked over to the table. Renee wore a fresh change of yoga clothes. Denny wore a newly pressed Pendleton plaid of reds and oranges with blue suspenders and had assumed the posture of a king who sits among his people. Gabe said, "Mind if we join you?"

"Hey, there they are," said Uncle Denny. "Please. Renee and I would be honored. And help yourself to the buffet. It's on the house. Just don't tell the uniforms—they'll report me to HQ."

Gabe and Liv went to the buffet and filled their plates with scrambled eggs, fresh fruit, bagels toasted via a conveyor-belt toaster, yogurt, and cinnamon rolls. They returned to the table and sat down.

"Good. You got the cinnamon rolls," said Denny. "House specialty. I eat one a week. One cinnamon roll a week. One beer a night. One meal of red meat per week. One meal of walleye per month—they got those forever chemicals in 'em now. Shouldn't even eat that much. And three miles on the treadmill every day except Saturday. Plus my late-night patrol walks. I bought all sorts of wireless security equipment but I haven't opened one box. I like doing things the old-fashioned way. I'm a man of routines and self-imposed limits. Can't help it. That's just the way I am."

Renee smiled and took Denny's hand. "He's predictable and dependable. Nice qualities in a partner."

A young woman approached the table and said, "So are these my lost-long cousins?"

"Liv and Gabe," said Denny, "this is our daughter, Winona. I think the last time you saw her was at Mack's wedding. She was just a little tyke then. Six or seven."

Gabe and Liv said hello to their first cousin they hadn't seen since she was a young girl. Winona Ahlstrom looked like her mother. She was magazine beautiful. Brown skin, deep dark eyes, a strong chin, and a stout but perfectly proportional nose. She wore a heather-gray PENN sweatshirt and matching sweatpants. Her pin-straight hair was pulled back into a ponytail. Her smile revealed straight, white teeth.

"Good morning, honey," said Renee. "How did studying go last night?"

"Okay." She turned toward Gabe and Liv. "Sorry about Mack."

"Thank you," said Liv. "What are you studying?"

"Business. I'm getting my MBA at Wharton. I always come home for reading-week before finals. There are no distractions around here this time of year. Plus maybe I'll win the ice-out raffle, which is getting so big it's practically start-up money. Is it okay if I join you?"

"Of course," said Gabe. "We apologize for not visiting before."

"No worries," said Winona. "Leech Lake must be a painful place for you, losing your parents when you were so young." She threw a warm smile to each of her cousins and then added, "I'll be right back." Winona left for the buffet.

"She's stunning," said Liv. "And Wharton? She'll do very well."

"Did her undergrad at Cornell—University, not the other Cornell in Iowa—and majored in electrical engineering. No shortage of ability in that one," said Denny. He tucked his thumbs under his suspenders and smiled. "She comes from royal blood on both sides, you know. Renee's great-great-grandfather was Chief at Red Lake, and my grandfather, your great-grandfather, founded Ahlstrom's."

Liv and Gabe laughed.

"What's so funny?"

Liv said, "I don't think you can equate being chief of an Ojibwa tribe with founding a resort."

"Sure, I can. They're both something to be proud of."

Renee smiled and said, "I think what Denny's saying is, Winona comes from strong stock on both sides. We started so late that we were only able to have one child. I thought I'd be a nervous wreck with only one, putting all of our eggs in one basket so to speak, but Winona was such a capable child, I never worried about her. And her future certainly seems bright. She has eleven job offers already."

A man with long dark hair and a scarred face dollied a beer keg with a side-to-side sway to his gait. He said, "The beer delivery is here. You want to sign the invoice, Denny, or should I?"

"You go ahead, Raymond. And hey, there are some people I'd like you to meet. Raymond Lussier, this is my niece and nephew, Liv and Gabe Ahlstrom."

Liv and Gabe said hello and nice to meet you. In response, Raymond lifted his chin but said nothing. Didn't smile. Just looked at them with black eyes.

"Raymond is Renee's baby brother. Been working here for what is it now, eight years?"

"Nine," said Raymond. He took one last look at the siblings then wheeled the keg in the direction of the bar.

"Sorry about Raymond," said Renee. "His social skills aren't always the best."

"Must be nice to have your brother in town," said Gabe.

"It is," said Renee. "Especially when I miss the rest of my family in Minneapolis. And Raymond's had some tough breaks, so I'm glad things are working out for him here."

Winona returned with her breakfast. Fruit, non-dairy yogurt, and oatmeal. She pulled out a chair and sat next to Renee.

"Oh," said Liv. "Before I forget"—Liv removed her mother's skeleton key necklace from her neck—"does this key look familiar to you, Uncle Denny?"

"Sure," said Denny. "It's an old skeleton key. When I was a boy, a lot of locks still used those. They were considered old then, but they worked. They were mostly used for interior doors. You know, to lock a bathroom or bedroom."

"Did the house you grew up in use these?"

"Yep," said Denny. "Most of the old houses did."

"Where did that come from?" said Winona.

"We found it in our mother's jewelry box," said Gabe. "Ed stored all of our family's old things in Cabin 14."

"I know," said Denny. "I keep telling Red Pines corporate I need that space for storage. When they object, I remind them I own fifty-one percent of the resort and what we do with Cabin 14 isn't up to them. Can you believe they want to turn it into a meditation center? We already have yoga and oat milk. Now they want meditation. Isn't that what fishing's for?"

"That's my dad," said Winona. "We'd all be driving a horse and buggy if it were up to him."

"Traditions are meaningful," said Denny. "Generations of families vacation at Ahlstrom's. No need to scare 'em away with a meditation center."

Renee took a grape from her daughter's plate and said, "He's not the old grump he pretends to be." She popped the grape in her mouth then mock whispered, "He wears expensive Tommy John underwear."

"It's comfortable!" said Denny. "A man achieves a certain status in the world, he's earned the right to wear comfortable underwear."

Liv said, "Do you remember my mother wearing this necklace?"

Denny said, "I don't think I do. I was only twelve when Bette married my brother so I didn't pay too much attention. She might have worn it but I didn't notice."

A gaggle of Outboard Motor Association members passed by carrying trays of breakfast and wearing matching Evinrude sweatshirts.

"We never saw her wear this key either," said Liv. "But she's wearing it in a photograph with Ed when she was sixteen. It's so good to see Ed again, and it's very nice of you to let him live here."

"Thank you but nice isn't the word. I'm legally obligated. Mack wrote it into the contract when he sold me the resort. Ed gets to live here for the rest of his life. Even if I sell Ahlstrom's, he's part of the deal. But no complaints here—I'm happy to have him around."

Thirteen retirees walked by carrying their breakfast trays while humming "The Battle Hymn of the Republic," each wearing a yellow windbreaker that read *The Funsters* on the back.

Gabe stifled a laugh and said, "Who are The Funsters?"

"Local club," said Denny. "They're like a gang of teenagers but in old bodies. Mostly they like to snowmobile in the winter, drive around on their ATVs in the summer, stand on their Fourth of July float during the parade, or cruise around the lake on their pontoon boat. Sometimes they host polka dances as fundraisers."

"You didn't get invited to be a Funster?" said Liv.

Denny shook his head. "I don't qualify. You have to be retired and they don't accept anyone under seventy."

Gabe had a hard time taking his eyes off The Funsters as he said, "Denny, do you think someone else could have given that key to our mother? Do you remember if she dated anyone other than our dad back then?"

"I don't think so," said Denny. "Bobby and Bette were together since they were fifteen. My brother didn't let her out of his sight. And who could blame him? Bette was quite the looker."

"What my father is so eloquently trying to say," said Winona, "is that if a woman is attractive, who wouldn't stalk and possess her?" Winona smiled.

"Now don't go twisting my words, Winona. Sheesh, every time I open my mouth around you I'm afraid of getting hauled off by the PC police. All I'm saying is Bobby and I didn't have much in common, but we were both frogs who married princesses."

"Not true," said Renee. "I think you're very handsome."

Winona sighed and shook her head. "Young love."

Denny winked and said, "It's the suspenders."

Gabe and Liv walked back to Cabin 14 after breakfast, the warmth of the April sun on their faces, the paved paths stained wet with melting snow.

"Mom was kind of a babe when she was sixteen," said Liv. "Dark hair and those blue-blue eyes. Long legs and buxom. She must have drawn a lot of unwanted attention."

"What are you saying?"

"I'm saying, wondering actually, if maybe she attracted the wrong kind of boy. Or man. Maybe someone much older than her. And . . . I don't even like to contemplate this but . . ."

A squirrel dug up an acorn and ran off with its treasure.

"You think she might have been raped?" said Gabe.

"It's possible, right?" Liv pushed her hair behind her ears. "And back then, especially if it was a man in power, she might have kept quiet about it. Even if it was just another kid in her class, there was so much shame back then. About everything really. Maybe she got pregnant, and Dad stepped in to help her save face by marrying her."

"You know what you're suggesting?" said Gabe. "That Mack's biological father was a rapist."

"I'm brainstorming here," said Liv. "So let's assume for a minute that's what happened, yeah? And let's also assume that Mom and Dad never told Mack. He just grew up thinking Dad was his biological father. Like we did. But then maybe something happened. Maybe someone who was around back then told Mack the truth."

"Like who?" said Gabe.

A porcupine waddled across the path twenty feet in front of them, its quills brushed straight back as if it had been driving in a convertible.

"I don't know. Someone who knew about the rape somehow. Or what if Mack used one of those ancestry DNA companies and saw that he had a close relative in the Leech Lake area who wasn't Dad and Mack figured it out himself? Could have happened. And Mack contacted the person and asked him about it, but the guy wanted to keep it covered up after all these years, so he killed Mack."

"But if that happened," said Gabe, "Mack would have known who was trying to kill him."

"Yeah-yeah, that's true," said Liv. "But what if the guy pretended to be nice so Mack didn't see him as a threat?"

"It sounds kind of far-fetched," said Gabe.

"I agree. But again, we're just brainstorming. Even if it's a stupid idea, something worthwhile might come from it. Wait a minute. Was that a porcupine that just walked by?"

"Yes."

"Are we safe?" said Liv. "How far can a porcupine shoot its quills?"

"Seriously?" said Gabe.

"What?" said Liv.

"Porcupines can't shoot their quills. That's a myth. How could you not know that?"

Liv felt something she wasn't used to. Embarrassment. Shame. Inferiority. "I don't know. I guess I haven't seen one in twenty years. I forgot. But the quills can stick in you, right?"

"If you touch them," said Gabe, "yes. So don't touch one. And your theory that Mack's father was a rapist and Mack found out about it so the rapist murdered him . . . we'll put that on the list of things that might have happened."

"We have a list of things that might have happened?" said Liv.

"We'll start one," said Gabe. "The last thing I want to do is throw a wet blanket on your ideas."

Their phones dinged. Gabe looked down at his, relieved to see it wasn't another email from Mack. "We just got a text from Andrew Otsby. He came back with his parents and he's inviting us to their house for lunch."

Liv checked her email to see if anything was blowing up at work. Nothing was. She said, "I suppose we should go. Andrew might have more to tell us about Mack. Do you want to text them back and—What's wrong?"

Gabe pointed toward Cabin 14's front door and said, "There's an envelope on our door."

Liv stepped up to the cabin's porch and removed the envelope. "It's blank," she said.

"Open it."

Liv tore open the envelope and removed a single sheet of paper that read:

Leave now. Your lives depend on it.

· CHAPTER 15 ·

"Okay, that's two warnings to leave," said Gabe, stepping into Cabin 14. "One from our dead brother, and the other from the last person on earth who uses a typewriter."

"I'm not afraid of a typewriter," said Liv, right behind him. She shut the door and added, "Or this note. Someone feels threatened by our presence here. And I think that's a good thing. It means we're close. To what I don't know, but we're close."

"I know what we're close to," said Gabe. "Close to getting killed."

The cabin smelled of pine and last night's burned firewood. The morning sun cast crisp lines of light and shadow across the floor. The siblings endured another of their unendurable silences. Liv was about to remind Gabe he was free to leave when they heard a knock on the door. Gabe said, "Who is it?"

"Winona."

Gabe opened the door, and Winona Ahlstrom said, "Do you two have a minute?"

Winona had freed her hair from its ponytail. It fell long and dark and shiny, the way hair does in shampoo commercials featuring people under twenty-five, all of whom have shiny hair even if they wash their hair in dish soap. She stepped into the cabin and said, "I've never been in here." Winona sat in a teak chair with blue cushions and added, "This furniture must be worth a fortune."

"I know, right?" said Liv. "It belongs to your family. But if you don't want it, we'll buy it."

"Interesting you should say that because that's kind of what I want to talk to you about."

"Furniture?"

"No," said Winona. "The future of the resort."

Gabe looked to Liv to see if she knew what Winona was talking about, but Liv just shrugged. They moved into the living area and sat on opposite sides of the couch. "We have nothing to do with the future of the resort," said Gabe. "Your dad bought it when I graduated from high school."

"Yes, but have you seen the purchase agreement?"

"No," said Liv. "I assume it's a standard real estate transaction."

"Hardly," said Winona. She brought her hair over one shoulder, removed an elastic hair band from her wrist, and bunched it back into a ponytail. "And that's not unusual when one family member sells to another family member. Like with the Ed clause. Him getting to live in his little cabin for the rest of his life is atypical of most real estate deals but that kind of thing is fairly common in family-to-family deals."

"Do you have a problem with Ed living here?" said Liv.

"Not at all. Ed's wonderful. He's like a grandfather to me. He took me fishing. He fixed my bike. Made kites for me. I hope he lives here forever. I want to talk to you about another clause in the contract. A clause that could affect my future."

Gabe and Liv shared a look. Gabe said, "What clause is that?" He felt quite comfortable in the cabin and realized how much he'd missed this kind of place. Simple. Bucolic. Made from the very things found on the grounds on which it was built.

Winona crossed her legs and said, "Did you know my father can't sell the resort without giving you first right of refusal?"

"No," said Liv. "We had no idea."

"Nor can he give up controlling interest without offering it to you. So I'd like to know what your intentions are."

"Our intentions?" said Gabe. "I don't think we have any intentions."

A woodpecker hammered away on the cabin's exterior. Neither Gabe nor Liv nor Winona flinched. It was like hearing a siren in New York City or a car with oversized subwoofers in LA. It was part of the natural soundscape.

"Then let me tell you about my intentions," said Winona. "My MBA thesis explores low-wattage, independent power stations that serve rural communities. The power stations liberate those communities from the grid, where cities take the bulk of the power, and where tens and even hundreds of miles of power lines are required to transmit that power out to rural areas. Those power lines are terribly inefficient—a large percentage of power is lost in the process. And they're ugly. And the source of that electricity still relies heavily on fossil fuels. My power stations would generate electricity solely by wind and solar, there'd be almost no loss in transmission, and local communities would own the stations. The short of it is, rural residents' power bills would be cut in half, and their energy would be clean, sustainable, and renewable."

"And how would you make money?" said Gabe.

"Building the power stations. The concept would be profitable for me, profitable for rural communities, and money-saving for those living in rural communities. The only losers in the deal are the legacy power companies."

Liv said, "That sounds wonderful."

"Thank you. I agree. But my father does not."

"So what? What does it matter what he thinks? Unless you want to use the resort as the site for the power station."

The woodpecker stopped its hammering.

"Well, yes, actually," said Winona, "I do. One great unique thing about Ahlstrom's, as opposed to most resorts, is our great-grandfather had the foresight to buy the land surrounding the resort so no one could build another resort or homes or anything near it. It's part of the place's charm. It also makes the property quite a large parcel, and perfect for both a wind and solar farm. But you heard my father at breakfast. He doesn't like change. He values tradition. He has no objection to the idea of the power station, but he has no interest in razing the resort to locate it here."

Gabe felt a chill on the back of his neck. "You want to raze the resort where we grew up?" he said. "Where we learned to fish and climb trees and chase lightning bugs and ride bikes and—"

"I know there's an emotional element," said Winona, "but—"

"An emotional element?" said Liv. She could feel herself going into business mode. Her back straightened. Her shoulders tensed. "More like an emotional foundation. And not just for us. You want to raze a resort hundreds of thousands of people have come to for almost a century."

A Northwoods silence filled the room, a silence that is never truly silent. Birds chirped outside. Wind rushed through the pines. Branches brushed against the single-pane windows.

"Again," said Winona, "I know lots of people have emotional ties to this place. Especially you. And especially me—I grew up here, too. But there are tons of resorts around here. Tons of places where memories can be made. And I'm offering a practical and ecologically friendly solution to support the people who live and work here year-round. That way people from all over the world can continue to visit and enjoy this part of the world."

"Okay," said Liv. "I hear you. That makes sense, from one point of view anyway. So what are you proposing?"

"If my father sells his fifty-one percent, I'm hoping you'll pass on your option to buy it. Then I can buy the resort."

Liv said, "Does your father want to sell? He's what, sixty-three years old? He doesn't seem like he's wanting to retire anytime soon. And he looks to me like he's in his element here."

"He doesn't want to sell," Winona said. "Not yet. But my mother really wants to move back to Minneapolis to be near my grandparents. She moved here for my dad, now she wants him to return the favor. That's why I'm here. If my dad sells, he has to offer the resort to you first. That's the way Mack set it up. All three of you had to agree unless one was deceased, of course. Again, sorry about Mack. He was a good guy."

"How well did you know Mack?" said Liv.

"Not well. But he visited a few times. He wasn't the stranger you two have been."

Gabe crossed his arms over his chest and said, "Doesn't your dad's corporate partner have the next option to buy if we pass?"

"No. Red Pines is third on the list. When my father bought Ahlstrom's from Mack, Mack insisted that if he sold, you three had the first option. I was a kid then, and my dad thought if your family wanted the option to keep Ahlstrom's in the family, then I should have the option to keep Ahlstrom's in the family. It's an odd contract."

"Maybe it's odd," said Gabe, "but the contract stipulates that Ed can live here for the rest of his life. How would that happen if Ahlstrom's was razed to build a power plant?"

"I'd honor the contract, of course," said Winona. "Ed would continue to live in his cabin and he'd continue on as groundskeeper."

Liv felt her guard go up. "But without all the people around?" she said. "Ed would be living here without Denny. Without the dogs. Without the guests."

"Well . . . ," admitted Winona. "Yes. Not nearly as many people."

Gabe shook his head. He, too, felt he was making up for lost time when it came to Ed. "And is it even safe to live near all that electricity? I don't like it, Winona. I think you should build your power plant on some other piece of land."

"I've been looking," said Winona. "But Judith Otsby has bought up everything. She's trying to surround this place and choke us out. But if it were to become a power plant, her whole plan would backfire."

"Fifty-one percent of Ahlstrom's must be worth millions," said Liv. "Even with the family discount. You can afford that?"

"I have VC and private equity people interested," said Winona. "I'm confident I can raise the money. And fifty-one percent means Red Pines has no say. They're a hospitality company. Not a power company. They'll probably want out and then I'll own the land free and clear." Winona challenged Gabe and Liv with her dark eyes. She had the confidence of youth that's rewarded in the academic world and untested in the real world.

Gabe met his cousin's gaze, refusing to look away, and remembered when he was eight years old, when he and two friends set out to catch one hundred frogs. They each carried a bucket as they traipsed through the slough stalking frogs that were seemingly painted in green and brown camouflage. It took all day, but by dinnertime, the boys had caught 137 frogs. It's the kind of thing they would have Instagrammed had Instagram existed back then. Then they dumped their buckets, and the frogs hopped away in all directions. It was an accomplishment of no significance other than thirty years after the fact, Gabe remembered it as if it had happened yesterday. Finally, he said, "I don't know, Winona. I'm not inclined to sign the death warrant on this place."

· CHAPTER 16 ·

"Do you still want to leave?" said Liv.

"I don't know," said Gabe, sitting in the Tahoe's passenger seat as Liv drove a black road through a white birch tree forest, the trunks bold and bright even under a cloud-gray sky. "I'm starting to feel a bit territorial. Someone's trying to scare us away. Winona wants to demolish our childhood home to build a power plant. Kind of makes me feel like staying and fighting."

Liv smiled. "I knew you had it in you."

Gabe noticed a dead raccoon on the side of the road and said, "And it's weird Winona knew Mack, isn't it?" said Gabe.

"It's not so weird Winona knew him, but that we didn't know that Winona knew him. But that's our fault. We're the ones who haven't come back. We're the ones who made no effort to see Winona since she was a little kid."

Gabe knew Liv was right and it pained him. "Winona's power plant is a nice idea," said Gabe. "I agree it would benefit the community, but I think Denny would want the resort to continue as a resort even if he doesn't own it rather than have it all torn down to make room for solar and wind farms. Or at least that's what I want."

"So do I," said Liv. "I'm all for Winona's power plant—there has to be another location she can make work."

The sun emerged from behind a cloud and bounced off the pavement, wet with melted snow. Now the birch trees looked neon against the dark pines behind them. Liv reached into the center console, fetched her sunglasses, and put them on. "Wow. Heat wave. Sixty-two degrees on the dash. And I've counted three dead raccoons since we left the resort. I thought raccoons were supposed to be smart."

"Well," said Gabe, "you know the old joke. Why did the chicken cross the road? To show the raccoon it could be done."

Liv laughed as she started up the driveway toward a lake mansion. John and Judith Otsby no longer lived at their resort. They'd built a colossus on a piece of lakefront property south of Otsby's. The house didn't fit the lake resort theme. White clapboard siding, white pillars out front, and a porch that jutted out around the entire building. It had black shutters and a third story under a red roof topped with a widow's walk. It looked like it belonged in *Gone with the Wind* far more than *Fargo*.

"No lawn jockey," said Gabe. "I'm surprised."

"Judith probably stores it until summer," said Liv, knocking a brass knocker on a door painted gloss black with heavy brushstrokes as if the home had been built in 1820 rather than 2020.

Andrew answered the door and said, "Please excuse the hammering and sawing. They're working in back to make the house wheelchair accessible. My mother has taken a few tumbles. She'll be safer in a chair. And be warned. She's in a particularly bad mood today."

"I live in New York," said Liv. "A difficult Minnesotan in a foul mood is your average maître d'."

"I live in Los Angeles," said Gabe. "We call them producers."

Andrew led the siblings into the dining room, which, like the home's exterior, was dripping with antebellum charm. That is, if you lived in Savannah or Charleston. In northern Minnesota, it felt out of place. A platter of sandwiches rested on the table. Turkey. Tuna. Roast beef. All on white bread. A squeeze bottle of mustard. Another of mayonnaise. A third of nuclear green relish. Sliced tomatoes, lettuce, and an assortment of Kraft singles, individually wrapped. A separate tray held cans of Coke, Diet Coke, Sprite, and bottles of water. Judith Otsby and her husband, John, were already seated, a paper cup filled with a dozen of Judith's pills between them.

"Gabe and Liv are here!" said John. "So nice to see you both! Help yourself, everyone, and dig in!"

"The Ahlstroms have arrived," said Judith Otsby, taking a roast beef sandwich. "Back after twenty years of living abroad. That's what I call Los Angeles and New York. Foreign countries because if you haven't noticed, lots of foreigners live there. So, Ahlstroms, how do you like your old family resort now?"

Judith sat at the head of the table wearing a loud floral print, pink flowers on a field of black. Her nasal tube led to John, who sat around the corner next to her oxygen tank.

"Ahlstrom's has changed," said Gabe. "A lot."

"I didn't ask if it's changed," said Judith. "I know it's changed. I asked how you like it?"

"Not so much," said Liv. "Ahlstrom's has lost its up-north feel. Seems more like a resort that could be anywhere."

"Ah," said Judith, "you're one of those. You get to go off to New York City and your life changes in all sorts of big and marvelous ways, but we little peons back in northern Minnesota don't get to change. We have to remain in some kind of arrested state so you can feel nostalgic about your idealized memories. Well, I'll tell you something, Ahlstroms, we get to change, too. We get to grow with the world even though we still live in Minnie-snow-dah. I knew people in my parents' generation who moved away and came back to visit. They complained about running water and forced air heat. Not the same as it used to be, they said. Well, no shit. We like comfort, too."

Judith passed the tray of sandwiches to Andrew.

"Mother," said Andrew. "Be nice."

Andrew, Gabe, and Liv sat down at the table as the tray came their way.

"Truth and nice don't always go together, Andy. You're fifty years old—you should know that by now."

"If you're not comfortable at Ahlstrom's," said John, "you're welcome to stay here. Judith and I moved down to the first floor. It's better if she doesn't have to negotiate the stairs. That leaves the entire master suite vacant on the second story."

"People don't say master suite anymore, Dad," said Andrew. "It's owner's suite. Master is a reference to slavery."

Judith Otsby hammered the table with her plump fist. "Oh for Christ's sake," she said. "The list of things we can't say is longer than the list of things we can say. It's a goddamn master suite. It's not about slaves. It's about who owns the house. Master of the house. Nothing wrong with that unless we can't own inanimate objects now. You're tearing away our social fabric and leaving us nothing to hang on to. I swear, sometimes I think my poor health is my soul's way of telling me to get out while the getting's good. No reason to stick around for the shit show people call a kinder, gentler society."

"Honey," said John, "Gabe and Liv are our guests. They're here for lunch. Maybe go easy on the language."

"Eh," said Judith.

The doorbell rang. Andrew excused himself from the table to answer it. He looked relieved to get out of the dining room.

Liv struggled to unwrap a single slice of cheese. "It sounds like we'll have quite a few people at the memorial tomorrow," she said. "Denny's going to put out a big spread."

"And it will be great to see some familiar faces at Ahlstrom's," said Gabe, who had just attempted to put mustard on his sandwich and instead doused it in yellowish water. "And we've reconnected with our cousin, Winona. Hadn't seen her since she was a kid but she's grown into a very impressive young woman."

"Watch out for that one," said Judith.

"Because?" said Liv.

"I hear she's all over the County Land Use bureaucrats. Asking all sorts of questions about zoning and eminent domain and—"

"Mother," said Andrew, "Tyler Luther is here to see you. He says it's important."

Judith took a deep breath and said, "Get the hell in here, Tyler!"

All heads turned toward the entrance. Tyler Luther looked twenty-five years old. He wore a sweater vest over a white shirt and tie with khaki pants—all no-iron wash and wear. He had a vestige of hockey hair, blond and unkempt, a tad too short in the front and too long in the back.

"Sorry to interrupt your lunch," he said, carrying a manila folder, "but it's important you sign these documents asap. The other party would like to close the deal by three o'clock today."

"John," said Judith, "get my lucky pen."

John sprung up from the table and disappeared into the kitchen. Liv tried to inconspicuously spit out a piece of plastic wrapping that had stuck to her cheese. Andrew cleared his throat and said, "Tyler, these are our dear friends, Liv and Gabe Ahlstrom. They grew up at Ahlstrom's and are in town for their brother Mack's memorial service." Andrew looked at Liv and Gabe. "Tyler is Mother's lawyer."

"Oh hey," said Tyler. "Nice to meet you." His eyes dropped and he added, "And sorry for your loss."

"Thank you," said Liv, the piece of plastic wrapping now on her lap. "Did you grow up in the Leech Lake area?"

"Yeah. My whole life."

"Where did you go to law school?"

"It doesn't matter where Tyler went to law school," said Judith. "What matters is Tyler does what I tell him."

The kitchen door swung open and John entered carrying a red Montblanc pen. He handed it to Judith, and she popped off the

cap. Tyler set the documents before her, each labeled with SIGN
HERE Post-its, and Judith scratched her signature six times.

"Thank you," said Tyler, scooping up the documents. "I'll call
as soon as the other party signs." He smiled awkwardly and then
exited the room.

"Are you buying another resort?" said Gabe.

"Ha!" said Judith. "Maybe I am. Grow or die. That's the Otsby
motto. Growth offers peace of mind. Your uncle Denny's got all
his chickens in one coop. One lawsuit, one hostile takeover, and
he's out of business."

"There can't be a hostile takeover," said Liv. "Ahlstrom's Resort
is a privately held company."

"I know what Ahlstrom's is," said Judith. "Denny owns a controlling interest along with Red Pines's minority participation,
and he can't sell it without your and Gabe's permission." She
smiled, unaware that a smear of mayo streaked her chin. "Needed
Mack's permission, too, but he's no longer in the picture. My condolences, again." Judith coughed, and a speck of roast beef landed
in the middle of the table. Liv saw it and suppressed both laughter
and the urge to vomit.

"Judith," said John, "I'm sure we can find a more pleasant topic
of conversation."

"Pipe down, John," said Judith, chipmunking a quarter of a
sandwich in one cheek. "We're talking business. And you got some
mayo on that damn beard of yours. When are you going to shave
off that rat's nest?"

John's pale cheeks reddened. He did not mention the mayo
on Judith's chin. "I've told you, honey, I'll shave it off when the
weather gets warmer."

"It's sixty-something degrees out. How warm do you need it?"

"I'd like it to be a little warmer yet," said John.

"Beards," said Judith. "Any woman who says she likes them is
lying."

"I don't mind a man's beard," said Andrew.

"Andy. Please. Keep your private life to yourself. I hated Bill Clinton, but his Don't Ask, Don't Tell malarkey is starting to sound pretty damn good."

Andrew smiled and said, "She's the only mother I have."

Judith chomped some chips and kept her eyes on her plate. John offered his son a warm smile. Judith then swallowed and looked up at Gabe and Liv, as if Andrew had said nothing. "To answer your question, Gabe, I did buy another resort, at least partially. And I might as well tell you because you'll hear about it soon enough." She threw the cupful of pills into her mouth, dry-swallowed them, and added, "I just purchased Red Pines, your uncle's corporate partner."

· CHAPTER 17 ·

"Denny is going to lose his shit," said Liv as they drove into town to pick up groceries for Cabin 14. "Can you imagine having Judith Otsby as your business partner? She'll make his life miserable."

"It's a problem of his own making," said Gabe. "Denny never should have sold forty-nine percent to Red Pines. I don't know how big that company is, but I bet they'll soon have their hands in a lot of resorts now that Judith is at the helm. The question is, should we be the ones to tell Denny or just let him find out from Red Pines?"

"I don't know," said Liv. "I think—" Liv's phone rang. Cooper's name appeared on the Tahoe's touchscreen. "Sorry. I'm going to take this." She pushed the button on the steering wheel to answer the call on Bluetooth. "Hi, honey."

Cooper didn't respond.

"Cooper?"

They heard a horn honk through the car's speakers. And then a truck rumble by.

"Cooper? Are you there?"

"Hey, man, looking good," said a voice that was not Cooper's. Distant and muffled. "Want to feel even better? I can make that happen. Fifty bucks with no government taxes jacking up the price of prime weed."

"Not today," said Cooper, also distant. "Have a good one."

"God bless, brother."

"Butt dial?" said Gabe.

"He's walking home from Wall Street," said Liv. "I think he's in City Hall Park." They heard more voices and then a busker singing John Lennon's "Imagine," and then a bicycle bell. Liv touched the steering wheel and ended the call. "Sounds of lower Manhattan."

Gabe watched Liv grip the wheel so tightly he heard a faint squeak. "You all right?" he said.

"I think so," said Liv. "I suppose a butt dial from my husband is better than no call at all, yeah? At least I'm still in his contacts."

Seeing the town of Birchwood for the first time in full daylight, it seemed even more had changed. The water tower was painted like a fishing bobber. A shed-sized building sat under a sign that read TOURIST INFORMATION. The old fire station had been replaced by a Walgreens and a new fire station had been built halfway down the block. Liv pulled into the parking lot for the Super One and said, "Is that an EV charger? You got to be kidding me."

Inside, the supermarket had, like most supermarkets, white, almost blue, shadowless light. It was bright and public and about as safe-feeling as you could get, but both siblings kept their eyes open since receiving the typewritten note on their door telling them to:

Leave now. Your lives depend on it.

"What did Mack know that he didn't tell us?" Liv pushed the shopping cart down an aisle in the Super One.

Gabe grabbed a bear of honey and placed it in the cart. "Remember Diana said Mack talked about our family being broken? I think if he knew what broke it, he would have told us. Or he would have told Diana. He did tell her he had a different father. That could be the extent of it. Okay, we need coffee, tea, lemon, cereal, bread, and a trip to the liquor store."

They rounded the corner toward the produce section when a shopper approached from the opposite direction. He did not stop until the end of his cart bumped the end of theirs. He stared at

Liv and Gabe with onyx eyes. "Why are you here?" said Raymond Lussier, whom Gabe and Liv had met in the dining hall when Raymond wheeled a keg of beer by their table. Raymond's long dark hair fell straight, and his scars shined under the supermarket lights.

"To buy food," said Liv. "That's what supermarkets are for. Next we're going to the liquor store. Guess what we're going to buy there."

Gabe questioned Liv's tone and choice of words. If it was Raymond who stuck that note on their door, they might not want to aggravate him no matter how bright the lighting. And Gabe's concern seemed justified because Raymond Lussier didn't smile, didn't blink, and, it seemed, didn't breathe until he said, "Why have you come back to Ahlstrom's?"

"We grew up here," said Liv. "Our last name is Ahlstrom. Our older brother just died. Not that we need a reason . . ."

"You're not wanted at the resort."

Gabe took a more conciliatory tone. "If Denny asks us to leave, we'll leave," he said. "Do you have a problem with us?"

"Yeah, I do," said Raymond. "You don't respect Leech Lake. You don't care about the land. You don't care about the town of Birchwood. And you don't care about the people who live here."

"None of that is true," said Liv. "And thank you for your condolences about Mack. It was a pleasure running into you again."

Raymond Lussier stared at Gabe and Liv with a stillness that shook their souls. After what felt like half a minute, he pulled his cart back, steered around them, and continued in the other direction, his side-to-side gait swaying his hair like a clock's pendulum.

"Sweet guy," said Liv.

"He's my new best friend," said Gabe.

Liv opened another cardboard box in Cabin 14. This one held old sports equipment: ice skates, hockey pucks and gloves, baseball mitts, and a couple of Frisbees. "Do you think Raymond put that note on our door?"

Gabe sliced a new box and opened the cardboard flaps. "Maybe. He works at the resort so he has access. Also seems like the kind of guy who would have an old typewriter lying around." Gabe pulled out pots and pans. "Why did Ed save these?"

"Ed saved everything. The last box I opened had towels in it. Towels. From 1990. So gross." Liv keyed open another box and said, "I bet Raymond knows that if Denny sells the resort, he has to offer it to us first. I mean, his sister is married to Denny, right? Maybe he's trying to scare us off so Denny will sell to the next in line, Winona. I'm sure he thinks his niece wouldn't kick him to the curb, and it sounds like working here helped Raymond turn his life around. Maybe—" They heard a knock on the door. "Who is it?"

"Ed."

"Come in," said Gabe.

The door opened and Ed entered. He wore a flannel shirt and no jacket. "Hi, Gabe. Hi, Liv. Do you need more firewood?"

"Sure, Ed," said Gabe. "Thank you. And let me give you a hand." Gabe stood and followed Ed out the front door. A few seconds later, Ed and Gabe returned, each with an armful of logs. They carried them to the hearth, knelt, and set them down.

Ed stacked them on the pile and said, "Don't know how much you'll need. Still pretty warm outside. I'd say spring's coming, but whenever I think that, it snows. Don't know how the weather knows what I'm thinking."

Liv smiled. She loved Ed's outlook on life. "I don't think it's your fault, Ed," said Liv. "Once it snowed in June."

"Don't I know it," said Ed. "I remember. We had the snow-blower all emptied of gas and oil. I had to shovel everything by hand. Took all day. My back was sore for a week."

Gabe caught Liv's eye and pointed to his neck. Liv understood her brother's silent suggestion and said, "Ed. Do you remember seeing this key before?"

Ed stacked the last log on the pile, stood, and walked toward Liv, who held the key out from her neck. He studied it for a moment then said, "Oh, sure. Bette used to wear it around her neck just like you are now."

"That was a long time ago. You remember that?"

"Uh-huh. She wore it in that picture I brought over. She wore it every day. And then she stopped wearing it."

"Did she ever tell you why she stopped wearing it?"

"No," said Ed. "She never did."

Gabe brushed wood debris from his shirt onto the hearth and said, "Did she tell you what the key was for? Did it open a lock?"

"Oh, sure. It's a key. Keys open locks."

"Do you know which lock, Ed? Was it the house she grew up in?"

"Oh, no. Not a house." Ed pulled a brush and dustpan from the fireplace set and swept the hearth. "That key is for a lock on a box."

"Let me do that," said Liv, taking the brush and dustpan from Ed. "Do you mean like a padlock?"

"Yep. A padlock. That's what it's for."

Liv dumped the debris into the fireplace. "A padlock from 1900? Not exactly a fortress of security."

"Maybe it wasn't for security," said Gabe. "Maybe the lock and key were just decorative."

"Decorative?" said Ed. He folded his arms across his chest, and his eyebrows scrunched toward one another.

"For decoration," said Gabe. "For how it looked. Like a piece of jewelry. Just how Mom wore the key."

"No," said Ed.

"No?"

"The key is for a lock on a box that holds secrets."

Liv stood. "Secrets? Bette told you that?"

"Yes," said Ed. "The lock is for a box that holds secrets."

Gabe looked at his sister then swiveled his eyes toward Ed. "What kind of box?" said Gabe.

"A pirate box."

Gabe and Liv looked at each other again. Liv said, "Like a treasure chest?"

"Yes," said Ed. "That key is for a treasure chest."

Gabe went to the refrigerator and said, "Want a Coke, Ed? I got the tiny cans. I remember you used to like those."

"Oh, sure," said Ed. "I still like 'em. Thanks, Gabe."

Gabe popped the top on an eight-ounce can of Coke, handed it to Ed, and said, "I don't remember seeing any kind of treasure chest when we were growing up."

"Me either," said Liv. "Ed, do you know where the chest is?"

Ed sipped the Coke and said, "Ahhhhhh," the way he'd seen people do in commercials decades ago. "Oh, sure. I know where the chest is."

Liv walked toward Ed, and said, "Would you please tell us, Ed? Where's the chest?"

"It's a secret," said Ed. Sip. "Ahhhhhh. I'm not supposed to tell anyone."

Another knock on the door. "Shit," said Liv.

"That's a bad word," said Ed.

"I know. You're right. I'm sorry. I'm just frustrated." Liv turned toward the door and called out, "We don't need housekeeping."

"I'm not housekeeping," said a voice from the other side of the door.

"It's Winona," said Gabe. He sighed, went to the door, and opened it.

Winona walked in with the golden retrievers and said, "There's been a development you need to know about—Oh, hey Ed. I didn't know you were here." The dogs ran to Ed, and he knelt to pet them.

"I brought more wood," said Ed.

"Thank you. I'm sure Liv and Gabe appreciate it."

"And Gabe gave me a Coke."

"That's nice," said Winona. "Ed, may I please talk to Liv and Gabe in private?"

"Oh. You want me to leave."

"I'm sorry," said Winona.

"Okay, I can—"

"No," said Liv. "Winona. We'll join you for dinner. We can talk then."

"Ahhhhh," said Ed.

"I'm not comfortable talking in the dining hall," said Winona. "Meet you in the bar at five? My father will be setting up the bonfire then."

Gabe and Liv agreed. Winona nodded, called the dogs, then left. Gabe went to the window to make sure she was out of earshot then turned back and said, "Ed, I know Bette told you to keep the treasure chest a secret. But we're her children. Little Gabe and Little Liv. She'd want us to know where it is."

Ed turned from Gabe to Liv with questioning eyes.

"Gabe's right," said Liv. "Bette would want us to know. Because we're her children and she loved us, right? Bette wouldn't want to keep a secret from her children." The strain on Ed's face remained. Liv added, "Did Bette tell you to keep her secret from me and Gabe? Did she say never let Liv or Gabe see the treasure chest?"

Ed shook his head.

"She only wanted it kept secret from other people, Ed. Bette was our mother—she shared everything with us." That wasn't true, of course. If Bette had wanted to tell Gabe and Liv about the chest, she'd had plenty of opportunity. She'd kept the secret of Mack's father, as well. But Liv hoped Ed was more focused on the present than the past.

Ed nodded. "Bette loved her children."

"That's right," said Gabe.

"Mothers are supposed to love their children," said Ed. "People mothers and animal mothers."

"Yes," said Gabe.

"That's why you should never go near a baby bear." Sip. "Ahhhhhh. The mother will protect it."

"Like Bette protected us," said Liv. "Where's the treasure chest, Ed?"

· CHAPTER 18 ·

They traipsed through the forest over a path that looked like a game trail, unpaved and only wide enough for single-file traffic. It was a ten-minute walk to Ed Lindimier's cabin that sat nestled in the woods behind the resort, the woods Gabe and Liv's great-grandfather had had the foresight to purchase along with the original resort property.

The cabin itself was tiny. Ed had a twin extra-long bed, a nightstand made of a throw blanket over a crate, a two-burner stove that ran off an external propane tank, a vintage farmhouse sink with a built-in washboard, a Formica dining table with one chair, and a stone fireplace. There was a loveseat and an old CRT television topped with an aerial antenna in front of a wingback chair and ottoman. Two naked lightbulbs were mounted in the overhead rafters. A radio sat on the windowsill. Ed's bathroom included a toilet and, next to it, a shower just big enough to stand in. The cabin was paneled in knotty pine, had pine plank floors and a small closet. The entire place looked immaculate and smelled faintly of ammonia.

"Ed," said Liv, "do you realize that I've never been in your cabin?"

"I don't get visitors," said Ed.

"It's very nice," said Gabe. "Cozy and clean. I like it. Who ran the pipe all the way out for running water?"

"Bobby did. When they tore down the old school in town, it was full of copper pipes. Bobby brought them here and dug a trench with a machine so the pipes wouldn't freeze in winter and connected them so I'd have running water because cleanliness is next to godliness," said Ed. "I love it here. I don't want to live anywhere else. Ever."

"You won't have to," said Liv. "It's in a contract. This is your home for the rest of your life."

Ed smiled.

"Is the treasure chest in the closet?" said Gabe.

Ed shook his head. He walked to his bed, sat down, removed the lamp from the nightstand, and took off the throw blanket. The crate was not a crate but a square chest secured with two hasps and two padlocks, each appearing to be over a hundred years old.

"May I open it?" said Liv.

"Bette would want you to," said Ed. "You're her child and mothers love their children."

"That's right, Ed. Thank you." Liv walked to the nightstand, knelt, and removed her necklace. She inserted the key into the left lock, twisted it, and the lock popped open. She looked at Gabe with raised eyebrows. Liv removed the lock from the hasp, set it on the floor, and inserted the key into the lock on the right hasp. She twisted, but it wouldn't turn. She jiggled it and tried again, but again it wouldn't turn.

"What's wrong?" said Gabe.

"It's stuck."

"No," said Ed. "It's not stuck. That lock needs a different key."

Liv's head dropped.

"Maybe we'll find the other key in the boxes back in Cabin 14," said Gabe. "That's where we found the first key."

"It'd be quicker to get a bolt cutter, right?" said Liv. "Ed, do we have a bolt cutter in the toolshed?"

"Oh, sure," said Ed. "We have a bolt cutter. I used to cut the bolts on the dock when they got rusty."

"Could you please get it?"

"Oh, sure," said Ed. "I could get it. But if you want, I can give you the other key."

Liv laughed. "You have the other key? Why didn't you say so?"

"You didn't ask if I had it."

"Ed," said Liv, "do you have the other key?"

"Oh, sure." Ed went to his tiny kitchen, opened a cupboard, and removed a cardboard cylinder of Quaker Oats. "There's not oatmeal in here. It's a trick." Ed popped the lid off and pulled out a key that looked like Bette's key.

"That's a good trick, Ed," said Gabe.

Ed smiled. "Yeah. No one ever found it." Ed handed the key to Liv, who inserted it in the padlock on the right and turned. The lock popped open.

Gabe felt his pulse quicken. Half an hour ago, he didn't know his mother had kept a locked, secret chest. Now he was about to see what was inside. Liv was right, he thought, you never know what you'll discover if you persevere. Mack's last email and the note on the door made Gabe want to quit. But he didn't quit and now he was about to reap the reward.

Liv removed the lock from the hasp and opened the chest. "Holy sh . . ." Liv caught Ed's eye and said, ". . . sheepers creepers."

Gabe stood over her and stared at the chest's contents. A half-empty bottle of Hennessy X.O cognac. A pink camisole. Dried purple flowers. A bottle of Crabtree & Evelyn Lily of the Valley perfume. And a bundle of letters in their cut-open envelopes bound together by a pink ribbon.

"It's like a love kit," said Gabe.

"Something like that," said Liv. She looked over at Ed, who kept his distance from the chest. "Ed, did you know what was in here?"

Ed shook his head. "No. I never looked inside the chest before."

"So you never opened it?"

"No," said Ed, "I only had one key."

"You must have known where the other one was," said Liv.

"I didn't look in Bette's private things. I don't look in people's private things. That would be bad. I'm not bad."

"Of course you're not bad," said Liv.

"We know you don't do bad things," said Gabe. "We're just curious who else knows what's in this chest."

"No one knows," said Ed. "Only Bette did. She gave me one key because she said it was safer if she had one and I had one. But I never opened it. That would be bad. I am not bad."

"You're very good, Ed. Did you ever see any of these things before Bette put them in the chest? Way back a long time ago before Liv and I were born?"

"No," said Ed. "I've never seen any of those things before. Sometimes I see purple flowers like that in the woods or the meadow. But they're in the ground and alive. Not dead."

Gabe looked at Liv and then back at Ed. "Can we take this chest back to Cabin 14, Ed? Would that be okay with you?"

Ed nodded. "I didn't look inside. I don't do bad things."

"We know, Ed." Liv shut the box. "You're very good."

"I'll get it," said Gabe, who squatted and lifted the box by its leather end handles. "We have to find you a new nightstand, Ed."

"There's a wooden box in the storage shed. It used to hold lawn darts, but we don't have those anymore. They're dangerous and we shouldn't play with dangerous toys."

Liv and Gabe looked at each other. They had no idea what lawn darts were. "Okay," said Liv. "We'll take this if you're sure it's all right with you."

"Bette would want her children to have it. Mothers are supposed to love their children."

"Ed," said Liv. "Is it okay if I hug you?"

"Oh, sure."

Gabe had to set the box down three times to rest on his walk back to Cabin 14. It was still above sixty degrees. The clouds had moved in, blanketing northern Minnesota in the day's warmth. Gabe put the chest on the kitchen table, opened it, removed the bundle of letters, and said, "You ready for this?"

Liv took the bundle, untied the pink ribbon, and removed one opened envelope from the bunch. She pulled out the letter inside. Her hand trembled. She looked at it and said, "It's a love letter."

"In Mom's handwriting?"

Liv shook her head. "It's typed. It's to Mom. Not from her."

"Typed or printed from a computer?"

"Definitely typed. Some letters are darker than others and they're not all even."

"Is it from Dad?"

"I'm not sure. What do you think?" Liv handed the letter to Gabe.

He read the letter then reread it and said, "Why would someone type a love letter in 1969 or whenever it was? Why not write it by hand?"

"To hide their identity," said Liv. She set the letter on the table. "That's why it isn't dated. No return address on the envelope. Or postmark. It must have been hand-delivered. And the signature is just a typed *Your Q*."

Gabe pulled out a chair and sat at the table. "Hardly anyone's name starts with a Q. There's Quentin, there's . . . that's all I can think of."

"Maybe it was a nickname," said Liv. "Or maybe it stands for Queen."

"A woman was in love with Mom?"

Liv shrugged.

"But a woman couldn't have been Mack's father."

"True," said Liv. She opened another envelope, removed the letter inside it, and read. "Same stuff. *Dearest Bette . . . I miss you . . . I can't wait to be with you again . . . I dream of you . . . I hate this ocean between us . . . Be my wife and I will walk away from everything for you . . . Just be my wife. I love you with all my heart. Your Q.*"

Gabe interlocked his fingers behind his head and sighed. "So either these are from Dad, or Mom was seeing someone else. Or these letters could be from someone before Dad."

"When Mom was fifteen?" said Liv. "People didn't get married at fifteen years old. Not in 1971. It probably wasn't even legal, right?" She shook her head. The great chest that promised to answer so many questions seemed to be asking more than it answered.

"I don't know," said Gabe. "I think we'll have to read them all to see if there's any revealing information. There must be over a hundred letters in the bundle."

Liv sat across the table from Gabe. "We have an hour before we have to meet Winona at the bar, yeah? Want to make a dent?"

Gabe and Liv began to read, each taking one letter at a time, each blurting out "nothing new" or "same old" every few minutes. But just after four thirty, Gabe said, "Here's something. Wow."

"What?"

"*Are you really going to let Bobby believe our child is his?*"

"That's it," said Liv. She stood and walked around the table to read over Gabe's shoulder. "That's Mack's biological father. It has to be, right?"

"*Leave him, Bette. Let's take our child and build a new life. I hate this ocean between us. Let's go far away and never come back. I love you. Yours, Q.*"

"Someone around here has to know who this person is. Or

was," said Liv. "How do you carry on an affair in a town as small as Birchwood without anyone knowing?"

Gabe handed the letter back to Liv and said, "Grandpa and Grandma are dead. Mom was an only child. She didn't seem to have many friends other than Dad. But maybe Denny knows. Or Ed. Or someone in their high school class. Let's look for a yearbook in these boxes or at the library, or maybe her high school class has a Facebook page."

Gabe got up from the table, walked over to the front window, and looked outside. "I wish we could see the letters Mom sent to whoever this is. I bet that would reveal who the guy was."

Liv stood and pulled another letter from the bundle. "The answer has to be somewhere in this chest. Maybe in the letters. Maybe in the dried flowers. Somewhere."

"You know," said Gabe, turning back toward his sister. "There's another possibility for Mack's father."

"What do you mean?"

"Maybe it's not someone in the Leech Lake area. Maybe it was one of the resort guests. Mom worked here at the resort in high school before she and Dad got married."

Liv thought about that and said, "But their affair was ongoing. These letters look like they were written over at least a couple of years. That means it's someone local, right?"

"Not necessarily," said Gabe. He returned to the table. "He could have been a frequent guest. And/or Mom traveled to see him, too. Hey, I wonder if Denny kept all the old guest books. Everyone used to sign those."

Liv finished scanning another letter and said, "Mom and Dad used to keep the guest books in the basement of the office." She started pacing the room. She was in problem-solving mode. Literally thinking on her feet, as if moving her legs pumped extra blood to her brain to tap all its knowledge and creativity. "If we can find the guest books from about a year before Mack was born through the following year . . . This is great, Gabe. This is huge. Because it seemed Mack might have been delusional when he told Diana he had a different father. But according to this chest, Mack was right—he did have a different father. And if he was right about that, then maybe he was right about someone trying to kill him."

Gabe shut his eyes and gripped his forehead between thumb and forefinger and winced as if he'd just been walloped by a headache.

"What?" said Liv. "What's wrong?"

He walked to his suitcase so fast he almost broke into a run. He unzipped the outer pocket and pulled out an envelope and then the sheet of paper it contained. He held it toward Liv and said, "Does it match? Is it the same typewriter?"

· CHAPTER 19 ·

Liv took the sheet of paper from Gabe and laid it on the kitchen table next to one of the letters. "Holy shit," said Liv. "The person who put this note on our door, the person who wrote *Leave now. Your lives depend on it*. That person is Mack's biological father."

"Yeah," said Gabe. "Here we are trying to find him but, apparently, he's found us. And he's not happy we're here." Gabe left the kitchen and went to the mid-century couch. His instinct to quit was overpowering all other feelings and thoughts. "Damnit, Liv," he said. "This feels dangerous. This feels really fucking dangerous."

"Maybe it is," said Liv, studying the note they'd found on the door one more time. "But whoever wrote this, he doesn't know we have his love letters. He might not even know Mom saved them. So right now, we know more than he does. We're getting closer, Gabe. We're getting so much closer to finding him." She held up the typewritten threat. "Because this letter tells us Mack's father is still alive. And if he's still alive, he could have killed Mack."

"Leave if you want," said Liv, dodging a puddle of snowmelt on the asphalt path that led to the bar. "But I can't just ignore what I know and go on with my life as if I didn't know what I know."

Gabe thrust his hands in the pockets of his fleece. It might be warm for Minnesota in April, but two decades in Los Angeles had thinned his blood. "Mack's father, whoever the hell he is, threatened us," said Gabe. "And if he's the kind of guy who goes around threatening people, there's a good chance he killed Mack. Why don't you take that threat seriously? I mean, he probably hates us because Mom stayed with Dad and then we came along and cemented the deal."

They passed a playground with a small climbing wall, swings, a slide, and a contraption that looked like a grueling test on an obstacle course. All the equipment was mounted on a sponge-like surface designed to cushion the falls of stumbling children. The playground equipment of Gabe and Liv's childhood, death traps in comparison, was long gone. A metal merry-go-round that spun with such centrifugal force that it launched kids onto hard asphalt. A tall swing set positioned in the perfect place so an aggressive swinger could fly off and land on a nearby barbecue. And a teeter-totter that the bottom person could hop off and send their partner hurtling to the ground with a butt-breaking crash.

Liv felt grateful for a playground that taught her how to navigate danger. Yeah, it took a few victims, but that was life. The old playground helped prepare her for the real world. "Remember in high school," said Liv, "when you played guitar in the jazz combo, and what's-her-name's uncle was visiting from Boston and came to a concert and afterward told you how good you were and that you should apply to Berklee College of Music?"

"Kelsey Swenson."

"Yeah," said Liv. "Kelsey Swenson's uncle. And you were so excited. For about a week. And then you started making excuses why you wouldn't apply to Berklee."

"I didn't have the training the kids from the cities had," said Gabe. "They would have blown me away."

"You're still doing it, yeah? My God, Gabe. What about success scares you?"

"I'm not afraid of success," said Gabe, looking straight ahead, his jaw set firm. "I wasn't then and I'm not now. I'm afraid of getting killed. There's a difference."

"Bullshit," said Liv. "You think Mom's lover has something against us? We came along over ten years after Mom's affair. We had nothing to do with her decision to stay with Dad. That's just a wild hypothesis to justify your running away. Again."

"Fuck off, Liv. Seriously. Just fuck off. It's looking more and more like Mack was murdered and we could be next. This isn't a game. This isn't a psychological exploration of why you're more successful than I am. This is real." Gabe waited for Liv's response but it didn't come so he continued. "You were a bully when we were kids and you're a bully now. If I'm at all fearful it's because of you. So how about this? How about we just not pretend we're going to get along? How about we just agree to not agree on anything and everything and we'll be as polite as possible about it and go our separate ways after the memorial service tomorrow and get back to our very separate lives?"

Liv felt her brother's eyes on her but didn't meet his gaze. "Fine," she said. "Fine by me. We'll just agree to disagree and move on with our lives."

Gabe and Liv walked another thirty seconds in silence then entered the bar. It was a welcome relief from each other and a total surprise. When they were growing up at the resort, guests could buy canned beer, and only canned beer, Miller or Miller Lite, at the office along with a selection of individual bags of potato chips. Now the bar was a whole room in the same building as the dining room, off to the right from the main entrance, and it tried its best to create a Northwoods feel. The taxidermy was fake but excellent facsimiles. Walleye, crappies, bass, and northern pike. Deer heads—does with soft eyes and bucks with racks of antlers—bear heads, and porcupines. A bald eagle, wings spread, hung from the ceiling by monofilament, as if scanning the customers before diving down and scooping one up for a meal.

Neon signs for Minnesota breweries: Portage, Modist, Bent Paddle, Indeed, Mad Musky, and Summit. Winona sat alone at a table, her long black hair reflecting the beer signs' pink, yellow, blue, white, and red light. Liv joined Winona as Gabe continued on to the bar.

The walls were made of faux pine logs, the tables laminated in faux wood Formica, and the floor was maple plank under heavy coats of polyurethane. The bar itself was made of knotty pine and topped with copper. The place was three-quarters full, everyone waiting for the first outdoor dinner of the season prompted by the mild weather. Through the window, Liv could see the resort's chef standing with two giant paella pans over wood fires. Kegs of beer sat in garbage cans of ice. Denny stacked a pyramid of wood for a bonfire, the golden retrievers pulling out individual sticks. Ed stood on a ladder, running string lights between the pines. Raymond Lussier set up folding tables and chairs.

Gabe approached Liv and Winona carrying three cocktails in lowballs and a bucket of popcorn, its metal handle draped over one forearm like a purse. He set it all on the table and sat next to his cousin, sandwiching her between himself and Liv.

"What are these?" said Liv.

"My own creation," said Gabe. "Wherever I work, they add The Gabeson to the cocktail menu."

"Is it like a Gibson?"

"In name only. It's bourbon, brandy, rum, Madeira, and bitters. Don't ask me what brands and in what proportions because I'll never tell. Dana at the bar let me mix them myself."

They toasted each other then each sipped Gabe's eponymous cocktail. Gabe and Liv made eye contact as their glasses met, and their agreement was formalized. Agree to disagree and make the best of each other until one or both of them left northern Minnesota.

"It's good to have a mixologist in the family," said Winona. "God, this is good. You're welcome at all gatherings."

"Whoa, Gabe," said Liv, setting down her lowball. "You're in the right business."

Gabe managed a smile. "I made a pitcher. So drink up."

They did and chatted for a few minutes before Liv said, "Winona, do you know if your dad still keeps the old guest registry books in the basement of the office?"

"I'm not sure," said Winona, "I haven't been down there since I was a kid. But he used to. Why?"

Liv smiled the smile of a liar. "Gabe and I are feeling a bit sentimental. We wanted to look at the old registry books to rekindle our memories. Can you get us down there?"

"Sure," said Winona. "You keep feeding me cocktails like this, I'll give you keys to the whole damn place." She looked away for a moment and then said, "Speaking of the whole damn place, that's what I wanted to talk to you about. I heard some disturbing news today."

Gabe said, "We may have heard the same news you did."

"Really?" said Winona. "What is your source?"

Liv set down her lowball. "Are we talking about Red Pines?"

"We are."

An elderly man wearing a yellow Funster windbreaker motored by on an electric scooter. A tall, orange safety flag was mounted near the rear wheels, and the front basket was filled with bottles of beer.

Liv sipped her Gabeson and said, "Our source is the new proprietor."

Winona whispered, "Judith Otsby told you?"

"We were over there for lunch today. Her lawyer showed up with paperwork for her to sign. Does your father know?"

Winona shook her head. "He's going to freak when he hears. He'll still own a controlling interest, but Judith Otsby will make this place hell for my dad. And if that happens, it'll be the last straw for my mom. She'll insist they move back to Minneapolis, which would probably be the best for my dad because if he doesn't bend to Judith's will, I'm afraid she'll choke off the resort with a price war. She owns three resorts in this area. If she drops her prices for a season or maybe even a year, that will force my dad to drop prices and the place will no longer be profitable. Judith Otsby can weather that storm—my dad can't."

More Funsters, clad in their yellow windbreakers, waltzed in pairs in one corner of the room, as if there were music playing, but there wasn't.

"We know you want this place for your power plant," said Gabe. "But maybe you should look for another location."

"I have," said Winona. "Don't forget I grew up here. I know the area. I know the people in local government. And I know it'll be so much easier and more profitable if I build it on this property. None of the local resort owners will fight me if I eliminate Ahl-strom's from their competition, especially now that Judith Otsby is part owner. But if I try building on another piece of land, the other resort owners will complain about the wind turbines as an eyesore and bird killer." Winona helped herself to a few kernels of popcorn. "In the long run, maybe even in the short run, an independent power station is in their best interest, but for some reason, people have a difficult time seeing anything but immediate transactional value. Not just here—all over the country. It's kill-ing America's place in the global economy."

Liv swirled the ice in her drink and said, "Can you even build it on this property with Judith Otsby as your partner?"

"Judith Otsby is a nightmare. But she's had it easy—no one has ever fought back. If I owned fifty-one percent of this place, I'd bring in good lawyers. New York lawyers. They would tie her up in so much legal muck she'd want out. I'm sure of it."

Gabe said, "We met Judith's lawyer today. Tyler Luther."

"What?" laughed Winona. "Tyler Luther is Judith's lawyer? He was two years ahead of me in high school. He's an idiot."

Annabel Johnson, the front desk clerk, approached wearing her gray vest, name tag, and white shirt. "Hello, Gabe and Liv," she said. "I was going to call you but I saw you sitting here. I'm wondering if you know when you might be checking out."

"I didn't know we were checked in," said Liv.

"Yes. You are. For legal reasons." Annabel flashed her hospitality-degree smile. "Even though Cabin 14 is not technically available, Red Pines accounts for all guests on the property."

"We don't know when we're checking out," said Gabe. "Tomorrow is Mack's memorial service. One or both of us could leave right after that, or it might be another couple of days."

"I will make a note of that. Please let me know if your plans change. Hope you're enjoying your stay at Ahlstrom's." Another smile from Annabel Johnson and she left.

"If your dad can put up with her," said Liv, "he can probably handle Judith Otsby."

"Annabel's a trip," said Winona. "We're the same age and every time I'm home she wants to hang out with me. Fortunately, I have studying as an excuse."

Liv took advantage of Annabel's interruption and changed the subject. "Winona," she said, "does your father ever talk about our parents?"

"What do you mean?" said Winona.

"Does he ever say anything disparaging about them as individuals or about their marriage or about our family?"

"Not really." Winona grabbed more popcorn. "He's always said your dad was a great big brother. Bobby was kind to him. He's said that many times." Winona dropped her eyes and added, "But once he was talking to my mother. It was Bobby's birthday, I think. My dad always mentioned Bobby on Bobby's birthday. And always positively. They were cleaning up after dinner. I was in the living room doing my homework—I'm pretty sure they didn't know I could hear them. It's an only-child thing. Your parents want adult time, which leaves you alone and lonely. So I did a lot of eavesdropping. I must have been nine or ten. And I heard my dad say your dad deserved a better wife or something to that effect. Sorry. I'm sure that's not fun to hear."

"It's okay," said Gabe. "Thanks for telling us."

"Why do you ask?" said Winona.

"Hey cutie." This from a woman Funster holding a bottle of Mad Musky in each hand. She was addressing Gabe. The left breast of her Funsters windbreaker was embroidered in cursive— *Donna*. "You want to dance?"

"Uh . . . ," said Gabe. He noticed both Liv and Winona trying to suppress smiles and failing. "I'm sorry, I can't right now. But thanks for asking." And then he added in the most genuine voice he could muster, "Maybe later?"

Donna stared at him. She looked more angry than disappointed. "Yeah, sure." Then she left.

Gabe turned red. Winona and Liv took a moment to let the laughter out of their systems then Liv said, "Winona, we're just trying to piece together our childhood. Fill in the missing gaps we don't remember. I think it's because Mack died. And because we're back here for the first time in twenty years. We're both feeling really sorry we haven't seen you again until now. Kind of embarrassed, actually."

"Sorry and embarrassed and guilty," said Gabe. "And that old Funster woman isn't making matters any better."

"Well, if you change your mind and get over there," said Liv, "and you two hit it off, at least you won't have to worry about her getting pregnant."

Maybe it was the Gabesons. Maybe it was the timing. But Liv

and Winona had a good laugh at Gabe's expense then Winona reached into her jacket pocket and took out a ring of keys. She removed one and said, "This key opens the walkout entrance to the office basement. Hopefully, something down there will help piece together your childhood." She slid the key across the table. "Or if you and your new lady friend need a place for some privacy, Gabe."

"Are you guys done?" said Gabe.

Liv picked up the key and said, "Oh, and one more thing. I collect old typewriters. Do you know anyone around here who has one? I pay top dollar."

"I don't think so," said Winona. "I haven't seen an old typewriter . . . maybe ever?"

"What about your Uncle Raymond? Does he have an old typewriter?"

"Not that I know of. But there might be one in the basement."

"Denny knows about Mom's affair," said Liv. "I mean, from what Winona said, he has to know, right?"

"He has to," said Gabe. "Why else would he say Dad deserved a better wife? We have to ask him about it. We have to ask him and not back off until he tells us who Mom was seeing."

"Maybe we'll get a glimpse of him tomorrow," said Liv.

Gabe walked a few more steps to consider what Liv said but couldn't figure it out. "What do you mean?"

"Tomorrow is Mack's memorial. Maybe Mack's father will show up for it."

"Yeah," said Gabe, not quite sure if that would be exciting or terrifying or both. "Maybe he will."

They stood in the office basement, which had changed little since they were kids. The floor was concrete and the joists overheard were exposed where fluorescent tubes hung in metal fixtures. The kind that take half a minute or so to blink themselves to life after flicking on the switch. Gabe and Liv did not find an old typewriter but did find Denny's security equipment—wireless cameras, lights, a home base hub, and a video monitor that it all hooked up to—that sat unopened because he didn't want to give up his late-night patrol. And they found the guest books on the shelves where they'd last seen them. It took about two minutes to locate the volumes for the year leading up to Mack's birth. Half an hour later, they'd identified one person who'd visited Ahlstrom's six times that year.

"Who is Alan Cohen from Highland Park, Illinois?" said Gabe.

Liv's face was already in her phone. "There's an Alan Cohen from Highland Park who was born ten years before Mom."

"How do you know that?"

"He has a Wikipedia page."

"Really?" said Gabe. "Maybe it's him."

"I think it's a pretty safe bet. Listen." Liv read, "Alan Cohen. Born in Highland Park, Illinois, in 1946. Worked his entire career at Marshall Field, first as legal counsel and eventually becoming CFO. He retired at the age of fifty in 1996.'"

Gabe said, "Why do you think he's the Alan Cohen we're looking for?"

"Because," said Liv, "he's lived right here on Leech Lake since 1996. And according to this, he's never been married and he's still alive. He must be seventy-eight years old. Look, here's his picture."

Gabe studied the picture and said, "I remember that guy. He bought that big stone house on the north end of Steamboat Bay. Used to eat dinner at the resort by himself. I waited on him. I'm sure of it."

"Yeah," said Liv. "I remember him, too."

Gabe said, "I wonder if he owns a typewriter. Mom died in 1996. Alan Cohen could have moved here to say goodbye. To spend some time with her before the end. Let me see that picture again."

Liv showed him the photo. "Pay him a visit tomorrow?"

Gabe hesitated. Was it a good idea to pursue the man who could be threatening them? Who might have both fathered and killed Mack? He didn't think so but since agreement didn't seem to be possible with Liv, he offered a noncommittal, "We'll see."

· CHAPTER 20 ·

Ten minutes later, Gabe and Liv stood in the warmth of the bonfire. The string lights Ed had hung lit a stretch of lawn that would
soon be green and smell of freshly cut grass. The lake ice looked
more gray than white, a sure sign it was on its way out and spring
was on its way in. The facsimile car still rested atop the ice, but its
falling through was days, not weeks away.

It seemed the entire town was gathered. Ahlstrom's first cookout of the season was open to the public. Twenty dollars got you
all the food and beer you could consume and your hand stamped
so you could come back for more. The resort's excellent view of
the car on the ice helped draw a crowd, as did Ahlstrom's chef,
who had a knack for making foodie-grade fare for a Northwoods
palate. Tonight it was paella made of wild rice with venison, cran-
berry, onion, and wild peas all mixed together with seasonings
that were pointedly mild.

Parents carried and strolled their young children. Teenagers
roamed in packs, talking above each other in an effort to establish
a social hierarchy. The Funsters preferred to stand in one spot,
plastic cups of beer in hand.

"Anyone need a drink?" This from Andrew Otsby, who approached in a knee-length Canada Goose down jacket despite the
mild weather. He held a silver flask in his right hand and added
with a smile, "Don't cut your mother off. Don't end the relationship unresolved. That's what my therapist keeps telling me. I'm
trying. I am determined to be a superhero son and turn Judith

Otsby from evil to good, but like with all superheroes, it takes a toll. I am paying the price." He took a swig from his flask and offered it to Gabe.

"I'm good for now," said Gabe.

"Same," said Liv. "Tough staying with the folks?"

"Oh, not too bad," said Andrew. "My father is excellent at running interference. Always has been. He saved my life, in a way. But sometimes it wasn't enough. I remember hanging out with Mack at your house when I was in middle school. I wasn't out yet. No one was back then, at least in this town. I didn't even know I was gay. My mother had her suspicions and called me all sorts of names. But my father and your parents were always kind to me. Bette and Bobby Ahlstrom made me feel welcome. I'll always appreciate them for that. Good people, your mom and dad."

Another flock of Canada geese flew their flying V north, the setting sun illuminating their white breasts from below as they honked away like a bunch of gossips.

"Yeah," said Gabe, "Bette and Bobby Ahlstrom were nice people."

"The best," said Andrew, who was beginning to sound tipsy, as if he'd downed and then refilled his flask before leaving the house.

"It's nice to know that you and Mack reconnected," said Liv. She and Gabe made quick eye contact—they'd discussed Andrew and now was as good a time as any. The sun was slipping below the horizon, and the warm light from the bonfire softened everything it touched.

"Me, too," said Andrew. "Mack was a good friend when we were kids and an equally good friend over the last year. I hesitated when he asked me to be his doctor. I didn't want to blur any ethical lines but then I figured doctors are friends with their patients all the time."

"Were you the one who diagnosed his diabetes insipidus?" said Gabe.

"No. He'd seen a dozen doctors before finding one who figured out why he was always thirsty and urinating all the time. The other doctors had all tested him for sugar diabetes and when he tested negative, all those doctors told him to drink less water. That was terrible advice. Dangerous advice. Mack couldn't go longer than half an hour without having to pee and he had an unquenchable thirst. He told me he had to sit on the aisle at movie theaters. He couldn't get a decent night's sleep." Andrew sipped from his flask and added, "But he finally found one doctor who diagnosed him correctly. Fortunately, she'd had some experience with diabetes insipidus. It's pretty rare to have it for no reason. No head injury. No brain tumor. But I guess she'd seen a patient like that when she was a resident, so she sent Mack to an endocrinologist and they ran the test and sure enough, that's what it was. They gave him an MRI to make sure he didn't have a brain tumor, and he didn't. All Mack had to do was take a little pill four times a day, and he was back to normal. He told me it changed his life.

"He was so grateful to that doctor. When she retired he was concerned because naturally, he didn't trust other doctors. That's when he came to me. I checked his sodium and potassium and everything looked good. The medication was doing its job. The dosage was correct."

"So what happened, do you think?" said Liv. "Did he just stop taking his medication?"

"Possibly," said Andrew. "But I saw him a week before he died. He seemed fine then."

Gabe looked at Liv. She gave him the slightest head nod. Gabe said, "Did Mack ever mention to you that he thought someone was trying to kill him?"

Raymond Lussier approached the bonfire with a dead, dried-out Christmas tree. He heaved it toward the bonfire and it burst into flames in midair. The crowd cheered.

"What?" said Andrew. "What do you mean someone was trying to kill him?"

"Yeah, weirdest thing," said Gabe. "He sent Liv and me a couple of posthumous emails."

Liv explained about Mack's outbox, raising her voice to compete with the din of the crowd and roar of the fire.

When she was done, Andrew said, "No. He never mentioned anything like that to me. All that sounds a bit out there. Maybe Mack was having some mental health problems." He said this from a faraway place, looking out at the lit-up car on the frozen lake. He took another sip from his flask and added, "So many people have had a hard time. The pandemic. The political polarization. People pretending social media is a real connection. Families disintegrating because of all of the above. It's taken a heavy toll on otherwise mentally healthy people. Very sad."

"We agree," said Gabe. "And mental health issues would explain why Mack might not have taken his medication. And it would explain his paranoia. Could an imbalance of sodium and potassium cause that?"

"I don't know," said Andrew. "You'd have to ask a psychiatrist. I have a colleague who—"

Someone yelled, "Get the hell off my property!" Gabe and Liv turned in the direction of the shouting. The place went quiet except for the bonfire that now seemed louder without its competing din of hubbub. "I mean right now! Get out of my sight!" It was Uncle Denny, arm extended, index finger pointing. He stood near the paella pans, his ire focused on Judith Otsby. "Leave now or do us all a favor and take that oxygen tank closer to the fire!"

"Uh oh," said Liv. "I think Uncle Denny just found out Judith bought Red Pines and became his corporate partner."

"Oh, Mother," said Andrew, more to himself than to Gabe and Liv as he sipped again from his flask.

"We'd better get over there," said Gabe.

Gabe and Liv started toward the paella pans, where even at a distance they could make out Judith Otsby's girth leaning forward on her cane, calmly deflecting Denny Ahlstrom's wrath. John stood near his wife, her wheeled oxygen tank at his feet.

"You have no right!" said Denny. "No right at all! Does your greed know no bounds?! You will not force me out! This resort is my birthright!"

"Denny," said John. "Business is business. This is not personal."

"Dad," said Winona, approaching her father. "Walk away. Come on. This isn't the time or place."

"Judith Otsby, you are a lowly troll. A miserable, hateful, spoiled witch. The entirety of northern Minnesota hates you. Even your own body can't stand you. Look what it's doing. I hope you choke on your own tongue!"

"Uncle Denny," said Gabe from ten feet away. "Let's go. There's nothing you can do right now."

"I can make her leave! I can get her the hell out of my sight!"

"No, you can't," said Judith Otsby. "You may still own controlling interest in Ahlstrom's, but as your co-owner, I have contractual rights. And one of those rights is to be present at the property whenever I wish."

The crowd formed a circle around Denny and Judith but stayed twenty feet back from the fracas either because the distance implied a false sense of respect for Denny and Judith's privacy or, more likely, they just got a better view, as in the sixth row at the theater is better than the first row. Some of the teens had their phones out and pointed at the combatants, a miniature version of the scene playing on their screens. The Funsters took advantage of the spectacle to refill their cups at the keg now that it had no line.

"Mother," said Andrew, emerging from the flickering shadows of the bonfire. "There's no need to make this harder on Denny than it already is."

"What's so hard?" spat Judith. "Because of me, Denny finally has a competent partner instead of a gaggle of corporate stooges." She turned her heavily lidded eyes toward Denny. "You should be thanking me, not cursing me. I just saved this place. Saved it from fading into obscurity. Saved it from your sentimentality. Sure, you've built some new buildings and paved some paths, but your mindset is in the last millennium. And if you weren't intent on ruining your business, Red Pines was. Between your folksy hooey and their gross mismanagement, you were ripe for picking. Just be glad it's me buying the place and not your parasitic daughter. She wants to turn this dump into a power station!" Judith Otsby punctuated her outburst with a wrenching cough. John pulled a fresh handkerchief from his pocket and held it to Judith's mouth. "Get that away from me, John!"

"You make me sick!" said Denny. "Absolutely sick. And you," he said, pointing at John Otsby. "You're a toad of a man. Or maybe just a plain toad. You deserve everything that's coming to you!"

Renee stepped into the circle and said, "Denny." She took his arm. "Let's go home. She's not worth your energy."

Denny Ahlstrom turned toward his wife and said, "You don't know what this means. It's over. Over!" He pulled his arm away from Renee, wiped a tear from his face, turned his back on the crowd, and walked away. The din of the crowd returned as if someone had pushed an unmute button.

Liv said, "I may need another one of your cocktails, Gabe."

"The Gabeson," said Winona. "Count me in."

Andrew approached and said, "I'm so sorry. So sorry she does things like this. And I'm sorry my father doesn't stand up to her. No one does. I try but she doesn't care what I think." Andrew's mind wandered away for a moment, perhaps all the way to his childhood. Then he snapped out of his trance and said, "Hi, Winona. How are you?"

"All right, I guess. Nice to see you, Andrew."

Judith screamed, "God damnit, John! Stay close to me!" She and John made their slow trek to the parking lot. "You're going to yank this tube out of my nose!" Judith stopped and turned back toward the crowd. "Andy? Where are you? Get the hell over here!"

Andrew sighed and said, "I'm going to go tell her I'll find my own ride home. Meet you in the bar?"

Winona and Andrew walked away. Liv and Gabe started toward the bar when Tyler Luther, Judith Otsby's young lawyer, approached. He wore a Ski-Doo jacket and held a can of beer in a cozy that said OTSBY'S. "Hey, guys, catch up with you in a bit." This he said to a group of friends his age, high school hockey buddies whose muscles had morphed to fat. He then turned his attention toward Liv and Gabe and said, "Glad you were here for the show."

"That's what you thought that was," said Liv, "a show?"

"Judith Otsby does not tread lightly. Just remember that."

"It's hard to forget," said Gabe. "And is that a threat?"

"No." Tyler smiled, waving his beer around. "Do I look threatening?"

"You do," said Liv. "The combination of youth and subservience is always threatening."

"Ooh," said Tyler. "Subservience. Big word. But as a lawyer, I know big words are nothing more than a smoke screen. Consider me unimpressed."

"That's too bad," said Gabe. "Because we want nothing more than to impress Judith Otsby's stooge. Is stooge a small enough word for you?"

"Be careful," said Tyler Luther. "This isn't your turf anymore. You don't know how things work. Here's my friendly advice: do not cross Judith Otsby. She gets what she wants. One way or the other, she gets what she wants. So might as well give it to her. No need to take the hard road—it won't matter anyway."

"That's your friendly advice?" said Liv.

Tyler Luther glared at the siblings. Glared at them for ten seconds before saying, "You're not one of us anymore. Don't forget that. You're not one of us." He finished his beer, dropped the can on the ground, and walked away.

· CHAPTER 21 ·

Liv and Gabe had a late night, closing the bar at midnight with Winona and Andrew after several Gabesons each. They arrived back at the cabin too tired to continue going through their mother's chest but vowed to pick up where they'd left off first thing in the morning, which came earlier than they'd hoped when they were woken by voices outside Cabin 14. Gabe covered his head with a pillow and said, "What the hell is going on out there?"

Liv got out of bed, went to the window, and peeked through the curtains. "People are walking toward the lake. I bet the car fell through the ice."

Gabe emerged from under his pillow and sat up. He grabbed his phone, scrolled for a few seconds, and said, "You're right. The Birchwood Facebook page is all abuzz about it. I wonder who will win the raffle."

They fired up the kettle for pour-over coffee, dressed, brushed their teeth, and carried steaming mugs of coffee down to the lake, where over a hundred people had already gathered and looked out at where the car used to be. Now they saw a dark gray area of slush, out of which ran a steel cable. Ed was busy running a long, orange extension cord from the dining hall to an electric winch. He plugged it into the machine, flipped a switch, and the winch hummed. The cable pulled taut, stopped for a moment, then the winch, geared down to glacial speed, turned. It would be the most exciting twenty minutes of boredom anyone there had ever seen. Bystanders stood with paper to-go cups of coffee, the bulk of conversation consisting of dates and times, most stated with the resignation of loss, but a few hopeful that the car had at least fallen through on the day they'd chosen, whether it was yesterday before midnight or today in the predawn hours.

The onlookers were mostly resort guests. The Outboard Motor Association would be checking out by noon, but they had all purchased ice-out tickets when they booked the resort last fall. A few locals pulled into the parking lot, having read the news online or having heard it via town chatter. This was arguably the most exciting day of the year on Leech Lake. Yes, there were the fishing and hunting openers, waterfowl and deer, the water ski show, and Pine Cone Days, a weeklong summer celebration that included the Best 4th of July Fireworks Show in the Upper Midwest®, but ice-out day provided an extra element of drama because of the international purchasing of ice-out raffle tickets. Yes, word had spread to Manitoba.

"Thank God this is happening before Mack's memorial service," said Liv. "If the car fell through the ice during the service, no one would be able to think about Mack. Hey, you want a cinnamon roll?"

"Yeah," said Gabe. "Thank you."

"Save my spot."

The dining hall was half-empty with so many potential breakfasters outside waiting for the car and its stopped clock to be winched out of the lake. Liv overheard snippets of speculation about how twenty-five thousand dollars could change a person's life. And she heard at least three people comment on which boat they'd buy. Liv went to the register and ordered two cinnamon rolls to go in separate bags so they didn't stick to one another as cinnamon rolls do, and two fresh cups of coffee. She scanned the patrons while waiting and didn't see anyone she knew. She guessed Renee was teaching her first yoga class of the day and Winona was still sleeping. Twenty-four-year-olds were able to sleep through anything, even a mass of clattering onlookers not far from their bedroom window. And Denny was probably too embarrassed to show his face after his outburst at the bonfire. A shouting match like that in New York City was forgotten as soon as it ended. But in mild-mannered northern Minnesota, a public lapse in stoicism was remembered for years and might even be chiseled into one's headstone. For most New Yorkers, the goal was to claw their way to the top. For most Minnesotans, the goal was to not stand out, good or bad. Just blend in and carry on as if you're embarrassed to be alive.

But most Minnesotans didn't mean all Minnesotans. Judith Otsby had no desire to fit in. She didn't care what others thought of her. She didn't care what they said behind her back or to her face. Andrew had spoken about his mother over cocktails last night. "She was a climate change denier for years," he said. "Until she realized that climate change would mean an increase in property values in northern Minnesota. All of a sudden, she couldn't stop talking about California being on fire or washed away in the rains, Florida being swallowed by rising sea levels, and Texas and Arizona's oven-like summers. She said all those people would have to move. After that Judith Otsby was not only on the climate change bandwagon, she was driving it. And she started buying property as if she were playing Monopoly. I'm sure that's what's behind her purchase of Red Pines, which owns or co-owns twenty properties," said Andrew, "including forty-nine percent of Ahlstrom's."

A server approached Liv and said, "Sorry for the delay, ma'am. We have a fresh batch of cinnamon rolls coming out of the oven. It'll be just a few more minutes."

Ma'am? thought Liv. *When did I become a ma'am?* The girl must have been sixteen, and she reminded Liv of herself at that age. Working at Ahlstrom's, living in the only town she'd ever known. Liv at that age was full of dreams and aspirations. She couldn't wait to leave. She belonged to the first generation that grew up with the World Wide Web. It existed from her earliest memories. Long before social media, it was Yahoo, AOL, and MySpace that showed her a world she couldn't have imagined. Most everyone she'd grown up with had moved away in search of that bigger, brighter, shinier world.

Gabe stood alone, waiting for the sunken car to be winched out of the water and for Liv to bring him a cinnamon roll. His phone dinged. He looked at the screen and saw a text from his neighbor Carly:

Grabbed a bite after work with coworkers and thought I'd be the first to wish you a good morning. Hope the service today gives you some peace and that you and Liv are finding a way to get along.

Gabe looked at the time. 7:15 A.M. 5:15 California time. That was the fate of a nightclub bartender. Last call at two A.M. Get out of there at three A.M. Then a couple of hours to unwind before you can even think of falling asleep. What kind of life was that for Gabe as he neared the age of forty? Not only for him but for Carly, who was a year older than he. A fantasy crept into Gabe's head about him and Carly somehow buying out Uncle Denny, moving to Ahlstrom's, and settling down together. They would concoct the best cocktails in the five-state area. They could start their own micro-distillery with locally grown wheat, corn, and barley. They could start a family. Gabe would get a do-over on Leech Lake. All this flitted through his mind in a matter of seconds before returning Carly's text.

Good morning! I'm standing by a lake filled with slush waiting for a car to get pulled out. A big event on Leech Lake! (No one drove into the lake—it's a tradition—explain later.) Gabe hesitated before hitting send and then thought maybe there was some truth in what Liv had said—he did allow his fear to seed excuses for not going after what he wanted. Maybe he did throw a wet blanket on life. Gabe thought, *What the hell?* and added: *Miss you, Carly.*

Liv said, "Fresh cinnamon roll right out of the oven and piping hot coffee." Gabe looked up to see his sister holding out a white, grease-stained bag, and a to-go cup of coffee.

Liv buying coffee and a cinnamon roll was a simple gesture. It was something she'd do for a mere acquaintance. But given their history and rough start in Chicago, seeing Liv extend the bag toward him, Gabe felt extraordinarily grateful for Liv and something akin to warmth. "Thank you." He reached for his breakfast when he heard:

"There it is!" from a woman standing nearby. "There's the car!"

Gabe took the cinnamon roll and coffee from Liv and turned toward the lake where the car's roll bars emerged from the slush. His phone dinged in his hand. He was afraid to read Carly's response. She was a kind person. She wouldn't tell him to back off or worse. But if twenty years of auditioning as a guitar player and sending out demo tapes had taught Gabe anything, it was how to read a rejection when that rejection lay between the lines. A band might say, "You're a good player, dude. Just not our style." That, of course, was bullshit. As was, "We like the demo, we just don't know how to market it." Also bullshit.

He could imagine Carly's polite rejection. "Yeah, you've been gone too long." Or "The sidewalks of Santa Monica aren't the same without you." Or the worst: "It's important you're taking this time to be with your family." Gabe built up his nerve to look at Carly's response when he heard a scream. He looked at the car rising from the water, its wheels rolling up and onto the beach, and saw a body strapped behind the wheel, its head slumped forward.

CHAPTER 22

The cinnamon roll. The coffee. Carly's response to Gabe's text. They would all have to wait. The lakeshore buzzed with dour speculation. "Horrible, ghastly, tragic," people said although no one looked away, even for a minute. Even The Funsters stood silent, transfixed on the dead body strapped behind the wheel. Ed kept the winch turning, and the car rolled up from the beach, water, slush, and ice falling from its open frame. The human body appeared frozen stiff. It was pitched forward against the steering wheel. No one moved. No one knew who was in charge.

"Is anyone here a doctor?" someone finally called out.

"Call 9–1–1!" said another.

But everyone could see it was too late for a doctor. Too late for anyone other than the county medical examiner.

"Who is it?" said someone else. "Who's in the car?"

"I'm a doctor," said a woman who approached the open-framed imposter of a car. She removed her gloves and, without looking at the person's face, held two fingers to the neck. She waited for almost half a minute before shaking her head, which surprised no one.

"Come on, Gabe," said Liv. "Let's get out of here."

Gabe looked at his sister with raised eyebrows. "Don't you want to see who it is?"

Liv hesitated then said, "I know who it is."

"How? You can't see the person's face."

"You don't have to see the person's face," said Liv. "Look at the slush on the shoulders. It's just translucent enough to make out what's underneath—red suspenders." She began to cry. "It's Denny. Damnit, Gabe. It's Denny."

"No . . . ," said Gabe. But he knew it was true. The world seemed to spin. He felt lightheaded. He looked at Liv and they pulled each other into a hug. The emotion of the moment was too much, not because Denny was dead—they barely knew the man—but because Gabe and Liv felt yanked back in time. Back to when their mother had died at this same resort. Back to when their father dropped dead from a heart attack on this very patch of lawn. Leech Lake felt haunted if your last name was Ahlstrom.

The doctor said, "I think we should wait for the police before touching the body."

And as if on cue, they heard sirens in the distance.

"Maybe we shouldn't have come back here," said Liv in a flat, monotone voice meant to mask her terror.

Gabe resisted the urge to say *I told you so* and simply said, "Yeah . . ."

"We'd better postpone Mack's memorial service. I'll make some calls . . ."

They turned and looked as police cars, vans, and an ambulance pulled onto the property, drove through the parking lot, and rolled out and onto the lawn. Rank-and-file officers exited their vehicles and dispersed the crowd. Crime scene investigators erected a white tent over the car and body. Despite Liv's desire to return to the cabin, she and Gabe stood outside the yellow tape.

Fifteen minutes later, a uniformed police officer in her late sixties emerged from the white tent, removed a pair of blue latex gloves, and spoke into a walkie-talkie. She stood tall and thin and angular with gray hair and gray-green eyes. Another uniformed police officer escorted her outside the yellow tape. This one younger, shorter, and male. Liv and Gabe watched the two cops make their way under the yellow tape and through the crowd. They continued walking toward the home of Denny, Renee, and Winona Ahlstrom.

"Do you think Denny killed himself?" said Gabe.

Liv shrugged. "I don't know . . ."

"Do you think Denny found a note on his door?"

Liv looked at Gabe. Looked at him a long time then said, "Come on. Let's go back to the cabin."

Liv and Gabe returned to Cabin 14. There was nothing they could do now except wait for confirmation that Uncle Denny was dead and learn whether he'd taken his own life or was murdered. Gabe grabbed the chest off the dining room table and set it down in the middle of the living room.

"Kill some time?" he said.

"Poor choice of words," said Liv.

"Yeah . . . Sorry."

"But a good idea. We need a distraction." Liv sat on the floor, where she and Gabe read the remaining letters. It seemed an impossible task to divert their attention from the throngs of people outside, the emergency vehicles, and knowing police were breaking the news to Renee and Winona, but the letters to their mother were up for the challenge.

"This is sad," said Liv, holding one of the letters. "You can see the relationship dying, yeah?"

"Yeah," said Gabe. "It's hard not knowing Mom's side of it, but this person keeps asking her to leave Dad and marry him. Each letter is more desperate than the last. Like the guy will die if she won't change her mind."

"I just can't get over how the person wrote such intimate letters and still hid his identity. I can only guess it's because he was afraid the letters might fall into the wrong hands or at least be read by the wrong eyes. But what could that mean in the Leech Lake area? Was this guy protecting himself or was he protecting Mom?" Liv picked up the pink camisole, hesitated, then held it to her nose. "I remember this scent. This is how she smelled." Liv shut her eyes and felt her heart pound. By scent alone, it felt as if her mother had come back to life, and Liv had been gifted the chance to say the things she couldn't say at the age of fourteen. When she opened her eyes, her vision was blurred with tears because Liv knew she would never get that chance. She extended the camisole toward Gabe, who was about to take it when he felt his phone buzz in his pocket. He glanced at the notification on the screen and saw a text from Carly:

I looked at the Birchwood newspaper online to read about the car falling through the ice and OMG, they found a body in it! Did you know the person?

Gabe had never looked at Carly's previous text, her response to Gabe's *I miss you, Carly*. It was all he had cared about until the car rolled up onto land with dead Uncle Denny strapped behind the wheel. After that, time stopped. The past and future skipped away and the present stomped all over everything like a monster in a 1950s horror film. Gabe took a deep breath and scrolled up:

I miss you, too, Gabe. Hurry home. Hurry, hurry, hurry.

Gabe's heart felt like it was splitting in two. A tragedy pulled one way. A glorious miracle pulled the other. He shut his eyes for a moment in an effort to center himself and then replied:

It was my Uncle Denny. Police are investigating. I wish I'd never left California. I wish I'd never left you.

Carly replied with a simple, red heart.

"You don't want to smell your mother's skimpy sleepwear?" said Liv.

"What?" said Gabe, as if yanked out of another world.

Liv shook the camisole. "It smells like Mom."

"Oh. Sorry. Look." He turned his phone toward Liv so she could read his text exchange with Carly.

"Gabe, that's fantastic." Liv's eyes shined. Her smile was free of sarcasm or jealousy. "I'm thrilled for you. She's the one you were telling me about, right?"

Gabe nodded as they heard a knock on the door.

"Police," said a voice. "Please open the door."

· CHAPTER 23 ·

Birchwood Chief of Police Julie Haaland stood six foot tall, wore no cap, and kept her shoulder-length gray hair clamped behind her head. Her gray-green eyes were set in weathered white skin. They sparkled when she smiled. She wore the uniform as an act of solidarity with her subordinates and came off more as a shepherd than a cop. Julie Haaland knew most of the full-time Birchwood residents. Knew them and their parents and their children and their stories, from uplifting to tragic.

"Hello," she said after entering Cabin 14. Julie Haaland introduced herself as the Birchwood chief of police. "And this is Officer Hunter Schmidt," she added, referring to her colleague. Hunter Schmidt was short and squat with no visible neck. He wore his police cap atop his large head with a pie-shaped face that featured a brown mustache under a flat nose and brown eyes. "We're sorry to inform you that—"

"We know," said Liv. "We know it was Denny." Off Chief Haaland's quizzical look Liv added, "I recognized his suspenders under the slush."

Chief Haaland nodded. "We're sorry for your loss."

"Condolences," said Officer Schmidt, who tried to counter his bulldog appearance with kind eyes and a reverent demeanor.

"We'd like to ask some questions," said Chief Haaland, "if you have a few minutes."

Liv eyed the police officers with a mix of curiosity and indignation. Why did they want to talk to her and Gabe? They had nothing to do with Denny's murder. And thank God they wanted to talk to her and Gabe—they might find out what happened. "Of course," said Liv. "Would you like a cup of coffee?"

The police officers accepted Liv's offer, and she heated up the kettle as Gabe showed them to the kitchen table.

"Is it okay to start?" said Chief Haaland. She smiled and nodded toward Officer Schmidt, who took out a notepad and pen.

"Yeah-yeah, go ahead," said Liv. "I'll be there in just a minute."

Chief Haaland intertwined her fingers and rested her hands on the table. "When was the last time each of you saw your uncle?"

"If you mean when was the last time we saw him alive," said Gabe, "it was at the bonfire last night. I'm sure you've heard about that."

"Yes," said Chief Haaland. "We have." She smiled a reassuring smile. "But we'd like to hear your version."

Gabe wondered why the police hadn't separated Liv and him to question them individually. That's what the police did on TV cop shows. He hoped it was because neither were suspects, but also wondered if it was a trick to see if they'd agree with each other no matter what, as if they'd expected this visit and had prepared for it.

"I last saw Denny when he walked off in a huff," said Gabe. "He seemed mad at everybody. He yelled at Judith Otsby. Said she had no right to muscle her way into Ahlstrom's, which he said was his birthright. And he accused her husband, John, of being a toad, and deserving it."

"No-no," said Liv as she removed coffee filters from the box. "Denny didn't say John deserved to be a toad. He said John deserved whatever he had coming to him."

"Did he?" said Gabe.

"That's what I heard," said Liv. "Milk or sugar?"

"Both please," said Chief Haaland.

"None for me, thank you," said Officer Schmidt, still writing in his notebook.

Liv removed a carton of milk from the refrigerator and set it on the table along with a box of individually wrapped sugar packets.

"Did Denny have words with anyone else?" said Chief Haaland.

"He accused his wife of not knowing what this meant," said Gabe. "*This* meaning Judith buying Red Pines. And he wouldn't listen to anyone who tried to calm him down. Not us. Not Winona. No one. Then he walked off by himself."

Officer Schmidt scratched down the rest of what Gabe said then looked up at Chief Haaland, signaling he was ready for more.

"When is the last time you saw your Uncle Denny, Liv?" said Chief Haaland.

"Same. Gabe and I were there together. After Denny walked off, Andrew Otsby approached us and apologized for his mother buying Red Pines and asked if we wanted to grab a drink at the bar. We were already headed there with Winona, so the four of us spent the rest of the evening there until it closed at midnight."

"And where did you go after that?" said Chief Haaland.

Liv placed coffee filters in two plastic cones and said, "Right back here."

"Gabe?"

"Yeah," said Gabe. "We both walked back here. We'd had a few. Maybe one or two more than we should have."

"Or two or three," said Liv, pouring hot water from the kettle over the coffee grounds.

"True. It was a stressful night and we weren't driving so we indulged ourselves then we walked back here and crashed."

"And Winona and Andrew Otsby?"

"What about them?" said Liv.

"Where did they go after the bar?"

Liv shrugged. "Home, I assume." She carried the two cups of coffee to the table and sat.

"Thank you," said Chief Haaland. "Did Winona and Andrew each consume as much alcohol as the both of you?"

"I think so," said Gabe. "We had a big pitcher of cocktails and I remember pouring for everyone."

Chief Haaland sipped her coffee and smiled. "Strong," she said, "and very good."

"Mmm," said Hunter Schmidt in agreement.

"Andrew Otsby had come to the cookout with his parents," said Chief Haaland. "But Judith and John Otsby left after the altercation. Do you know how Andrew Otsby got home?"

Gabe and Liv looked at each other and shrugged. Liv said, "No clue. Did Winona give him a ride?"

"According to Winona, she did not. She also said she felt quite drunk when the bar closed. She walked home and went straight to bed. Her mother confirmed this. And neither of you drove Andy Otsby home?"

"No," said Liv. "We walked straight to Cabin 14 like we said. Neither of us were in any condition to get behind the wheel. Maybe someone else at the bar gave him a ride, yeah? Or one of his parents came and picked him up. Or he grabbed an Uber."

"Both Judith and John Otsby said they did not leave the house once they returned home. We have two rideshare drivers in the area. I've checked with both and both said they had no clients last night. I've verified that with Uber and Lyft."

Chief Haaland sipped her coffee. Officer Schmidt's pen scratched away at its pad. Liv and Gabe shared a look of impatience then Liv said, "Well, I don't know how he got home."

"Me either," said Gabe. "Did you ask him?"

"We did." Chief Haaland smiled. "We're not at liberty to share his answer at this time." Chief Haaland took another sip of coffee, and Liv regretted offering it to her. She should have learned her lesson with Detective Ryan Fitzpatrick in Chicago. "Now," said Chief Haaland, "this next part is completely voluntary—at least for now—but would you two be willing to let us examine your cell phones?"

Gabe and Liv looked at each other. And then Liv said, "Uh . . . are you allowed to do that?"

"Like I said," said Haaland, "it's voluntary. We can get a warrant if we need one but—"

"It's fine," said Liv, "have at it. I have nothing to hide. Except Julia Roberts's phone number. Please don't write that down."

Chief Haaland didn't react to Liv's name drop. "Gabe?"

"Yeah. No problem. Just don't beat my high score on Angry Birds."

Nor did she smile at Gabe's joke. "Thank you," she said. "If you'd please unlock and hand your phones to Officer Schmidt."

Gabe and Liv each handed over their cell phones as Officer Schmidt slid the notepad and pen to Chief Haaland.

"Do either of you own a firearm?" said Chief Haaland.

"A gun?" said Liv. "Uh, no."

"Me neither," said Gabe. "Is that how Denny died? A gunshot?"

"Yes," said Chief Haaland. "One round to the center of the forehead from a small-caliber firearm. Did either of you hear anything unusual last night after you'd returned from the bar?"

"Like?" said Gabe.

"Arguing. Crying. Screaming. Appears to be a .22 caliber wound so more of a popping sound than bang."

Liv shut her eyes and couldn't help visualizing Denny being shot in the forehead. And she kept her eyes shut as she said, "I can only speak for myself, but I pretty much conked out a few minutes after we got back to the cabin." She opened her eyes and said, "You'll see on my phone that I texted my husband and fell asleep."

"And I fell asleep right after I brushed my teeth," said Gabe.

"Your husband still hasn't responded to your text," said Officer Schmidt, his face in Liv's phone. "Is that unusual?"

Liv's jaw tensed. She took a breath, opened her eyes, and said, "How is that relevant to Denny's death?"

"You don't have to answer the question if you don't want to," said Chief Haaland.

Liv wanted to appear cooperative. Her simple trip to Chicago to attend Mack's funeral had morphed into what was looking like a weeklong stay in northern Minnesota. She didn't want things to get even more complicated. She sighed and said, "It's unusual for us to be apart this long. Cooper's a hedge fund manager on Wall Street and works ungodly hours. But we usually see each other every morning and every night. And I still don't know what this has to do with anything unless you're planning on asking me out."

Officer Schmidt ignored Liv's comment and said, "Is it okay if I take his contact information from your phone?"

"Cooper's in New York," said Liv. "Why would you want to talk to him?"

"Well," said Chief Haaland, eyes on Liv's phone, "you also texted your husband this morning to tell him that your uncle Denny died, and he still hasn't responded. That seems odd to me."

"It's odd to me, too," said Liv. "I don't know what to tell you."

Chief Haaland said, "You don't have to give us his contact info if you don't want to. We have other sources."

Liv folded her arms. "Go ahead. Help yourself."

"Appreciate it," said Chief Haaland. "I know this all seems strange and nonsensical. We're just trying to be thorough, which brings me to your visit. I understand your brother Mack passed away and you're here for a memorial service that was scheduled for today and has since been postponed for obvious reasons. I'm terribly sorry for both of your losses."

"Thank you," said Gabe.

"Was Denny murdered?" said Liv. "Or did he take his own life?"

"We don't know the answer to that question yet," said Chief Haaland.

Liv and Gabe looked at each other for what they realized was too long. Now they had to say something. If it hadn't been for Mack's emails, they would assume Mack and Denny dying so close in time to one another would have been an unfortunate co-incidence. But now they weren't so sure. "As long as you have our phones," said Liv, "you'll see a couple of emails we received from Mack after he died."

Chief Haaland looked up from her notes. Officer Schmidt looked up from the phones. Julie Haaland said, "After he died?"

"Apparently you can write an email and schedule it to be sent at a later date," said Liv. "It just sits in your outbox until its designated departure time. I didn't know you could do that, but Mack obviously did. He'd had a couple of near misses. He was almost hit by a car. A bullet grazed his jacket. He was mugged. Mack thought those incidents were connected and that some-one was trying to kill him. You'll see it in the emails. He said if he died, no matter how it looked, we should suspect he was murdered."

Chief Haaland had a quizzical look on her face. She didn't un-derstand.

"The way it worked," said Gabe, "is Mack scheduled the emails to be sent the next day." He continued with the explanation and then added, "There were two emails. One came the day after he died and one came the day we arrived here."

The woodpecker returned to the outside of the cabin and started in with its *rat-a-tat-tat* as if it were sending a message in Morse code.

"I heard Mack died of a seizure," said Chief Haaland.

"He did," said Gabe. "You should probably just read the emails."

"I am most curious to read those," said Chief Haaland. "Was the second email the same as the first?"

"No," said Gabe, "the second email warned us to stay away from Leech Lake."

Again both Chief Haaland and Officer Schmidt looked up at the siblings.

"We didn't think much of his concern until yesterday when we found a note on our door warning us to leave town. And then again this morning when we saw Denny come out of the lake strapped into the car."

Liv said, "I don't want to speak for Gabe, but I'm looking forward to hearing your opinion about those emails."

"Oh," said Gabe, "so am I."

Chief Haaland said, "May I please see the note you found on your door?"

Gabe went to his luggage and returned with the white envelope. Both Chief Haaland and Officer Schmidt read the note.

Leave now. Your lives depend on it.

Chief Haaland said, "Do you have any idea who wrote this?"

"No," said Gabe, "but we found some love letters to our mother that look like they were written on the same typewriter. Apparently, she'd had an affair before Mack was born."

Chief Haaland pushed her chair away from the table as if Liv and Gabe's information was too much for her to handle. She hesitated and then said, "That's news to me. And you have no idea who she had an affair with?"

"No," said Gabe, "we weren't even born yet."

Chief Haaland nodded and pursed her lips then she and Officer Schmidt read the emails Mack had written to Gabe and Liv. Chief Haaland then scooched her chair back up to the table and said, "Okay. We'll consider Mack's emails along with the note on your door as we investigate your uncle's death. Do you mind if we take this to run it through the lab?"

"I took a photo of it," said Liv. "It's all yours. Do you think Mack was delusional?" Liv blurted it out without thinking.

"I don't know," said Chief Haaland. "But his claim that something wasn't right with your family is most interesting. Especially after you just told me about your mother's affair. We'll want to see those letters, too. You didn't know about the affair but Mack might have. Kids are perceptive. They can sense something even when they don't know it. I'd say especially when they don't know it. Without all the distractions of adult life, kids are very in tune with the emotions of people around them. Especially family. My guess is Mack didn't know any details. Otherwise, he would have told you and maybe he would have understood why he felt threatened. Mack visited here only a few times since he moved away. And I hope it's not impertinent of me to say that you two must have felt family strife, as well, because as far as I know, neither of you has visited your hometown in twenty years. And that's a bit strange." She turned to Officer Schmidt and said, "Hunter, what is that saying about Minnesotans?"

"We're like salmon," said Officer Schmidt. "No matter how far away we go and for how long, we always come back home."

Chief Haaland smiled. "Yes. I think that's true. I have to remember that saying." She turned back to Gabe and Liv and said, "Just a couple more things. I know this might be an inconvenience, but I'd like you both to stay in town for a few more days. It would make our job a lot easier if we have more questions. I know it's a big favor to ask, and I could go to a judge to force the issue, but I'd like to avoid that. We like to keep things as friendly as we can."

Liv shut her eyes and sighed. "Yeah-yeah, I can stay. Thank God for Zoom, yeah?"

Gabe pursed his lips. "So can I. I do have to get back to work soon, but if I can be of any help in your investigation of Denny's death . . ." Gabe trailed off and sighed.

"Okay," said Chief Haaland. "Thank you. It's much appreciated. The other thing is, do either of you remember me from when you lived here?"

The siblings shook their heads.

"I had blond hair then and was a bit plumper than I am now. But when your father died, I was the Officer Schmidt to then Police Chief Chuck Anderson. I was here the day Bobby Ahlstrom died, asking you the same questions."

"How . . . ," started Liv. "How could we not remember that?"

"It was a stressful time. You'd lost your mother eight years earlier. Mack hadn't arrived from Chicago yet. It was just the two of you, suddenly orphaned. You were probably in a state of shock." Chief Haaland smiled a warm smile. "I'm sorry for what you've been through. Then and now."

"Thank you," said Liv.

"Yeah," said Gabe. "Thanks."

"Hey," said Liv, "do you know if Alan Cohen still lives on the north end of Steamboat Bay?"

"Alan Cohen who used to work for Marshall Field?" said Chief Haaland. "He sure does. Nice man but kind of sad. Lives in that big stone house all by himself. Stays here all year—doesn't even head south for the winter. Why do you ask?"

"Being back in Leech Lake sparks a lot of memories," said Liv. "Alan Cohen was a regular guest at the resort, and after he moved into that house, he used to eat dinner here all the time. I remember he was a nice guy."

"He's a lovely man," said Chief Haaland. "Donates quite a bit of money to local charities. But very solitary. Alan Cohen likes his alone time. Well, we won't take up any more of your day. We have a long list of people to talk to. Oh, and if you have a chance to make copies of those letters to your mother and drop them by the station, we'd appreciate it." Chief Haaland shook her head. "Hell of an ice-out day, huh?"

"Yeah," said Gabe. "I almost forgot it was ice-out day. Do you know who won the raffle?"

"Raymond Lussier," said Chief Haaland. "Do you know him?"

"We've met him a couple of times," said Gabe. "He wasn't very friendly."

Chief Haaland smiled. "Sounds like Raymond."

CHAPTER 24

Shortly after Chief Haaland and Officer Schmidt left, Liv and Gabe walked across the resort to offer Renee and Winona their condolences. They'd never been in the house before—Denny and Renee built it after they took possession of the resort. They found Renee on the living room floor being consoled by the dogs. The house was already a revolving door of those paying their respects and dropping off food. Renee told the siblings she'd like to have a family-only dinner that evening, and the Ahlstrom Irish twins asked what they could bring. *Nothing* was the answer. The kitchen couldn't hold any more food as it was.

Liv and Gabe returned to Cabin 14 and the chest on the living room floor.

Gabe said, "Any word from Cooper yet?" Liv shook her head. Gabe hesitated. He didn't want to ignite another argument, but there's that thing with family members—it's okay to treat each other horribly, but it's not okay if an outsider does. "What's going on, Liv?" said Gabe, his eyes kind and his tone deferential. "Seriously. Cooper not getting back to you—it's not right."

Liv looked off at nothing for ten seconds then said, "Things haven't been good for a long time. I mean, they're not horrible. They're not even exactly bad. That's the confusing part, right? We don't fight. Cooper's nice enough to me. We have sex once in a while. But the older I get, the more I realize something's missing. There's no passion. And I don't mean physical passion necessarily, but there's no zeal for each other. Or our marriage."

Gabe unstoppered the bottle of perfume and smelled it. "Has it been that way from the beginning?"

"Yes and no. Yes in that I think that's how Cooper has always felt about me. Kind of blasé. But no in that I was madly in love with him. I thought about him all the time. Did nice things for him. Initiated sex. Initiated romantic trips. Intimate dinners. I was so passionate about Cooper and our marriage. But I think . . . I think at some point I just got tired of initiating everything and Cooper rejecting me a lot of the time and eventually . . . well, eventually, I just gave up. Then no one initiated anything. And that's been going on for a couple of years."

Gabe returned the perfume bottle to the chest and picked up the cognac bottle. "Do you and Cooper remind you of anyone?"

"What do you mean?"

"Polite. Passionless. Civil. And married. That doesn't ring a bell?"

Liv said, "No. Should it?"

Gabe uncorked the cognac bottle and passed the liquor under his nose. "I think so. Mom and Dad. At least that's how I remember them." He turned it upside down just to make sure.

Liv wiped a tear from her cheek.

"Sorry," said Gabe. "I didn't mean to upset you."

"It's okay. You're right. Cooper and I *are* like Mom and Dad." Liv laughed through tears, "My therapist will be very excited. Seriously, it's going to be the highlight of her year." Liv held up one of the letters and said, "Well, someone had a lot of passion for Mom. Maybe that's why she kept these letters. And the camisole he possibly gave her. And the perfume. And cognac. And dried flowers. I suppose we should be happy about that, yeah? For our mother anyway. Our mother who died way too young."

"Sorry," said Gabe. "Sorry things suck with Cooper."

Liv forced a smile. "Thank you." Liv returned the letters to the chest and exhaled as if she were trying to push out her sadness. "We have time to drop in unannounced on Alan Cohen if we hurry over there. See if he has an old typewriter lying around. What do you think?"

"You think it's safe going over there?" said Gabe. "I mean . . . you know what I mean."

"I'll call Chief Haaland and say, *In case we disappear* . . ."

"Great," said Gabe. "That makes me feel so much better."

Alan Cohen lived in a house of stones cut from gray granite. The front of the house was set back a couple of hundred yards from the main road, and the back looked out on the north end of Steamboat Bay. Gabe rang the doorbell. He and Liv heard movements behind the large, oaken door. A full minute later, the light behind the peephole darkened, and then the door swung open.

A small man, gray-haired with stooped shoulders, dressed head-to-toe in sporty Orvis garb, khaki pants and a blue and white checked fly-fishing shirt, stood in the foyer.

"Hello, Mr. Cohen," said Liv. "We're—"

"Nope," said Alan Cohen. "Don't tell me. I've been taking memory supplements and I want to test if they're working. Not that I've had any memory problems but one must be on the look-out for these things at my age."

"I don't think you'd recognize—"

"You're Ahlstroms. You used to work at the resort when you were children. It's the shape of your eyes and the distance between them." He smiled and added, "You look like your mother."

Gabe said, "You're right. Gabe and Liv Ahlstrom. We're back in town after being away a long time."

They shook hands and Alan Cohen said, "Come in, come in, please. Ahlstroms are always welcome in my home."

Liv and Gabe stepped into a foyer floored in slate. The home was large and open—even from the front entrance you could see all the way through to the back wall of windows that looked out on Steamboat Bay. The place had a Northwoods feel with its timber posts and beams, but none of the Northwoods kitsch that often accompanies it. There were no hunting or fishing trophies mounted to the walls. No duck decoys carved from wood. No buffalo plaid throw blankets. No framed needlepoint signs saying BLESS THIS HOME or PLEASE MIX YOUR OWN or NAP QUEEN. The furniture was upholstered in brown leather. And the television was so big you expected to smell popcorn and Milk Duds in its presence.

"Please come sit." Alan Cohen led the way to the big room that overlooked the lake. He sat in his recliner. Gabe and Liv chose the couch.

"We're back in town," said Liv, "because—"

"I know. So sorry to hear about Mack's passing. Tragic. He was still a young man. I remember when he came back after your mother died and stayed a whole year. That was very kind of him. And I heard your Uncle Denny was found dead this morning. Terribly sad. I'm mostly retired, but I've done some legal work for him."

Gabe tried not to show his surprise. "I didn't know that."

"If I really like a person," said Alan Cohen, "I'll help them out from time to time. I'm so sorry to hear about what happened this morning."

"Thank you," said Liv. "It was quite shocking when the ice car was pulled out of the lake and we saw Denny strapped behind the wheel. Shocking and terrifying."

"And the biggest news around here in years," said Alan Cohen. "I've received over a dozen calls about it. People liked Denny, but some folks are wondering if he was up to something that got him killed. And some folks are worried he wasn't up to anything and what happened to Denny could happen to them."

Gabe and Liv had discussed the intent of their visit with Alan Cohen while driving north on Highway 371. They had decided to do nothing more than feel out the situation. They would neither ask nor accuse Alan Cohen of having an affair with their mother, Bette. Nor would they accuse him of being Mack's biological father. If he offered information voluntarily, great. But otherwise, they'd smile and do their best to make Alan Cohen feel at ease. If he asked why they'd come to visit, they'd tell him a half-truth. They were going through the old guest books and noticed how frequently he'd stayed at the resort and they were curious about how he was doing since moving to Leech Lake.

"I was planning on coming to Mack's memorial service today," said Alan Cohen, "but I understand why you canceled it."

"Did you know Mack well?" said Gabe.

"I've never known anyone in the Leech Lake area well," said Alan Cohen. "That's my choice. I left Chicago to live a life of solitude. And for over a quarter of a century, that's exactly what I've done."

"But you came to eat at the resort quite often," said Liv. "I remember."

"Yes. I loved Ahlstrom's. Still do, although I prefer the resort before all the changes. It was my go-to vacation spot. Loved it so much I decided to move here when I retired. I've continued to eat at the resort because it reminds me of the time I spent there on vacations, the food is as good as it gets around here, and it's nice for me to be around people once in a while. I can go weeks without seeing another soul. I've read there's a spectrum on the introversion/extroversion scale. My guess is I'm on the far end of the introversion side. I like people. I have social skills. But I'm so much more comfortable and energized when I'm by myself."

"I hope we're not infringing on your privacy," said Liv.

"Not at all. I enjoy visitors. Once in a while." He winked.

"So you never hoped to run a resort of your own one day?" said Gabe.

"Oh, God no," said Alan Cohen. "Loved being a guest but I would hate to run a resort. Too many people to manage. Too much chitchat with the guests. Your Uncle Denny was a master at that. So was your father. Your mother was more the quiet type. Liked to keep to herself. Very attractive quality in my eyes."

A silence hung in the big house. And silences can be more telling than words, a fact both Gabe and Liv intuited so neither were inclined to break it. They waited it out until . . .

Alan Cohen said, "It's very nice to see you again after all these years, but I'm curious. Is there a particular reason you drove up to visit me?"

Liv launched into their planned excuse about going through guest registry books and remembering Alan fondly and wondering how he was doing. Especially after Mack's and Denny's deaths, she said, both she and Gabe wanted to reconnect with their pasts at Ahlstrom's.

Alan Cohen smiled. "That's a lovely sentiment. But it sounds like complete bullshit."

Liv smiled, looked at Gabe then back to Alan Cohen. "For not spending much time with people, your people-reading skills are excellent."

"Remember," said Alan, "I am a lawyer. I'm trained in sniffing out the truth. And then obfuscating it." He laughed. "And I used to spend a lot of time with people, which is why I don't now. So what can I do for you? Do you have a question you need answered? Are you raising money for something? Do you need a kidney? What is it?"

"All right," said Liv. "Fair enough. We'll come clean. Are you okay with that, Gabe?"

Gabe shrugged. "Why not?"

"Well, now I'm most curious," said Alan.

Liv said, "We have reason to believe our mother was in love with a man other than our father. This would have been long before we were born, but around when Mack was born. And we're wondering if the person she was in love with was you."

"Me?" said Alan, a wry smile on his face. "What gives you that idea?"

"We weren't lying when we said we went through the guest registry books. You visited Ahlstrom's frequently when you were a young man. And you moved here when our mother got sick. We're wondering if that's a coincidence or if you chose to live closer to her when she was dying."

"Because I was in love with her?"

"Yes."

Alan Cohen smiled a sad smile. "It's flattering to think a person as beautiful as your mother could have been in love with me, but that was not the case."

"So your moving here when she was dying was a coincidence?" said Gabe.

"I'm afraid it was."

Liv smiled. "And you started coming here in your twenties? By yourself? That seems a bit unusual."

Alan Cohen exuded the calm confidence of a man who knows and accepts himself. "Not for me. Look at where I live. I could have chosen anywhere. This is where I'm happy. Living alone but never lonely."

"And you didn't have any kind of romantic or physical relationship with Bette?" said Liv. "Not even a flirtation?"

"None. Why do you think she had a relationship with another man? She and your father seemed quite happy together."

"A couple of reasons," said Liv. "One is that before Mack died, he told his wife that he had a different father than Gabe and me.

And second, while going through some old family things, we found a chest. A secret chest our mother kept. And in it, among other things, were a number of love letters from whomever it was our mother was seeing then. Typed letters. Neither signed nor dated."

"We thought the man might be someone in town," said Gabe, "or he might be a frequent guest at the resort. That's what you were, and that's why we're here."

Alan Cohen's eyes lit up and his lips moved almost imperceptibly. Liv guessed that he was talking to himself, running over his argument in silence before saying it out loud. "Well," said Alan Cohen, "that I believe." He smiled. "You may not guess it from appearances, but I have had many love affairs in my life. I made a conscious decision not to marry or have children so I could fall in and out of love as many times as my heart could take. It's what I was born to do. I adore women. There are only three words in that sentence, and the most important word is women. Not woman. Women. Plural. I know that may make me sound like a monster or pig, but I have always been upfront with the women I've dated. I've told them from the get-go that I do believe in love and lust but I don't believe in monogamy or marriage. So your instincts are correct: I could have fallen in love with your mother—but the evidence suggests otherwise. For instance, I don't write love letters. Never have. To me, love letters are like reading a review of a movie before you see it. Best to feel what you feel in the moment without any preconceptions going in.

"I see that face, young lady. You think I have memories of grandeur. But let me tell you something. If a man is single after forty years of age, can communicate in full sentences, has a job, doesn't look like he fell into a vat of molten lead, and—this is the most important factor—is attracted to women his own age, he'll have quite the advantage in the world of dating. So many middle-aged and even elderly men run around chasing younger women. Idiots.

Women age like fine wine. I'm only telling you this so you understand that I'm not some broken heart living in the woods on my own, albeit quite comfortably, because I'm still pining for Bette Ahlstrom. Although I will admit that if she hadn't been married, I would have been most interested."

"All right," said Liv. "Thank you for your candor. It was worth a shot."

"Of course," said Alan Cohen. "One must take their shots. But now that you've asked me a question, may I ask you one?"

"Sure."

"After the tragic death of your uncle, what will happen to Ahlstrom's?"

Gabe shrugged. "We haven't even thought about it." He went on to explain that he and Liv had first right of refusal to buy a controlling interest. If they didn't, Renee would probably sell the resort to Winona, who would then battle her minority partner, Judith Otsby, in an effort to redevelop the property as a renewable energy power plant.

"That would be a shame," said Alan Cohen.

"We agree," said Liv. "But I don't want to run the resort or move back here."

"I might," said Gabe, who couldn't shake the idea, or perhaps the better word was *dream* of running the resort with Carly.

Liv turned toward her brother. He expected to see disapproval or at least disbelief on her face but instead he saw curiosity. "Are you seriously considering buying the resort?"

"I don't know," said Gabe. "It's just a thought. There would be a lot of logistics to work out. I'm sure it would be an expensive endeavor."

"Well, Gabe," said Alan Cohen, "if you'd like to run the resort, and you want a financial partner, one who stays far, far away from the day-to-day operations, give me a ring. I would be most interested in saving Ahlstrom's."

CHAPTER 25

Renee's kitchen counters were covered in food. Casseroles (aka hotdish in Minnesota), Jell-O, potato salad, coleslaw, dinner rolls, cakes, pies, cookies, a ham, hamburger patties, sliced cold cuts, pasta salad, green salad, three-bean salad, another ham, and tater tots in glass, foil, tins, melamine, and plastic containers with matching lids labeled with masking tape and Magic Marker. The labels did not indicate food but the name of the person who'd brought it so they could pick up their hopefully empty vessel in a week or so.

After hugs and tears and more tears, Gabe, Liv, Renee, and Winona filled their plates and opened one bottle of red and another of white and gathered in the dining room, the chair at the head of the table conspicuously empty.

Liv raised her glass of wine and said, "To Denny."

"He was a good man," said Renee, who had cried herself dry. "It's why I fell in love with him. He was just good. It was undeniable. What a horrible last night for him. What that awful Otsby woman did to him."

One of the golden retrievers in the living room sighed. It was a tragic sight, seeing them both curled on the floor at the foot of Denny's recliner.

"He was always kind to us," said Gabe, which was true even though he skipped over the fact that he and Liv hadn't seen Denny in twenty years before finally returning to Leech Lake.

"And a good dad," said Winona. "We didn't have much in common. We didn't really appreciate the same things and had different interests. But he was always supportive of my activities and aspirations. I will miss him every day." She said this as if she were talking about a goldfish, not a human being, and certainly not her father.

Liv took this in, the matter-of-factness of Winona's postmortem. The lack of emotion. She saw the same concern flicker in Gabe's eyes. Liv wanted to confront Winona about the dissonance between her words and the tone in which they were delivered, but this was neither the time nor the place. Tonight was about honoring Denny's life and comforting Renee.

Gabe said, "What can we do to help? Either personally or with the resort. We're not going anywhere in the next few days."

"The police want you to stick around, too?" said Winona.

"They do," said Gabe. "But we don't mind."

"Thank you," said Renee. "In the short term everything will be all right. Denny was more of a figurehead than anything else. He liked to talk to the guests. He liked to take them to his favorite fishing spots. But he hadn't run the place in years. I guess Red Pines will keep doing what they've been doing as far as the day-to-day goes. I don't see Judith Otsby changing that, at least for a while. Raymond and Ed will take care of maintenance. I don't know if Denny's death, specifically how it happened, will affect business. Could go either way or both ways with some people wanting to stay away and others who hadn't planned on coming all of a sudden being interested. There is that side of human nature I don't understand. Like when there's an accident on one side of the freeway, cars on the other side slow down to have a look."

"And in the long run?" said Liv. "What do you think will happen to Ahlstrom's?"

"I think that's up to you," said Renee. "I am not going to keep the resort. It's time for me to move back to Minneapolis. Especially now. There's no life for me here without Denny . . ." She took a moment to let the sadness ripple through her.

Winona jumped in. "Liv and Gabe, you have first right of refusal to buy controlling interest. Technically my mom owns it until you decide, so you either agree on a price or a mediator can set one. If you're not interested, then I'll buy the resort from my mom."

"Even with Judith Otsby owning forty-nine percent?" said Gabe.

"Yes. Judith can make all the noise she wants but I'd have controlling interest," said Winona.

"And if you didn't buy it?" said Liv.

"Then Red Pines has the option to buy the whole resort," said Winona. "And Judith Otsby would own one hundred percent of Ahlstrom's. If anything could bring my father back from the dead it would be that. And he would not be a friendly ghost."

The dogs wandered over, sat near Winona, and stared at her with unblinking eyes. Winona was eating chicken with her fingers, and golden retrievers are golden retrievers, no matter how sad they may be.

"Well," said Liv, "I have no interest in buying Ahlstrom's, but Gabe might, right, little bro?"

"Really?" said Winona. She was not smiling.

"I'd have to talk to a lawyer who would have to talk to Denny's lawyer, Alan Cohen. I'm not sure how much time I have to make up my mind."

"Thirty days," said Winona. "I've read the contract."

Gabe nodded, taken aback by talk of business on the day Denny died.

Liv said, "If you don't mind me asking, how did it go with the police this morning?"

Renee swallowed a bite of tater tot, green beans, and mushroom soup hotdish and said, "They mostly asked about Denny's state of mind lately. And if he'd ever threatened to take his own life."

"Had he?" said Liv.

"No. Never. Denny wasn't perfect—he had his challenges like

everyone else. But he was not prone to depression. He loved life. He loved people. It helped that he wasn't an existential thinker. He was smart, just not intellectual. He never wondered about the meaning of life. What's it all for? Why did he exist? What's our place in the universe? None of that. He wasn't political. He was a simple and lovely man. Simple in a salt-of-the-earth way. In an uncomplicated way. But the police did ask if he owned any small-caliber firearms."

Winona's phone rang. She looked at the caller ID and said, "I'm sorry. I have to take this." She stood, walked away from the table, and said, "Hello," as she exited the dining room into the kitchen.

Gabe and Liv watched her go as they heard Renee say, "He did."

"He did what?" said Gabe.

"Denny owned several guns including one .22 rifle and a .22 pistol."

"Are those guns where they're supposed to be?"

Renee looked down and said, "No. The pistol is missing. Denny sometimes took it on his late-night walk of the resort. What he liked to call his *patrol*. He said it was in case he ran into an angry bear or rabid raccoon. A dive team drove over from Duluth today and searched below where the car fell through the ice but didn't find it." Renee took a deep breath and shuddered. "It's all very strange. I feel I've lost my mooring. I'm just floating without Denny . . ."

Liv and Gabe shared a look. An uncomfortable silence hung in the air until Gabe said, "Are you sure you don't want the resort, Renee? Would it be too much change if you left now?"

Renee looked at her plate for a moment then lifted her eyes to Gabe. "Yes, I'm sure. When Denny asked me to move to Leech Lake, I thought it might be a way to feel more connected to my ancestral past. My grandparents come from the Red Lake tribe of Ojibwa. That's just over an hour north of here. I wondered if the water and wildlife, the trees and night skies free of city light would trigger something in me I didn't know I had. But it didn't. I think if things like that happened, everyone would move to the country because if you go back enough generations, we all lived off the land. Not just native people.

"The truth is, I've wanted to move back to Minneapolis for a while now. My parents are almost ninety. I miss my brothers and sisters and cousins and nieces and nephews. As soon as Winona goes back east, I need to go home. I need to be with family. Raymond is here, but he's not the nurturing sort. If you want Ahlstrom's, Gabe, I'll be most happy for you."

"Thank you," said Gabe. "That means a lot."

Liv cleared her throat and said, "Renee, did Denny ever say that he thought his life was in danger?"

Renee looked at Liv and then Gabe and then at nothing. "No. Never."

"You know," said Gabe, "we're asking because Mack felt his life was in danger."

Renee snapped out of wherever her eyes had taken her. She turned back toward the siblings and said, "Mack told you that?"

They explained Mack's posthumous emails, how they were sent, and when they received them.

"I don't think Denny had any close calls," said Renee. "He would have told me. Anything that gave him an excuse to tell a story." She smiled and added, "Such a talker, my Denny. I can't believe he's gone. It feels like he drove down to the cities for the day and will walk through that door any minute. But he won't. I'll never see him again. Ever."

Renee's tears returned. Liv reached across the table and squeezed her hand. Winona returned to the dining room, as if on cue, and said, "My financing is in place. That is if you don't want the resort, Gabe."

Liv looked at Winona with eyes that said, *Who cares about*

your financing? Your mother is grieving. And by the way, why aren't you? Winona seemed to get the message because she went to her mother and put her arms around her.

The doorbell rang. Winona released her mother and walked through the living room to answer it.

Liv turned to her brother. The idea of him buying Ahlstrom's and running it gave her hope. Hope for Ahlstrom's and hope for him. She didn't know why. Maybe it was that he'd stuck around after receiving Mack's email warning them to stay away from Leech Lake. Gabe had taken that warning to heart, felt genuinely afraid, and yet here he was. Even after the note on the cabin door, he cared about this place. And apparently, he cared about the Ahlstrom family. "If you really want to buy this place, Gabe," said Liv, "and you're not comfortable with the person who offered to back you, I'll co-sign a loan. If this is what you want, I'll do everything I can to make it happen."

Mack's and Denny's deaths coupled with Renee's grief and now Liv's generosity was too much for Gabe. He couldn't hold back tears. Liv wanted to help him. His sister, Liv, who had tormented him as a child and whose success continued to torment him as an adult despite three thousand miles between them. All he could manage to say was, "Thank you, Liv. I really appreciate that."

Gabe's acceptance of Liv's offer felt as magnanimous as the offer itself. Liv held a hand to her heart and said, "Of course."

"That's nice," said Renee. "You know, before you arrived, Denny warned me it might be awkward to be around you two. Said you fought all the time when you were kids."

"That's true," said Liv. "We did."

"Denny also said it wasn't your fault. And he never blamed you two for never coming back here. Too many sad memories, he said."

"It is sad for us here," said Liv. "And lovely. It's nice to see how the town has changed. Speaking of which, we were shopping today at the Super One that didn't exist when we were kids, and we ran into your brother, Raymond. He wasn't very welcoming toward us."

Renee smiled a knowing smile. "Raymond's had some bad breaks. Got involved with the wrong kids when he was a senior in high school. He was incarcerated for seventeen years in Stillwater."

"Seventeen years?" said Gabe. "What did they do?"

"Robbed a liquor store. The owner pulled a gun and one of the kids took it from him and it went off, killing the store owner instantly. Prison was hard on Raymond. He really was at the wrong place at the wrong time. But Ahlstrom's has given him a second chance. He's very protective of this place. Denny saved his life by giving Raymond a job and a purpose. It's one of the reasons I hope you buy the resort, Gabe. If you keep him on, you'll get to know him and love him the way I do." Renee took a moment to compose herself and then added, "But until then, ignore Raymond. If you stay out of his way, he'll stay out of yours."

"I heard he won the ice-out raffle."

Renee nodded. "Twenty-five thousand dollars is a lot of money for anyone, but especially for him. That money will make a big difference. It might even inspire him to smile." She laughed at her own joke, a welcome relief from crying.

"Excuse me," said a voice they didn't expect to hear. "We're sorry to interrupt your dinner." They looked up and saw Chief Haaland and Officer Schmidt standing with Winona. "We have two quick questions then we'll let you get back to your dinner."

"Of course," said Renee. "Would you like some food? We have enough to feed a football team."

"No, no," said Chief Haaland. "But thank you. First, we're wondering if any of you have seen Ed since this morning."

"Ed Lindimier?"

"Yes."

"No," said Renee. "I haven't."

"Me either," said Winona.

"Why?" said Liv. "Is Ed missing?"

"He's not at his cabin," said Chief Haaland. "We've checked several times. And he's not answering his phone. It goes straight to voicemail. Last time it pinged a cell tower it was in the general vicinity, but we don't know where he is."

"We haven't seen Ed since this morning," said Gabe.

Liv felt embarrassed and ashamed that she hadn't thought of Ed since seeing Denny's slush-covered body strapped into the ice-out car. She tried to sound more incredulous than outraged when she said, "You don't think Ed had anything to do with Denny's death, do you?"

"That brings us to our second question," said Chief Haaland. She reached into her jacket and removed a gallon-size ziplock bag. Inside the bag was a pistol. It was small and black. "Is this the gun that belonged to Denny?"

"I can't be positive," said Renee. "I don't know much about guns and I've only seen Denny's a few times, but that's what it looks like."

"Okay. Thank you. We'll run a ballistics test to get a definitive answer on whether or not this is the gun that fired the lethal bullet," said Chief Haaland.

"If it's a match," said Renee, her breath quickening and her eyes glossing over, "does that rule out suicide?"

"That is most likely the case," said Chief Haaland.

"Where did you find the gun?" said Gabe.

"Twenty minutes ago we went to Ed's cabin again. The front door was open. We could see this gun sitting on top of his table from where we stood."

"Ed had nothing to do with it," said Gabe. "He loves our family. He loved Denny."

"I'm inclined to agree," said Chief Haaland. "I've never known Ed to be anything but a sweet, gentle soul. But it's our job to investigate all possibilities. And with all the changes going on around here—"

"Ed knew he was contractually bound to his cabin," said Liv. "He knew he wouldn't have to leave no matter who owns the resort."

"I'm sure that was explained to Ed," said Chief Haaland. "But I don't know if he's capable of understanding that kind of thing."

"Mack might have been an obstacle to the resort being sold," said Liv. "Denny definitely was an obstacle to the resort being sold. Ed is an obstacle to the resort being sold because he comes with the property." Liv sat at the kitchen table in Cabin 14. "And I know Ed is not a complex thinker, but even the simplest mind would know to hide the gun they used to shoot someone, yeah?"

Gabe poured two glasses of the Tattersall rye they'd purchased in town and said, "Let's say Ed found the gun in the woods today." Gabe carried the drinks over to the table and sat across from his sister. "And Ed didn't know any better so he picked it up and brought it home to his cabin. Then he started thinking that someone killed Denny. Ed was at the bonfire last night. He heard all the commotion. Denny yelling at Judith Otsby, accusing her of trying to take control of the resort. Judith yelling at Denny, saying she was going to save the resort. And Ed came to the conclusion he was in the way of her taking over the resort. Just like Denny was. Naturally, he would fear for his life. So maybe he took off to hide somewhere and, in his panic to get out of there, left the gun on the table and the door to his cabin wide open."

"That's possible," said Liv. "But where would he go?"

"I don't know," said Gabe. "So much of the resort has changed. I do know one thing—he knows every inch of this property. Every building. And the woods: every tree and old deer stand and duck blind and old lean-to that once held stacked firewood. If Ed doesn't want to be found, it'll be damn hard to find him."

Liv sipped her rye and shook her head.

"What?"

"If someone hurt Ed just because he's tied to this property," said Liv. "And if that's why Mack and Denny died . . ." Liv took another sip but didn't finish her thought.

So Gabe finished it for her. "If that's why Mack and Denny died," said Gabe, "then we're in the way, too. At least we are until we waive our right to purchase the resort."

Liv stood from the table, went to the freezer, and returned with an ice cube tray. She twisted it until a few cubes popped up, then dropped one into her rye. "Maybe we should keep quiet about the idea of you buying this place," said Liv. "And maybe we should make sure we're always around people."

"Do you think we should get a gun?" said Gabe.

"I don't know how to use one," said Liv. "Do you?"

Gabe shook his head as his phone buzzed. Liv watched him look at the screen. He smiled and returned the text.

"Who is it, Gabe?"

He didn't seem to hear Liv. Then Gabe's smile faded to something serious. He stood. "What's going on?" said Liv. "Is it Ed?"

Gabe walked to the front door.

"Gabe?" said Liv. "What are you doing?"

Gabe hesitated, took a breath, and opened the door.

CHAPTER 26

"Gabe, what's going on?"

"I can't believe it," said Gabe. "How is this possible?"

"Gabe?" said Liv.

A woman stepped into the cabin. She looked about their age with long dark hair and brown skin, a carry-on suitcase in one hand and a small dog in the other. "You sounded like you needed a friend," said Carly. "Ca-kaw." She smiled and handed Ms. Ramirez to Gabe. The dog wiggled and snorted with glee.

So much for going to bed early that night. After Carly explained that she flew out of LAX at noon and landed at MSP at five o'clock then rented a car and drove straight north to Leech Lake, Gabe lit a fire and the three humans and one dog sat around the dancing flames. Gabe and Liv told Carly everything that had happened since they first arrived in Chicago. About their lunch with Detective Ryan Fitzpatrick. About Judith, John, and Andrew Otsby showing up at Diana's apartment. About seeing Denny's wife, Renee, and their first cousin, Winona, for the first time in seventeen years. About their reunification with Ed and the skeleton keys and the chest Ed had kept all these years for their mother. They told her about the calamitous bonfire last night and waking up that morning to excited voices because the car had fallen through the ice. And how that excitement turned to horror when the car was reeled out of the lake and they saw the body of Denny Ahlstrom strapped behind the wheel.

As they filled in the rest of the day, Gabe and Carly went from sitting near each other on the mid-century modern couch to sitting next to one another. One hip of Gabe's touching one hip of Carly's, as if gravity had pulled them together. Ms. Ramirez lap-hopped back and forth, overwhelmed with her abundance of choices.

"Our sleeping arrangements aren't the best here," said Gabe. "I'm in that corner over there. Liv is in the opposite corner. The couch is available. We can also put you—"

"Gabe," said Liv. "Seriously. Stop."

"What?"

"Carly came all the way from Los Angeles to see you, right? Either give up your bed and you sleep on the couch, or just, I'm going to be blunt here, Carly can sleep in your bed with you. I mean, I'm tipsy and sleep-deprived, but am I misreading you two? I'm not saying you should have sex—I don't want to be in the room for that—but you're both pushing forty, you're both single, what the hell's the holdup?"

"Okay . . . ," said Carly with a warm smile in her eyes. "I've envisioned this conversation going a million different ways, but this is not one of them." She turned and looked at Gabe, and the two burst into laughter.

"I can wear my AirPods and crank Arctic Monkeys," said Liv. "You two can talk it out. I just think—"

Liv's phone buzzed. She looked at the screen. It was a text from Cooper: *Sorry I've been out of touch today. Two big deals blew up. Been putting out fires all day. So sorry about your Uncle Denny. How are you?*

"Excuse me," said Liv, "you two will have to fledge forward on your own. I have to deal with *my* relationship for a moment."

"We'll manage," said Gabe.

Liv: *I have had an eventful day. All unpleasant.*
Cooper: *Tell me.*

As Liv began thumb-typing everything she and Gabe had just told Carly, Gabe squeezed Carly's hand and said, "Want to take Ms. Ramirez for a walk?"

Gabe and Carly walked Ms. Ramirez on the resort's paved path, Gabe guiding the tour in the direction of the day's events.

"How come you've never told me about Ed?" said Carly as she let Ms. Ramirez sniff a clump of ornamental grass.

"I'm ashamed to say this," said Gabe, "but I never told you about Ed because I never thought about him. Not once. To tell you the truth, I was surprised to learn he's still alive. I don't know why. He's not even seventy. I guess I've compartmentalized my life at Leech and kind of sealed them up and never looked back on them."

Carly found Gabe's hand and said, "Is that as sad as it sounds?"

"I suppose it is."

There was no wind. The trees and shrubs stood perfectly still. Little points of light glowed around the resort and on the opposite side of the bay. The earth smelled of wet earth and dead flora.

"Well," said Carly, "I'm grateful I get to see the place where you grew up. I haven't seen it during the day, but so far it sure looks beautiful."

"It really is beautiful. I miss the green. I miss the seasons. December and January are fun. Then winter drags on after that. February, March, April, and sometimes even May are the months that make you appreciate summer. But somehow by August, you can't wait for fall, my favorite time of year. And the first snow is always exciting. And the first big snow is even more exciting. And then you do it all over again. There's a rhythm to it. Or maybe *cycle* is a better word."

"Do you want to move back here?" said Carly.

"I was considering it."

"Was?"

Gabe stopped and turned toward Carly. When she turned toward him, he caressed her cheek with his free hand. "I was considering moving back here before you showed up for what is the best surprise in my entire life. Now I'm hoping—oh, this is so weird to say—we haven't talked about anything yet—but unless my people-reading skills have completely gone to shit . . ."

"Just say it." Carly's eyes shined in the moonlight. "We've both not said things we should have. It's crazy I jumped on a plane to come here. It's crazy but it also makes sense because it wasn't a hard decision, Gabe. It wasn't even a decision. I knew I had to come here. I just knew it. So say what you're thinking. Please. Because Liv's right. We're both pushing forty—what's holding us back?"

"Okay. Total honesty." Gabe paused to breathe her in then said, "I thought moving back here might be the big change I need, but now I'm hoping that big change in my life is you. Where it happens isn't nearly as important." Carly's smile beckoned Gabe. He kissed her. Carly kissed him back. And that's how they continued the conversation for over a minute until they heard a door open and close.

Gabe looked in the direction of the noise. "Shit."

"What?"

"Sorry," said Gabe. "I'm not talking about you. That was wonderful. But someone just went in Ed's cabin."

"Was it Ed?"

"I don't know," said Gabe. "But we're going to find out."

CHAPTER 27

Gabe and Carly slipped into Cabin 14, expecting to find Liv sound asleep in her corner, but instead found her sitting at the kitchen table with two fingers of rye and tears in her eyes.

"You're awake," said Gabe.

Liv said, "Where were you?"

"Are you okay?"

Liv shrugged. "I just teed off on my husband for not returning my texts and a list of other offenses long enough to be written on a scroll. So no, I'm not okay. Neither is my marriage." She exhaled as if trying to expel her pain. "How much bad can happen in one week?"

"I'm sorry," said Gabe. "You deserve better."

"It's okay," said Liv. She straightened her back in a show of mock strength. "I'll persevere. I always do."

Gabe and Carly told Liv about their walk and what happened outside Ed's cabin.

"Any idea who it was?" said Liv.

"You tell me," said Gabe. He showed Liv the video he shot on his phone. "Sorry it's a bit grainy. I zoomed way in. Look at the walk."

"Is that Raymond Lussier?"

"I think so. He has that uneven kind of side-to-side gait."

"What the hell would Raymond be doing near Ed's cabin?" said Liv.

"No idea," said Gabe. "And why is he carrying what looks like a box?"

Carly was about to say something but couldn't because her teeth were chattering so badly. Gabe put his arm around her and pulled her tight.

Liv said, "You're freezing. Come over to the fire. We'll throw on more logs. And how does a hot toddy sound?"

"Like heaven," said Carly.

Gabe put the kettle on the stove as Liv, Carly, and Ms. Ramirez moved into the living room, where Liv lowered two fresh logs onto a bed of glowing embers. A moment later, they burst into flames. Carly inched closer to the fire. Gabe draped a wool throw over her shoulders.

"So," said Liv, "we think Raymond Lussier carried a box out of Ed's cabin. Now the question is, what do we do about it?"

"The way I see it," said Gabe, "we have three options. One, we go to sleep and deal with it in the morning. Two, we call the police and tell them what Carly and I saw and let them deal with it." Gabe poured rye into three lowballs and said, "Or three, we go over to Raymond's house right now, knock on his door, and ask him what the hell he was doing in Ed's cabin."

"Dude, I don't like option three," said Carly. "Not one bit. It sounds dangerous."

"And I am dead tired," said Liv. She stared into the flames and added, "But I can't fall asleep knowing Raymond Lussier might have something to do with Ed's disappearance. That would be like falling asleep knowing the stove is on, yeah? So I think we should either call the police or go over to Raymond's house and confront him."

Gabe squeezed the honey bear into the glasses and said, "I think we should go over to Raymond's."

"Because?" said Liv.

"Because Raymond might talk to us. He might reveal something, even if that's not his intention. But if the police knock on his door, the guy's going to clam up. Raymond served seventeen years in prison. He won't trust the police. I tend bar with this guy who served time. He has a completely different view of law enforcement than I do. I just think—"

"Excuse me." This from Carly, who was beginning to warm up next to the roaring fire. "I know I'm just getting caught up here, but from what I understand, Raymond not only served time in prison, but he might have killed Denny and is trying to frame Ed. You're going to put your lives in danger by going over to Raymond's, all for an old man who's lived most of his life? Does that make sense? I mean, Gabe, come on, dude, you just told me you loved me and now you're going to deliberately put yourself in danger?"

The fire popped and hissed. Gabe considered Carly's concerns. And Liv looked from one to the other with wide eyes. "What?" said Liv. "You told Carly you love her?"

Gabe brought one of the hot toddies over to Carly and said, "Yes. Seemed a bit overdue."

"Did she tell you she loved you back?"

"I did," said Carly. "Because I do. And I don't want either of you doing something rash whether you've told me you loved me or not." She sipped her hot toddy. "This is the best. Thank you."

Liv smiled. "Wow. Love. At least something good has happened this week." Then her smile faded. "But Gabe's right. Raymond will shut down if the police show up. How about this, Carly? If you don't hear from us by a certain time, you can call the police and tell them where we went and why. We'll build some talking time into the equation so we can try to reason with Raymond, but if something happens and you don't hear from us by, say, one o'clock, yeah, then you can call the police. How's that?"

Carly peeled herself away from the fire, walked into the kitchen, opened a drawer, rummaged through it, then opened another drawer. She removed a small filet knife in its leather sheath, pulled the blade, and scraped her thumbnail. "Not the sharpest knife, but it'll fit in your boot." She sheathed the knife and extended it toward Gabe. "I've seen you peel a lemon when they're standing six deep at the bar. You know what you're doing. Please take it. Just in case. For me."

Liv parked the Tahoe right in front of a small, single-story house sided with pink vinyl that sat half a block from Dairy Queen on Birchwood's main thoroughfare. Just as Ed had described it. It was past midnight on a weeknight. The streets were quiet. No one else appeared to be outside. Just shutting the Tahoe's doors seemed like disturbing the peace. Gabe and Liv heard a few dogs bark from inside dark houses, but no one came out, and no one turned on any additional lights.

They had made a plan to knock on Raymond's door. Not much more than that. Carly would call the police and ask for Chief Haaland or Officer Schmidt and tell them what they saw outside Ed's cabin and where Gabe and Liv were if she didn't hear from them by one A.M.

"I'm nervous," said Gabe.

"Yeah," said Liv. "Me, too. Remember we're doing this for Ed."

"I'm trying to."

They started up the front walk and made it almost to the first steps of the stoop when the front door swung open. Raymond Lussier stepped out of his dark living room holding a sawed-off shotgun. "Get in the fucking house."

CHAPTER 28

If Gabe could hear dogs bark from inside a house, someone inside that house would hear a shotgun blast. That was Gabe's reasoning, at least.

If Liv turned and ran, Raymond Lussier could shoot her on his property. She'd approached his home uninvited. Unwanted. Without warning. Just after midnight in rural Minnesota where the right to defend one's property was up there with the right to fry fish. That was Liv's thinking.

But thinking and feeling are two different things. Their logical brains took a back seat to their thumping hearts. Both siblings froze with fear.

"Now," said Raymond. His dark eyes and scarred face shined in the moonlight. "I'm not going to warn you again." He pumped the shotgun, and Gabe and Liv, though they had not been told, raised their hands. Twenty seconds later, they were inside Raymond Lussier's home.

The front door opened straight into the living room. No foyer. Nothing but a three-by-four-feet area of tile that abutted the hardwood. "Take your shoes off," said Raymond. "And put your phones on the mail table."

Both Gabe and Liv kicked off their shoes and set their phones on a small mail table near the front door.

Raymond kept the lights off and said, "On the couch. Both of you."

Streetlight and moonlight crept in around the pulled shades.

Their eyes adjusted to the dark room. Gabe and Liv walked to the couch painfully aware that Raymond followed them with the short barrel of the shotgun pointed at their backs. It didn't matter if the gun was loaded with birdshot or a deer slug—at that range, they were dead if Raymond pulled the trigger. Liv and Gabe sat on the old corduroy couch and kept their hands in the air.

Liv's mouth felt like dust. She had an inkling to reach for Gabe's hand but didn't dare. She told herself, *Think, stay present, do not fall apart, you're your best chance of survival.* It was how Liv handled difficult situations. She pushed down her feelings and let her head lead the way. Usually, it worked. At least in business. In her personal life, it may have doomed her marriage.

Gabe took a deep breath. He had never had a gun pointed at him but he had ridden out his first significant earthquake in 2008. Feeling the earth jolt beneath him, not knowing how long the shaking would last while sitting in a building that could collapse any moment so rattled Gabe that afterward, he had to have a talk with himself. The talk went like this: *If you're going to live in Los Angeles, you have to accept that earthquakes happen. If you accept that earthquakes happen, you might as well remain calm. Hardly anyone dies in American earthquakes. So stay calm and ride them out because panicking will put you in more danger than the shifting tectonic plates.*

Raymond pointed the shotgun between them and said, "What are you doing here? And no bullshit."

Liv cleared her dry throat and said, "A friend of ours is missing. We wanted to ask if you know where he is."

"You ever hear of a telephone?" said Raymond.

"Yes," said Gabe, "but—"

"Try telling the truth. Because so far, you're not off to a good start."

Liv was mulling over her options when she heard her brother say, "I saw you go into Ed's cabin tonight. And I saw you walk out of there carrying a box." Gabe was careful to say *I* and not *we*.

There was no need to put Carly in danger. "The police have been looking for Ed all day and haven't found him. But seeing you go in and out of his cabin, we thought you might know where he is. And that's what we came to ask you about."

"You know it's funny," said Raymond, "Denny Ahlstrom was doing just fine. Then you two come to town and he ends up dead. Murdered dead. And now you come here after midnight and tell me you're looking for your dear friend Ed. You ever think Ed might have done the math and figured it was safer to get away from you than stay near you? People say the man is slow, but I work with him every day. Know him like a brother. And he's got all sorts of smarts. Not book smarts. Instinct smarts."

"Does that mean you haven't hurt Ed?" said Liv.

"Hurt him?" said Raymond. "Why would I hurt Ed? I just got done telling you he's like a brother to me. And I look out for my brothers if you know what I'm saying."

"Good," said Liv. "We feel the same way about Ed as you do. We grew up—"

"Shut up," said Raymond. "You don't feel the same way I do about Ed. If you did, you wouldn't have disappeared for twenty years." He reached into his back pocket and removed four heavy cable ties. He held the gun in one hand, stepped forward, and tossed them onto Gabe's lap. "Zip your sister's hands together and then her feet. Then do your own feet."

"But we just told you—"

"I will shoot you right here and now. You think I give a shit about a little blood and guts in this rattrap?"

"People know we're here," said Liv. "If they don't get a call from us in a few minutes, they're calling the police."

"Too bad zip ties won't work on your mouth. I should have bought duct tape. Now get to work." Raymond stepped back and pointed the gun at Gabe, who did as he was told. When he was done securing Liv's feet and hands and then his own feet, Raymond said, "Now make a loop with the last zip tie, put your hands inside, and pull it tight with your mouth." Gabe followed Raymond's instructions.

Raymond set down the shotgun, approached the siblings, tightened each of the four cable ties, and stepped back. He walked to the front door and turned the deadbolt with a key, removed the key from the lock, and put it in his jeans pocket. "You two wait here. And I swear, if I hear one hop, one movement of any kind, I'll be back in here in three seconds and the last thing you'll see is a muzzle flash."

Raymond exited the small living room toward the kitchen. Gabe and Liv heard a door open and then Raymond descend the basement stairs.

"Damnit," said Liv.

"It must be getting close to one o'clock," said Gabe. "The police will be here five minutes after Carly calls."

"How do you think that will go? We'll be hostages in an armed standoff. We should have thought this through better."

"Or just listened to Carly because she was right," said Gabe. "We shouldn't have come here."

"Don't," said Liv. "Don't do that. You're here for Ed, yeah? We're here for Ed. Can you reach the knife in your boot?"

They heard footsteps ascend the basement stairs and stopped talking. The footsteps entered the kitchen and made their way into the living room. But when they turned their heads, it wasn't Raymond they saw.

"Oh hi, Liv. Hi, Gabe. Raymond said you came to visit."

"Ed," said Liv, "are you okay?"

"Oh, sure. I miss my cabin. But Raymond said I have to stay here for a little while because a bad person tried to make it look like I killed Denny."

Both Ed and Liv had managed their fear but now they let it go as Raymond Lussier stepped into the living room. In the dim light, they could see the shotgun pointing down at the floor. "Ed called me after Denny was found dead in the ice car. He told me what happened and said when he returned to his cabin, he found a pistol on his cabin floor, picked it up, and put it on the table. I told him not to touch it again. This all happened while the police were talking to Renee and Winona."

"The police think I did a bad thing," said Ed. "But I would not do a bad thing. I did not hurt Denny."

"We know that, Ed," said Gabe. "You don't do bad things. You don't hurt people."

"I know how cops think," said Raymond. "They don't like open cases. They like easy suspects, people that can be hauled away and incarcerated without a lot of hassle. No big protests. No fancy lawyers. They like low-hanging fruit. I smelled the barrel of the pistol Ed found in his cabin. It had been fired recently. I'm sure whoever planted it assumed Ed would pick up the gun and get his prints all over it. I thought of wiping it clean but if my prints or DNA somehow ended up on that thing I'd be looking at life without parole. Besides, that wouldn't stop the police from accusing Ed of wiping it clean. That's why I got him out of there. What you saw tonight was me going back for some of Ed's things."

"I brush my teeth twice a day," said Ed. "And floss. The dentist says I have to. And I use deodorant so I don't smell bad. And I need my pajamas to sleep in. And my slippers so I don't get a splinter in my feet."

"Ed," said Liv, "how do you feel about staying here at Raymond's?"

"I like it. Raymond is my friend. He made waffles for dinner. With maple syrup and bacon and orange juice. Just like breakfast but it was dinner. I liked that. And I have a room in the basement with a bed and a TV and there's a bathroom down there, too. Raymond said I have to hide so the police don't make me live in jail."

"I'm not trying to scare him," said Raymond, "but if the ballistics on that pistol match the bullet in Denny's head, well, like I said, the police don't like open cases."

"I know that's your experience," said Liv, "but I think Chief Haaland might be different."

"Could be," said Raymond. "But I also know Judith Otsby leans pretty heavy on the police. Bitch likes things to go her way. She wants intoxicated boaters pulled off the lake, but she doesn't mind intoxicated boaters if they're guests at her resorts. Fireworks are illegal in Minnesota, but Otsby doesn't want her guests getting citations for a little patriotic fun. God bless America, boom boom boom. So Judith makes police business her business. Gives plenty to the fund. Makes a big show of public support for law enforcement. So when Otsby the Terrible opens her big, fat mouth, the police listen."

"And you think Judith wants Ed in jail for Denny's murder?"

"Who else? I never really believed it was you. My niece wants that property so bad I don't know what she'd do but I'm pretty sure she wouldn't kill her own father. Or anyone else for that matter. Winona's got her sights set on big things. Big money. A big life. She's not going to do something stupid and ruin all the hard work she's put in at school. She's not going to ruin her future." Raymond ejected three shotgun shells and laid the shells and the gun on a chair across from the couch. "Judith Otsby exploits people who need money. She pays them to compromise their values. She sure as hell didn't wheel her oxygen tank into the back woods of Otsby's to plant that pistol in Ed's cabin. But someone did. Someone who might need to pay rent or a car payment or put food on their kids' plates. Plenty of people around Leech Lake need that kind of money."

"Do you have any names of who those people might be?" said Liv.

"I got a few," said Raymond.

"You mind sharing them with us?" said Gabe.

"I might mind," said Raymond. "I don't really know you."

"Shit," said Gabe. "What time is it?"

CHAPTER 29

Raymond allowed Gabe to call Carly at 12:58 A.M., and the siblings left with a promise to keep Ed's location a secret. Even if the police asked them directly again whether they knew where Ed was, they would lie. They understood that could get them in trouble, but they also understood Raymond Lussier would be in even more trouble for harboring a person of interest.

By 1:30 A.M., the siblings were back at Cabin 14. Carly remained by the fire, or rather the fireplace because the fire had again died down to embers. Gabe and Liv's hot toddies sat untouched, and Ms. Ramirez barely raised her head to say hello. Gabe and Liv updated Carly on Raymond Lussier and Ed, then Liv retired to her corner, and Carly fell asleep next to Gabe, curling her back into his chest, their hands intertwined, their dreams unable to compete with the physical reality of their nestled bodies.

They woke to a quiet cabin. Liv was gone, and Gabe found a note on the kitchen counter: *Went to Renee's to help her plan Denny's funeral and make some work calls. Back around noon.* Gabe had just finished reading the note when he felt Carly embrace him from behind, her lips finding the back of his neck.

"So we finally did it," said Carly. "We slept together."

They laughed as if it were the funniest joke they'd ever heard. Laughed for a good minute then stopped and started again. It was the kind of laugh two people share in a unique moment, like a couple of twelve-year-olds in a classroom after the teacher demanded silence. The kind of laughter that is unintelligible in the eyes of everyone except the two people sharing it.

Their laughter dwindled down and then Carly said, "Is Liv a master funeral planner or is her leaving an act of kindness to give us alone time?"

"I don't know," said Gabe. "I don't really know Liv anymore." Gabe turned around to face Carly. He kissed her forehead and added, "I'm so glad you're here."

Carly smiled. "Want to brush our teeth and see what happens?"

Gabe and Carly made love where they'd slept. Gabe's only desire was to please Carly. He listened to her the way a safecracker listens to a lock. Her breathing. Her vocalizations. No words were exchanged. Words had no place. Words couldn't convey what a shuddering body could, an arched spine, a hand gone rigid and then relaxed.

He had never felt so sure of his ability to read another person. It was as if there were an unspoken language that only used touch and Carly and he were the last two people on earth who knew that language, and they relished in each other's ability to communicate. Their love and commitment already existed, grown from walks in the neighborhood, talks at kitchen tables, binge-watching series together, drinks on balconies. For Gabe and Carly, sex was like a notary's stamp on a perfect document that had long existed.

Their connection felt holistically satisfying, and only when they were finished did Gabe wonder if Carly had felt the same fulfillment he had, if she'd made the same selfless effort as he, and somehow, two people back-burnering their own desires simultaneously created the most fulfilling experience possible.

They both rolled onto their backs and looked at the vaulted

ceiling of knotty pine, breathing in unison, until Carly broke the silent synchronicity by saying, "Wow."

"Yeah," said Gabe.

"Get a pen," said Carly. "Write down everything you did before you forget, so next time you can do it again."

Gabe laughed. "Don't worry. I won't forget. I won't forget one nanosecond."

"You'd better not."

"Goes both ways," said Gabe. "For every action, there is an equal and opposite reaction. I think I used to know what that was supposed to mean but I just learned what it really means, so you don't forget what you did either because I was just reacting to you. I've never experienced that before."

"Same," said Carly. "You know, I used to think, if anything ever happened between us, I mean romance-wise, that we'd be such good friends in our relationship that I could put up with mediocre sex. But now I feel like if what we just did is repeatable, then who cares about our friendship? All I need is you in a bed in a log cabin."

Gabe laughed. "I'm game for that."

His phone dinged. Gabe picked it up and read a text from Andrew Otsby. *My mother would like to see you both. Sorry for the short notice, but it's urgent.*

CHAPTER 30

Judith Otsby sat propped up in an adjustable bed. Oxygen fed her nose. A drip IV fed her right arm. Electrodes were taped to her neck and arms and additional wires wriggled under her gown. What little color she'd had was gone, leaving her round face somewhere between white and gray.

A doctor and two nurses fidgeted with the machines. Judith's husband, John, was no longer tethered to her via an oxygen tank, but remained physically close. He'd trimmed and combed his beard but had not shaven it off, as if he'd met Judith halfway with her request. He offered Judith a sip of water, holding a plastic cup and steering the bendy straw toward her puffy, dull lips. She turned her head away like a cat not wanting to be pilled then turned her head back toward Gabe and Liv and stared at them through her thick lenses.

"I know it looks like I'm dying but don't get your hopes up," she said. "Just going through a rough patch. If you don't go through rough patches, you're resting on your laurels. That's what people don't understand when they use the word *privilege*. Just because we're born with opportunity doesn't mean we have everything handed to us. It just seems that way because we don't revel in our struggles. We keep them behind closed doors where they belong." She turned her head in the direction of her husband and added, "Water, John."

John returned the bendy straw to her mouth. This time Judith sipped, breathed, and sipped again.

"Listen, you two Ahlstroms. I'm only going to make this offer once so pay attention. I'll give you forty-eight hours from five P.M. today to accept or reject the offer. And I mean accept or reject. I won't entertain any counteroffers. This is a generous play on my part so don't insult me. No word by Wednesday at five P.M., and I'm rescinding the offer. I have other ways to get what I want. But this path is the easiest for you and for me, although it's the most expensive. Once in a while, time actually is money, as they say, and in light of my health, I don't mind spending money to save time."

"Okay," said Liv, "we're listening."

"Good. Renee will offer you a fair price for her fifty-one percent. She wants out. She's moving back to the city."

"How do you know that?" said Gabe.

"It's my business to know," said Judith. "Now listen: Renee would sell Ahlstrom's to Winona but she has to offer it to you first. That's the language in the contract Denny made with Mack two decades ago. The point is Renee doesn't want Ahlstrom's so she's ready to deal." Judith Otsby wheezed to catch her breath. "Water, John."

John offered her the bendy straw and she suckled it.

"So you two make a deal with Renee. Now here's my offer. You won't need to write it down because it's simple. I'll pay you double what you pay Renee. She sells you her fifty-one percent for two million, I'll buy it for four million. She sells it for three, I'll buy it for six. All you have to do is sign the paperwork and you make a quick and hefty profit. Then you can fly away back home far wealthier than when you came here. You don't got to do nothin'."

"Except sell you the land that's been in our family for generations," said Liv.

"Yeah. That's what the easy money is for. An exchange of legal tender for all your precious memories." Judith almost smiled. Instead she coughed then said, "It's a fair deal. My lawyer is drawing up the contracts as we speak. He'll deliver them to Ahlstrom's by five o'clock today. Any questions?"

"I have one," said Gabe. "Why do you want Ahlstrom's? You have plenty of resorts."

"Because Ahlstrom's is right across Steamboat Bay from Otsby's. I'm going to join them so I have the first resort with a bay in the middle. I envision pontoon boats ferrying guests back and forth. Fishing competitions between Otsby's on Leech Lake East and Otsby's on Leech Lake West." Judith coughed. John offered her more water but she pushed it away. "Snowmobile races across the bay. Who knows? Maybe I'll buy a hovercraft. It'll be the first and only resort of its kind in the Upper Midwest. And when I see all that—when I have a clear vision of what I want to do—I'm never wrong. Ever. I've made a fortune on my dreams." Judith pushed a button and the bed propped her more upright. "Any other questions?"

"Yes," said Liv, "if we reject your offer, what are your other ways to get what you want?"

"I'm not telling you that," spat Judith. "That's proprietary information."

"But it's a fair question because the last person who had a controlling interest in Ahlstrom's ended up shot in the head."

"What are you implying?" said Judith, anger returning a hint of color to her face. "Are you accusing me of having something to do with Denny Ahlstrom's death?! How dare you?!" Judith struggled for breath. John again offered her the water and she yelled, "Not now, John!"

"Mother," said Andrew. "You need to calm down. Getting upset right now isn't helping matters."

"Damnit, Andy! Why don't you act like my son instead of a white coat? How about some support here! Don't you know I'm doing this for you and John?! So you have something when I'm gone!"

"I don't care about your money, Mother. I work hard to make

my own. And neither does Dad. We care about you. As difficult as you make it sometimes, we care about you."

"Eh," said Judith Otsby. "If you cared about me, you'd give me a grandchild. You know they have surrogates now. Buy a turkey baster. Hire a womb. Give me a reason to live! You know I'm the only girl at the club who doesn't have a grandchild! The only one!"

Andrew looked at Gabe and Liv, gave them the slightest eye roll, then said, "One does not bring a child into this world lightly, Mother. It's a different time."

"Oh, don't start your bellyaching about the glaciers. I was in kindergarten during the Cuban Missile Crisis. You think it was easy for my parents to send me off to school with nukes on the launchpad? Everyone's got to deal with something."

"We'll consider your offer, Judith," said Liv. Gabe gave her a *what the hell?* look. "Tell your lawyer we'll start a conversation with Renee and we'll be waiting for the contract."

"Good," said Judith. "Finally someone else around here is talking sense."

Andrew and John walked Gabe and Liv out of the room and down the long corridor toward the front foyer. The house felt so much like it belonged in the South, Liv had to look out the windows to see the half-frozen ground and leafless maples and aspens just to remind herself she was in northern Minnesota.

"Please don't judge Judith by her gruffness," said John. "I know it's off-putting. She comes off as an ornery old bear, but she's in a great deal of pain. It can't be easy being as sharp as ever only to have your body fail."

"No disrespect, John," said Gabe, "but Judith has always been like that. Even when she was healthy."

"I suppose there's some shade of truth in that," said John.

"It's not a shade, Dad," said Andrew, "it's a brick wall of truth. She's an unpleasant person. And to be honest, if she wasn't so sick, I'd cut her out of my life."

John sighed and shook his head, "No one else sees Judith's softer side. Her kind side. Yes, she is a tough woman because that's what her business demands. And don't forget she's a woman working in a man's world, so she has to be extra tough to hold her own."

"John," said Liv, "you're a patient man. Judith is lucky to have you."

"John!" yelled Judith from the bedroom. "Don't let those Ahlstroms leave! I have one more thing to say!"

"She has one more thing to say," said John.

"We heard," said Gabe, starting the walk back toward Judith's bedroom.

She made them go through the whole routine again. Looking from person to person as if it were the last time she'd see them, refusing John's offer of water and then half a minute later demanding water. Finally, she said, "Your cousin Winona has secured financing to buy her father's share of the resort if you do not."

"Yeah-yeah," said Liv. "We're aware."

Judith Otsby managed a smile. "But do you know who is backing her?"

"Does it matter?" said Gabe.

"It might matter to Liv."

"And why would it matter to me?" said Liv.

"Because Winona's financial backer is your husband, Cooper."

· CHAPTER 31 ·

"Wait a minute," said Gabe. "What does Cooper do exactly? I thought he ran a hedge fund." They'd just buckled themselves into the Tahoe.

Liv pushed the start button. "He does, but lately he's pivoted toward private equity and financing start-ups."

"So Judith could be telling the truth. Or do you think she's lying about Cooper funding Winona, you know, as a kind of gamesmanship?"

"Why would Judith make that up?" said Liv, pulling around the Otsby's circular drive. "It's easy enough for me to verify if my husband, my *fucking husband*, is financing Winona. I mean, what the hell, Gabe? Why wouldn't he tell me that?"

"And why wouldn't Winona tell you that?"

"Exactly! My brother's dead. My uncle's dead. We've been threatened. And now this?!" Liv put on her sunglasses and turned on the radio, scanned through a few stations, and then turned it off.

Gabe could see the tension in her jaw, her mouth small and firm. He said, "It was a shitty bit of theater on Judith Otsby's part, calling us back like that. I'm not even sure the point of it."

"The point of it is to rile me," said Liv. "And to stir things up between me and Winona. And to divert my attention toward my marriage. Or what's left of it. What a wrecking ball Judith Otsby is. Although you only use a wrecking ball to bring down a building that's obsolete so there's that unpleasant parallel."

The road around Steamboat Bay was smooth with dark asphalt

and freshly painted lines. Judith Otsby's influence at work, thought Liv. But the loop up and over the bay was a terribly inefficient way to get from one side to the other. Twenty minutes to drive what would be a three-minute boat ride. Maybe Judith planned on running a ferry between the two resorts, as well. She pulled onto the shoulder and said, "Would you drive? I need a moment."

"Yeah, of course," said Gabe. They each exited the Tahoe and walked around the front to exchange places. Gabe sat behind the steering wheel, adjusted the seat, and said, "Sorry, Liv. What Cooper and Winona did sucks. It really does."

"Thank you," said Liv. "But let's not let this distract us. I'll deal with Cooper and Winona, but we can't lose focus because the real question is, did Judith Otsby murder Denny because he wouldn't sell to her? And did she murder Mack for a similar reason, like he was going to buy the resort from Denny and not sell to her? Because she sure as hell seems awful enough to do a thing like that."

"That's what Raymond implied," said Gabe.

"He did," said Liv. "And Raymond seems pretty perceptive." The snow had melted in the ditches, and the wet rot of decaying plant matter found its way into the car. A smell Minnesotans do not attribute to death, but the life that will soon grow in the aftermath of winter. "By the way," Liv added, "I took a room in the main lodge so you and Carly can have a little privacy."

"You didn't have to do that," said Gabe. "We still have all that stuff to go through in Cabin 14. And the chest. There's something in there we're not understanding or seeing. I know it. I'd like you there to help figure it out. You're the smart one."

"Am I?" said Liv. "My cousin, who I'd practically forgotten existed, and my husband are allegedly working behind my back to buy the resort. If that's true, I'd say I'm the dumb one." Liv rubbed her temples. Between her uneven breathing and sniffling, Gabe knew she was crying. But one thing he also knew about his sister— she didn't cry for long. She had an uncanny ability to swallow her sadness and move forward. After a minute she said, "So . . . did everything go okay with Carly last night and this morning?"

"Yes," said Gabe. "Better than okay. I don't even want to say it out loud. I don't want to jinx it."

"You're not going to jinx it. Anybody can see just by looking at you two that there's something magical there. The only thing I don't understand is why you're not jumping up and down with glee."

"It's because I'm here," said Gabe. "Leech Lake makes me nervous. And because Mack died. And because Denny died. And because of the note on our door. And because Ed's hiding out in Raymond Lussier's basement. And because Judith Otsby is threatening to devour our resort. I think when I get far away from here, I'll be as giddy as a schoolboy."

"I hear you," said Liv. "That's why I'm not on the phone right now with Cooper. If he and Winona are going behind my back, it'll be only about the fifth-worst thing that's happened in the last week. But you know what? This isn't a bad place. This is a lovely place. It's just that it seems cursed for anyone named Ahlstrom."

"Yeah," said Gabe. "That is the confusing part. Our family is a small pocket of hell in a place that is otherwise heaven."

They didn't speak for over five minutes then Gabe broke the silence. "Sleep in the lodge if you want, but please hang out in Cabin 14. I have a feeling if we're together, we'll have a better chance of figuring this thing out."

"Agreed," said Liv. "And thank you."

"So," said Gabe, "the theatrics and betrayals aside, what do you think about Judith Otsby's offer? I mean, Renee doesn't want the resort. If we don't want it, Winona will use the land for a power plant. Or at least try to. What's better, razing the resort for a power plant or Ahlstrom's being replaced by yet another Otsby's?"

"You're not considering moving here and running the resort anymore?"

"It was a fantasy," said Gabe. "But the actual fantasy was Carly and me. And it looks like that's coming true no matter where we live. The dream of living back here—I don't know if I'm cut out for it."

They pulled into the resort and drove straight to Cabin 14 to find Carly sitting on the living room floor with the contents of the chest spread around her.

"Sorry we were gone so long," said Gabe, who bent down to pick up Ms. Ramirez. The dog wagged her tail and pressed her wet nose into Gabe's neck.

Carly looked up and said, "No need to apologize. I think I've figured out something. Something kind of big. You might want to sit down."

CHAPTER 32

Gabe and Liv sat on the floor with Carly and Ms. Ramirez and the open chest, its contents out and spread around the oval rug.

"I read through the letters like you suggested," said Carly. "Whoever wrote them was really in love with your mother."

"We agree," said Gabe.

"But something didn't feel right. It's so hard to know what without seeing Bette's letters in response. And as much as I racked my brain, I couldn't figure it out, man."

Liv forced a smile. "Welcome to Cabin 14."

"I took Ms. Ramirez for a walk, and when I came back, I took everything out of the chest and spread it out on the floor. I'm not sure why." Carly picked up the dried purple flowers. "I think I just wanted to see everything not connected to the things near it. So each thing would stand on its own. And that's when I noticed something." She set down the flowers, picked up the bottle of cognac, and said, "I've been a bartender since the day I turned twenty-one. I've bartended a lot of private parties. Catering companies call me in for special events. Whiskey tasting, wine tasting, and there's one group in Malibu that has a cognac event every year. They're a club of cognac enthusiasts and their annual meeting is always a catered event except the catering company doesn't provide the liquor, the cognac club members do. They all bring in a few bottles of whatever is most special to them.

"That old thing about people wanting to talk to bartenders about their problems is mostly a myth. Do you agree, Gabe?"

"I do. Maybe it was true before therapists were invented." Gabe looked at Carly. She was bundled up in a fleece and a scarf and a wool beanie and was impossibly cute. He was enamored with her and so damn honored she was diving into his family despite its problematic history and unanswered questions. He wanted to kiss her right there but didn't want to interrupt her momentum.

"But people do like to tell bartenders about other things," said Carly. "And they really love to talk about what they like to drink, how they make cocktails at home, what ingredients the bartenders use . . . And the cognac members would insist the bartenders try their special bottle. Of course, we couldn't because we were working. But a few years ago, an older man brought in his prized bottle and wouldn't stop talking about how much it meant to him because he bought it when his son was born. He stowed it away for the day his son turned twenty-one, when father and son would share their first drink together. Sadly, his son didn't make it to twenty-one. And so . . ." Carly hesitated, exhaled, then continued. "Sorry, it's such a sad story . . ."

"Understandably," said Gabe.

"Yeah," said Liv. "Take your time."

Carly nodded and regained her composure then said, "With his son gone, the man wanted to share that drink with me. The guy was way older than my father. Like he'd had his first kid when he was fifty. And if he wasn't such a sniveling mess when he told me the story, I might have thought he was trying to hit on me. But the guy was devastated. Really crushed, like something in him died when his son died. So when he offered me a drink from his prized bottle, I felt I couldn't say no. I poured two small snifters of cognac. We toasted each other and his deceased son and each took a sip. He took the bottle, corked it, slid it back to me, and said, 'Please. I want you to have this.' Then he got off his stool and walked away."

Liv leaned back on her elbows, relieved that Carly had taken the helm by examining the items in their mother's secret chest. Liv had long known that driving the ship was her greatest strength and her greatest weakness. She loved being in charge but it was exhausting. Intellectually and emotionally. Liv had a hard time letting go, but Carly seemed to be doing just fine without her. It made Liv feel taken care of, a feeling she didn't get to experience often despite her rich husband. A rich husband, she now realized, who had never taken care of her at all.

Carly said, "I took the old guy's cognac bottle home and occasionally poured from it. It took a few years, but I eventually finished it. But because of the sentimental value to that man, I kept the empty bottle thinking maybe I'd see the guy again and I could offer it back to him. I bartended several more events for the Malibu cognac club, but I never did see him again, so I put the bottle on a shelf in my apartment. It was so beautiful—like nothing I'd seen before—that one day I looked it up. Turns out some cognac distilleries make special bottles some years. So you can date the year by the shape of the bottle.

"And then sitting here today, I thought this cognac bottle also looks special. So I did some research online. This bottle is unique—and pretty special to me at least because they only made it the year I was born. Which is the same year—"

"That I was born," said Liv.

Cabin 14 grew quiet in the shadow of Carly's implication. Ms. Ramirez hopped out of Gabe's lap and went to Liv for the first time, as if the dog had picked up on Liv's distress and wanted to comfort her. Liv scratched behind Ms. Ramirez's ears and the dog snorted her appreciation.

Gabe said, "So according to that cognac bottle, Mom didn't have an affair the year Mack was born. She had an affair the year Liv was born."

"Oh, boy . . . ," said Liv, shaking her head, her voice quivering. "Oh, boy . . ."

"I know, man," said Carly, "it's huge. And I wasn't even sure I should say anything. I mean, maybe the bottle has nothing to do with the man your mom loved. Maybe it felt special to her because that's when Liv was born. But there's also the bottle of perfume. Some perfume brands change their bottle every few years. And I looked up that particular bottle of Crabtree & Evelyn Lily of the Valley. It's from the same year as the cognac bottle. Which isn't a guarantee but—"

"It practically is," said Liv. "Which means everything is turned upside down from what we thought."

Carly nodded. "And there's more. Did you read all the letters?"

"I think so," said Liv.

"Pretty sure we did," said Gabe.

"They're not dated, but you can kind of track a progression in them. In one that I think is from earlier in their relationship, the author of the letters says something about your mother having his child."

"I remember that," said Liv.

"But in another letter, which I think is toward the end of their correspondence, the writer of the letters says, 'And now two hearts from our love will beat in your home.'"

"Yeah," said Gabe. "I remember that one."

"Me, too," said Liv.

"At first I thought he meant Bette's heart and Liv's heart. But the way it's worded, *two hearts from our love*, and the fact that there are a couple of references to Christmas and a couple of references to spring and they appear spread out from each other time-wise, I think the affair lasted at least two years, maybe three, and I think, I could be wrong but I think, you're both children of that affair."

Gabe and Liv shared a look they'd never shared before. Liv pushed her hair back from her forehead and sighed. Gabe felt a rush of emotion. His eyes stung. His throat tightened. He swallowed it all down and cleared his throat.

Liv said, "So when Mack told Diana that he had a different father than us, he meant his father was the man we always believed was our father. Mom's husband, Bobby Ahlstrom. But really, Gabe and I are the ones with a different father than the man we called Dad. We're the result of Bette's affair. Not Mack."

Gabe stood, went to the kitchen, removed three lowballs from the cupboard, set them on the counter, and dropped an ice cube into each. He began to pour and said, "I've made a unilateral decision. Happy hour is earlier today. And it isn't all that happy."

"This is just a theory," said Carly. "I could be wrong."

"No," said Liv. "You're not wrong. Because if your theory is true, then a whole bunch of things that didn't make sense all of a sudden do make sense." Liv shook her head and said, "My God, Carly, you did it. You're a genius. You decoded the chest."

They showered and dressed and went to dinner in the dining hall, which was quiet with the Outboard Motor Association gone. It would get busier tomorrow when the Knitters of the Northern Plains gathered for their annual conference and knit-in. The special of the night was Minnesota Surf-n-Turf: roast chicken, deep-fried walleye, baked lake trout, and beef stew.

They talked little over dinner, Liv and Gabe still processing Carly's discovery, each in their own way. It wasn't until slices of blackberry pie arrived with vanilla ice cream that Liv said, "If Gabe and I have a different father, it has to be the reason Mack left home as soon as he could, right? He was twelve when I was born. Thirteen when you were born, Gabe. Mack was still a kid, but he was old enough to understand what was going on. He must have known Mom was in love with whoever wrote those letters, yeah? Maybe she was so consumed with the affair that Mom inadvertently abandoned Mack. He was probably right at that age when he wanted some independence from Mom and Dad but still needed their emotional support. And time. And love. But maybe Mack didn't get that time and love if Mom was having the affair that created us."

"And if your dad knew," said Carly, "man, that must have been so hard for him. He knew but he stuck it out. You both remember him as being a really good dad and a really good guy."

"He was," said Gabe. "But if Mack knew that our dad was aware of the affair, and our dad didn't do anything about it, or make Mom end it with the guy . . . If our dad just took it, Mack might have hated him for that. I mean, what kind of person lets their partner walk all over them? So then Mack would have hated Mom *and* Dad. And if Mack knew we were only his half-siblings, maybe he hated us, too. Not that he blamed us, but if Dad's not our biological father, Liv and I are kind of symbols of our parents' dysfunction."

Donna the Funster walked by, a pint of Mad Musky in hand, and when she saw Gabe sidled up to Carly, she glared at Gabe, shook her head, and kept walking.

"What I remember about Dad is him being so sweet to us," said Liv. "He always had a smile for me and for you, too, Gabe. Never hit us. Never even raised his voice. But what I also remember is he wasn't very involved. He worked a lot at the resort so he was always around, but now that I think about it, he didn't actually spend much time with us."

Three men in their seventies walked in carrying musical instruments. An accordion. An upright bass. And a bass drum that read *The Wally Kramarczuk Band*. They dropped their equipment on a portable stage set up under a mounted elk head then headed out for another load.

"We should do one of those genetic ancestry tests," said Gabe. "Maybe we'll get lucky. Maybe our bio dad or someone in his family did the test, and we can find out who it is that way. Or at least narrow it down. They catch serial killers from DNA left behind at the crime scene that way. Why not biological fathers?"

"Who very well might be a killer," said Liv. "But I think those tests take a couple of months. It's a good idea. I'm just saying we're not going to find out tomorrow."

"Do you need to find out soon?" said Carly. She put her arm around Gabe and ate a forkful of walleye off his plate.

"We do if our bio dad killed Denny and possibly Mack. We also need to make a decision about the resort soon. Whether we buy it and keep it or buy it and sell it for a profit to Judith Otsby or let it go to Winona so she can bulldoze every building and memory to build her power plant. Knowing what happened almost forty years ago might help us make that decision. And help us understand if Mom's affair is in any way tied to what happened to Denny."

"And Mack," said Gabe.

Liv nodded. "The way things are looking now, I'm inclined to let Winona wipe this resort off the map. A renewable power plant that serves the whole community is looking a lot better than our family history. And—"

"Hoped I'd find you here."

Liv looked up and saw Tyler Luther wearing a suit and holding a manila folder inch-thick with papers flagged with SIGN HERE Post-its.

Tyler Luther set the folder on the table and said, "Judith's contract. The offer rescinds Wednesday at five P.M. I have a pen if you'd like to sign it now."

"We'll have a lawyer look at it," said Liv. "Thank you."

"There's nothing fishy in the language. It's all straightforward."

"Thank you but save your advice for your client," said Liv. "You're working for Judith, not for us."

"I'll remind you what I said before. You can make this easy. Or you can make it hard. But Judith's going to get what she wants either way." Tyler Luther turned and walked away.

"What was that about?" said Winona, who approached carrying her dinner on a tray.

Liv said, "Please join us, Winona." And then added in a tone Gabe understood, "Gabe, Carly. Why don't you make us a pitcher of Gabesons. I could use a cocktail."

"Yeah," said Gabe. "We can do that."

Gabe and Carly headed toward the bar, and Winona sat like a lame duck on the opening day of hunting season.

CHAPTER 33

Liv stared hard at Winona and said, "I've heard your funding source is my husband."

Winona said nothing but her body language was loud and clear. Her shoulders slumped forward and she pulled her arms close to her body as if that made her a more difficult target to hit.

"But I didn't hear it from you," added Liv. "And I didn't hear it from my husband. So do you want to tell me what's going on?"

The three members of The Wally Kramarczuk Band returned, this time carrying amplifiers, mic stands, and a snare drum.

Winona had just sat down. Now it looked like she wanted to get up and walk away. She thought better of it, sighed, and said, "We were going to tell you."

"*We*," said Liv. "You're a *we*? Last time I saw you, you were seven years old. Now you and my husband are a we?" Liv took a few breaths to calm herself and added, "And what were you going to tell me exactly?" She wished she'd had one of Gabe's cocktails before this conversation. She wished she'd had two. But there was no way to put this off any longer.

Winona appeared like she, too, could use one of Gabe's cocktails. She looked down at the table, breaking eye contact with Liv. "I met Cooper at a Wall Street job fair at Wharton," started Winona. She picked up her fork and hovered it over her salad, but couldn't muster an appetite and set it down. "I didn't know he was your husband when I met him. There was this event where MBA students pitched their business ideas to VC and private equity and fund managers. It was ostensibly to give students practice pitching and developing business plans, but every year, a few students would actually land financing for their project." She looked up and faced Liv. "Cooper was very interested in my sustainable, rural power plants."

"Did Cooper know you were my cousin?"

"No."

"Really? I find that hard to believe. We have the same last name. If he asked anything about you, I'd think you'd mention you're from Minnesota, yeah? And then his natural response would be, 'Wow. My wife's last name is Ahlstrom and she's from Minnesota.' And then Leech Lake would come up and Ahlstrom's resort and the connection would be made. But you're telling me that didn't happen?"

"Testing, one-two," said Wally Kramarczuk into his microphone. "Testing . . . Testing . . . A yipidee da-doo. A yipidee da-doo."

Winona dropped her eyes again and said, "Well, eventually we made the connection."

"Yeah-yeah, but you didn't tell me. And Cooper didn't tell me. That doesn't look great, Winona. At least to me, the wife, it doesn't. In fact, it looks pretty bad. Really bad."

Winona looked up with her big eyes, nodded, and said, "I get that." She tried to swallow but could not. She reached for Gabe's water and took a sip.

"It also doesn't look good to me as the person who holds the first option to buy fifty-one percent of the resort," said Liv, who was feeling in complete control of this conversation and completely out of control of her life.

Winona grimaced. "Understandable."

"So what's going on? And I'd appreciate the truth."

"The truth," said Winona, "is that I don't know the truth. I don't know anything other than that Cooper said he'd be my angel investor to buy the property if you and Gabe pass."

"This was yesterday?" said Liv. "When Gabe and I came over to console you and your mother?" She bore her eyes into Winona, cold and unforgiving. "You excused yourself to speak to my husband about financing your purchase of my family's resort."

"It's *my* family's resort now," said Winona, fighting for the tiniest bit of moral footing, which slipped away as soon as she stepped on it. "But yes. That's when Cooper confirmed the deal. But we've been talking for months. And according to Cooper, you hate it here. Said you never wanted to come back."

Liv felt the sting of Winona's words. Mostly because they were true. Liv had no intention of coming back to Ahlstrom's or anywhere else in Minnesota. At least she hadn't until Mack died. "Still," Liv said in just above a whisper, "Cooper had no right to go behind my back on this. And you should have told me."

"Well," said Winona. "I'll tell you this. I don't know if Cooper's interest is strictly business or if he's also interested in me personally. And to be completely honest, if he's interested in me personally, I want to use that to my advantage. Nothing's going to happen between us—I have zero interest in him. No offense.

"And that's why I didn't tell you about Cooper. Because if his financial interest in me is tied to a romantic or sexual interest, I don't want to unburden him of that fantasy. I don't overtly flirt with him. I don't promise him anything he won't get. But I do flatter him. And I pretend I'm a little more in need of his financial expertise than I really am."

Liv sighed. "I understand your side of it. But Cooper's side of it . . . of course he's interested in you, Winona. That is, romantically and/or sexually." Liv shook her head and added, almost to herself, "Of course . . . And where there's smoke . . ."

"I need to get this power plant going, Liv. I need it for my career and we all need it because when it works here, then it'll work in India and China and Brazil and North Korea, not to mention the American Southwest where people die when the power goes out. The world needs this technology. And sorry to be so blunt here but I don't really care where the money comes from. The ends justify the means in this situation."

Liv glanced over at Gabe and Carly and with just a look told them *not yet*. She returned her attention to Winona and said, "I appreciate your honesty. Now I'm going to be honest."

"I'm a big girl," said Winona. "I can take it."

Wally Kramarczuk's drummer tested his kick and snare drums. *Boom-back-back. Boom-back-back.*

Liv said, "I wish you would have told me this earlier. Or more accurately, I wish you would have told me—period—instead of me hearing it from Judith Otsby."

"How does Judith Otsby know Cooper's financing me?"

"I have no idea, and that's a question we can explore later. But right now I want to say that I don't blame you for using your looks to your advantage. I mean, we haven't seen each other in seventeen years, right? And last time we did you were only seven years old. You don't owe me your loyalty. You don't owe me anything. That said, I would like to ask a favor."

"You can ask," said Winona. "But I can't promise anything."

"I would like you to keep doing what you're doing."

Winona looked not only surprised at what Liv said but surprised that she was surprised. She was used to feeling centered, but Liv had pushed her off-balance. "I'm not sure I understand."

"I would like you to carry on exactly how you have been and do not tell Cooper about this conversation. The fact that you're my cousin makes no difference to me . . ." Liv paused, knowing that Winona might not be her cousin after all. At least not by blood. But Winona didn't need to know that yet. ". . . But what does make a difference is that my husband has chosen to not tell me about his relationship with you, whether it's business or more aspirational on his part. That I do care about. Can you do that?"

"Not tell Cooper that you know?"

"Yes," said Liv.

"I can absolutely do that."

"Thank you."

This, too, threw Winona off-balance. Now Liv was thanking her. She took another sip of Gabe's water and said, "Am I misreading this, or are you not upset with me?"

"Your perception is accurate," said Liv. "I'm not upset with you, Winona. Like I said, my issues with Cooper and our marriage predate you."

"That is generous on your part," said Winona. "I appreciate it. And to reiterate, I have no interest in your husband. I promise."

"Even if you did, it wouldn't matter. I care about his interest in you. But I don't give a damn about the other side of the equation. So play it however you need to play it."

Winona said, "Does that mean you're leaning toward not exercising your option to buy the resort?"

"I don't know what Gabe and I will do. There are a couple of extenuating circumstances that I can't go into at the moment. But whatever happens between me and Cooper is not one of them."

Winona nodded and said, "Wow. Okay. And if you don't mind me saying so, you're taking this very well."

"I'm not taking it well, Winona. I'm actually quite upset. But I'm dealing with it like a grown-up. Emotions and actions are not mutually exclusive."

"Winona overheard Denny saying that Bobby deserved a better wife than Bette." This from Liv as she and Gabe stood in Renee's living room. The golden retrievers stood on either side of Gabe as he scratched the tops of their heads. Renee sat on the floor with Denny's belongings scattered about as she sorted through them. Her face was streaked with tears. All yoga classes at the resort had been canceled. "Did Denny say anything else along those lines?"

"No," said Renee. She placed a set of rainbow suspenders in a pile with the other suspenders and said, "These used to be Denny's favorite until he learned rainbows were a Pride symbol. Not that he had a problem with the queer community, but he didn't want people to mistake his orientation."

"So," said Gabe, "Denny never mentioned anything about Bette having an affair before we were born?"

"Why are you doing this?" said Renee. "Why are you pestering me with these questions?" The queen of calm lost her cool. "I'm mourning my husband! I'm mourning my home! My daughter is about to graduate from Wharton and move to God knows where! She's going to leave just like you did!" Renee caught her breath, sat on the couch, and let her face fall into her hands. "Denny's been murdered, his killer is still out there, and all you care about is something that happened forty years ago?"

Liv sat next to Renee and took her hand. "Gabe and I have good reason to believe that Bobby Ahlstrom, our *dad*, is not our biological father. And, Renee . . . and . . . we believe that whoever is our biological father . . . he may have killed Denny."

Renee lifted her face from her hands and looked at Liv. "Are you serious?"

"We are," said Gabe, "and we're terribly sorry to bother you with this, but if Bobby told anyone who our mother had an affair with, we think he might have told Denny. And maybe Denny told you."

Renee said, "I would never keep something like that from you. Denny never said anything other than that one comment about Bobby deserving a better wife than Bette."

Renee sniffled. Gabe handed her a box of tissues. She wiped her eyes and blew her nose. The dogs leaned into Gabe, demanding more scratches.

"What about this, Renee?" said Liv. "You've lived here nineteen years, yeah? How would someone pull off a multi-year affair without anyone knowing?"

Renee shook her head. "I don't know how that could happen. I love Leech Lake. I love the little town of Birchwood. But it's a fishbowl. Everyone knows everyone else's business. You can't go to a doctor one day without some random person the next day giving you a concerned look and asking how you're feeling. To pull off a multi-year affair that resulted in two children? I'd say that's impossible. So impossible that if I were you, I'd do one of those genetic testing kits. You just might find out you're Ahlstroms after all because for two people to have an illicit affair in this town, they'd have to be invisible."

CHAPTER 34

Gabe and Liv went back to Cabin 14, picked up Carly, and drove into town. They bought a cart full of groceries and brought them to Raymond and Ed. As Raymond put them away, they sat with Ed in the living room with the shades pulled. With Raymond's permission, Carly had carried Ms. Ramirez into the house. The dog took a liking to Ed and sat in his lap.

"Ed," said Liv. "We want to ask you a question about a long time ago, okay?"

"Oh, sure," said Ed. "I like questions. But not hard questions."

"It's not a hard question," said Liv. "And it's okay if you don't remember. Only answer it if you do remember. It's about Bette. Did she spend time with another man before I was born?"

Ed looked like he didn't understand. Raymond walked into the living room from the kitchen and said, "Did Bette have another husband or boyfriend?"

Ed shook his head. "No. Bobby was her boyfriend and husband. Only Bobby."

"Do you remember," said Gabe, "if Bette used to leave the resort a lot before Liv was born? Or before I was born?"

A truck rumbled down the street. Raymond went to the window and peeked out the pulled shade.

"No," said Ed. "Bette didn't leave. She worked at the resort like me and Bobby. She helped take care of the guests and their rooms and cabins."

"Ed," said Carly, "what did Bette say to you when she asked you to keep the chest with two locks? What did she say was in there?"

"She said it was secret. It was secret and only she knew what was inside. She said it was so secret, she didn't want anyone else to know about the chest. That's why she asked me to keep it because no one else visited my cabin."

"Right on," said Carly, "so do you mean, like, you're the only person who went into your cabin?"

Ed shook his head. "Only Bette and me went into my cabin. No one else. Only Bette and me."

Gabe looked at Liv and back to Ed and said, "What did you and Bette do in your cabin?"

Ms. Ramirez snorted up at Ed, who laughed and said, "Oh, you like it under the chin. You're a good dog."

"Ed?" said Gabe. "What did you and Bette do in your cabin?"

Ed said, "Bette and me didn't do anything in my cabin."

"It's okay," said Liv. "You didn't do anything bad. And we won't be upset with you. Even if Bette said it was a secret, you can tell us, Ed. Just like you gave us the chest. Bette was our mom, right? She'd want us to know."

"Me and Bette didn't do anything in my cabin," Ed repeated.

Liv looked at Raymond for help. But Raymond didn't respond so Liv said, "But Ed, you just said Bette's the only other person who went into your cabin. You must have done something together."

"No," said Ed. "I tell the truth. I don't tell lies."

"Ed," said Raymond, "they know you tell the truth. I know you tell the truth. Liv and Gabe and Carly are just a little confused because you said Bette was the only person other than you to go in your cabin."

"That's right."

"But you're also saying you and Bette didn't do anything

together in the cabin. Did you just sit in chairs and not talk to each other? Did you hold hands? Did you eat lunch? Did you watch TV? What happened when you were in the cabin together? That's what Liv and Gabe and Carly want to know."

Ed exhaled, rubbed his chin, and said, "Bette went into my cabin, but not with me."

Liv said, "Bette went into your cabin by herself?"

"Yes," said Ed. "She cleaned it for me even though I'm a good cleaner. Cleaning is important."

"When did Bette clean your cabin?" said Gabe.

"When Bobby and I took the guests out on the pontoon boat. We did that every afternoon. We would leave at two o'clock and come back at four o'clock. We'd help the kids fish for crappies and sunnies. Straight down from the boat near the bottom. That's where the fish go in the afternoon when the day gets hot. And when I would get back to my cabin, the dishes would be put away and my bed would have clean sheets and blankets."

"That's how Mom had an affair in a small town without anyone knowing," said Liv after shutting the Tahoe's driver-side door. "She used Ed's cabin. No one would have wondered why she was walking back there with cleaning supplies and a stack of fresh linens. And whoever wrote those letters must have approached from the back woods."

Gabe reached to the back seat over the center console and took Carly's hand. "If Mom carried on her affair in Ed's cabin while Dad and Ed were out on the pontoon boat, then the whole premise of what we're searching for is out the window."

"What do you mean?" said Liv.

"We've assumed someone in this small town had to know about Mom's affair. But maybe no one knew other than her and her lover. Maybe they were that smart about it. That careful."

Liv stopped at one of Birchwood's two stoplights. The locals were out in force to shop and eat and drink. Most wore shorts and T-shirts, exposing paper-white skin that hadn't seen the sun in six months.

"Why is everyone here dressed like they're going to a beach party?" said Carly. "It's only fifty-eight degrees. When it's fifty-eight degrees in L.A., half the town is wearing down puffers."

"Because," said Gabe, "fifty-eight degrees after a northern Minnesota winter feels like eighty-eight degrees. Got to enjoy the warmth while it lasts because it doesn't last long."

Liv waited for four Funsters to cross the intersection in a pedal car, each wearing a yellow *Funsters* T-shirt instead of their usual windbreaker. She turned onto Highway 371 and said, "If it's true Mom and our biological father, whoever he is, were able to keep their affair a secret, then we'll have to try the genetic ancestry route. It's just going to take a while."

"I have a thought," said Carly.

"Please," said Liv.

"I think it's strange that when you went to visit Alan Cohen he recognized you after all these years. He denied being Mack's biological father. But you never asked if he's *your* father. I don't know why he'd want to keep it a secret but he might have a reason. And if so, it would help explain two other things."

"Which are?" said Gabe.

"Why did Mack go to Chicago?"

"I don't understand," said Liv.

"It's possible Mack somehow knew about your mother and her lover. Maybe Mack saw them in the woods or something. And let's say that lover was Alan Cohen, who lived in Chicago. What if Mack pressured him for money, and Alan set up Mack in Chicago. Helped him get his first job. Maybe his first apartment."

"That doesn't sound like the Mack I remember but it's possible," said Gabe. "It's definitely possible. Mack was a kid from a small town. Going to a big city would have felt overwhelming. It did for me. What's the other thing it would explain?"

Carly said, "It would explain why Alan Cohen offered to back you if you choose to buy fifty-one percent of Ahlstrom's. Man, he barely knows you. He has no idea if you have what it takes to run a resort. No responsible business person would make that offer. But it is what a father would do for a son."

Liv's phone rang. She looked at the area code on the Tahoe's screen. "312. This must be Andrew." She answered the phone on Bluetooth. "Hello?"

"Liv?"

"Yes."

"This is John Otsby. I was wondering if you and Gabe wanted to meet for a drink. I have some information that you may find helpful."

"Helpful in what way?" said Liv.

"I'd rather explain in person if that's okay."

"Sure," said Liv, giving Gabe a *what the hell?* look. "We were just about to drive from town back to the resort. Gabe's girlfriend, Carly, is visiting from California. You okay if she tags along?"

"Don't mind at all. Meet you at Sven's Tiki Hut in half an hour?"

Sven's Tiki Hut was a mile out of town and tried its damnedest to create a tropical island atmosphere in a place that was about as far away from an ocean as you could get. They served drinks in plastic pineapples, tiki mask strung lights hung from the ceiling, anything that could be thatched was thatched, calypso music flowed out of speakers that looked like rocks, and Sven kept the thermostat at eighty degrees.

They left Ms. Ramirez in the Tahoe and found John sitting at a round table in a back corner under a thatched umbrella and with a pitcher of some concoction that looked like Windex. John stood

as they approached and greeted Gabe and Liv with the warmest
of smiles and handshakes that threatened to morph into hugs, and
was equally warm toward Carly.

"Thank you," said John, "I know this is last minute and I really
appreciate you coming."

John poured the blue liquid into four plastic pineapples and
added, "I don't know if you're hungry but I've ordered snacks.
Spicy pineapple and chicken skewers, crunchy rice balls, and coconut shrimp."

The drinks not only looked like Windex but tasted like a house-
hold cleaner, as well. Liv, Gabe, and Carly forced smiles as they
took their first sips.

"The reason I asked you to meet," said John, "is because I'd like
to encourage you to take advantage of that contractual clause and
buy a controlling interest in Ahlstrom's."

"So we can sell it to Judith," said Gabe.

"No," said John. "So you can keep it and run it yourselves."

"Yeah?" said Liv. "I'm surprised to hear you say that."

A server walked by wearing a necklace made of lit-up chili peppers. Gabe wondered if she knew chili peppers didn't fit the tropical theme. She might as well have been wearing a necklace made
of candy canes or cacti.

"Judith's been in an awful state lately," said John. "Her health
problems are getting worse. She's in pain. And, as you've seen, she
takes it out on anyone within earshot. If she knew I was here right
now talking to you without her permission, boy oh boy, she'd let
me have it." John smiled a sad smile. "But that's my Judith. She's
a darn tough businesswoman. Otsby's resorts are the finest in the
north. That's no knock against Ahlstrom's, but Ahlstrom's is one
property. Maintaining that quality across a dozen resorts is no
easy feat. Judith gets the credit for that."

John sipped from his plastic pineapple and said, "Mmm. Delicious." And then added, "But Judith is not right about everything.

I am not happy with her effort to muscle in on Ahlstrom's. Your family has done a hell of a job over the generations. And frankly, the competition is good for Otsby's. It's what drives Judith. I believe it's what's keeping her alive."

"Is that why you don't want controlling interest to go to Winona?" said Gabe. "Because she'd raze the resort?"

"Actually," said John, "I don't think Winona would raze the resort. I know she'd try, but the city and county would do everything in their power to stop her. And they'd do so with Judith's help. No one wants to see wind turbines and a solar farm on prime lakefront property. It'd be an eyesore for everyone out on the lake, bad for our Northwoods image, and bad for tourism. As a lifelong resident and lover of the Leech Lake area, I strongly believe Ahlstrom's should remain Ahlstrom's."

The chili pepper server approached and dropped off the food John had ordered. The crunchy rice balls and coconut shrimp were each skewered by a little plastic samurai sword—another insult to the tropical theme.

"But now that Judith owns a minority share," said Liv, "do you think she'll try to change Ahlstrom's and make it more like Otsby's?"

"She will try to change Ahlstrom's," said John. "Judith will scream and holler about what she wants, but without controlling interest, it's not her call. She'll get tired after a while and fade into the background. And more than anything," added John, "it would be good for Birchwood if both of you or at least one of you came back home. With Denny gone, Ahlstrom's doesn't have an Ahlstrom. Winona doesn't count because she wants to wreck the place and she wouldn't live here anyway. Birchwood needs you. Most of the young people have left. It's time some of them come home."

Gabe said, "Have you asked Andrew to come home?"

"Of course," said John, "every time I see him. But the last thing he wants is to be a small-town doctor. He's thrived in Chicago. I miss him to death, but there's no better feeling for a parent than knowing your child, even if he's fifty years old, is doing what he loves and is happy with life. This isn't the place for Andrew."

"And you think this is the place for us?" said Liv.

"I think Ahlstrom's is in your blood. And I think the resort and Leech Lake need you. That's all I wanted to say. Please consider it."

Liv reached for her plastic pineapple then thought better of it and said, "Sorry in advance for the indelicacy of this question, but what will you do, John, when Judith is gone?"

John said, "Unfortunately, I've had to think about that. My plan is to run Otsby's for a while longer, and then let Red Pines keep it going. They did fine before Judith. They'll do fine after Judith. Or maybe I'll sell Otsby's. Judith is such a force—I have no idea what life will be like without her. Who knows, maybe she'll defy the odds and stick around for quite a while by sheer determination. If anyone can, it's Judith."

CHAPTER 35

"What's going on?" said Liv. About twenty guests gathered in the parking lot at Ahlstrom's. They were all looking in the same direction, where Liv could see a faint glow of throbbing red light.

"The police are here," said a guest. "I heard they arrested someone who lives in a cabin at the back of the property."

If it weren't for the Windex in a plastic pineapple, Gabe, Carly, and Liv would have run to Ed's cabin. Instead, they quick-stepped along the single-file path and arrived at Ed's cabin to find three Leech Lake off-road vehicles parked out front, red lights flashing on the rooftop bars, and bright white lights pointing at the small wooden structure. Officers carried out neatly labeled plastic bags and loaded them into the police vehicles.

"What are you doing?" said Gabe. It came out more rude and aggressive than he'd intended.

Chief of Police Julie Haaland turned around. The friendly matron of the local police had shifted into another gear, a more serious, deliberate gear. "We found Ed. We've detained him along with Raymond Lussier."

"Detained them for what?" said Liv.

"Ed as a person of interest in the murder of Denny Ahlstrom."

"That's insane," said Gabe. "There's no way Ed—"

"And we've detained Raymond Lussier for harboring a fugitive." Julie Haaland stepped toward the siblings and said, "Would you like to tell me why you brought half a dozen bags of groceries to Raymond Lussier's residence earlier this evening?"

"That's what this is about?" said Gabe. "You've been following us?"

Chief Haaland repeated her question. "Why did you bring half a dozen bags of groceries to Raymond Lussier's residence earlier this evening?" There was no smile in her eyes, no light.

Liv didn't hesitate. "Raymond said he was feeling under the weather and asked if we could pick up a few things for him."

"That's the story you're going with?"

"It's not a story. Not the way you're implying. It's the truth."

Chief Haaland took one step toward them and said, "And you had no idea that Ed Lindimier was hiding out in Raymond's basement?"

"You found Ed Lindimier at Raymond's?" said Liv, who then turned to Gabe. "Ed was at Raymond's. Can you believe that?"

Chief Haaland took another step toward the siblings. "Listen, you two. I've always liked you. And your family. But that will not prevent me from doing my job. And if I find out . . . *when* I find out you knew of Ed's location and lied when I asked you about it, I will show no favoritism because you're Ahlstroms."

Liv said, "We had no idea—"

"Do not mistake me for some hick cop," said Chief Haaland. "I've been at this a long time. I know what I'm doing."

"And you've known Ed Lindimier a long time," said Gabe. "There's no way he murdered Denny or anyone else. He's decent. He's peaceful. He's kind to animals. He's kind to children. And he's kind to adults. If you found a gun in his cabin, then someone planted it there."

"It wasn't just any gun. It's the murder weapon that killed Denny Ahlstrom. The lab in St. Cloud has confirmed it. And yes, I have known Ed a long time. But like I said, I don't show favoritism to people I like."

"Who's paying you to do this?" said Liv.

Chief Haaland took a third step toward Gabe, Liv, and Carly.

She lowered her voice to just above a whisper. "I beg your pardon?"

"Judith Otsby? A hundred grand is nothing to her, right? But it's probably a hell of a lot to you."

"Don't you dare," said Chief Haaland. "Don't you even dare."

Liv took a step toward Chief Haaland and said, "Tell Ed his lawyer will be at the police station first thing tomorrow morning."

"Ed told me he doesn't have a lawyer. I've requested a public defender from—"

"Ed will have a private, criminal defense attorney at the police station tomorrow morning. And you better hope you've dotted every *i* and crossed every *t* because everything you did in your process of locking up a man you know is innocent will be scrutinized and re-scrutinized and examined and re-examined and I don't care if it costs me a million dollars in legal fees I will make sure justice is done."

Police Chief Julie Haaland took a few breaths to calm herself. She raised her shoulders then lowered them. "Ed Lindimier is entitled to the best legal representation he can get," she said. "If you're offering to bring in some big gun from Minneapolis or beyond, that's fair. That's the way our system works. I have nothing to hide nor to be ashamed of. I know Ed's your friend, Liv and Gabe. I know you grew up with him. But please don't make me out to be the bad guy here. I'm doing my job the best I can. Right now, Ed's being held on suspicion. If I arrest him, he'll get his day in court. Justice will be served. I promise you that. Now if you'll excuse me. I'm in the middle of a murder investigation."

Liv, Gabe, and Carly returned to Cabin 14. It took three phone calls for Liv to get the recommendation of a top criminal defense lawyer in the Twin Cities. It was almost ten P.M. when Liv's phone rang and that lawyer said, "Ms. Ahlstrom. This is Deena Petrocci. I understand you're looking for representation for a friend in a criminal matter."

The lawyer promised Liv she'd be at the Birchwood police station by 8:30 the next morning.

Gabe, Carly, and Liv sat around Cabin 14's dining room table drinking tea in hopes of flushing the Tiki Hut's Windex out of their bloodstreams.

"This situation is no longer tenable," said Liv. "Tomorrow let's force the issue, yeah?"

"Force what issue?" said Gabe.

"What do you two think of this? In the morning we go to Judith Otsby and tell her we're going to exercise our option to buy Ahlstrom's."

"Shouldn't we talk about that first?" said Gabe.

"Just hear me out. We tell her we're going to buy it, but we're not going to sell it to her. We're going to move back here and run it ourselves. It's all a lie, but that's what we tell her. Because there's no way it's a coincidence that John Otsby asked us out for a drink while the police were apprehending Ed and Raymond. Judith Otsby wanted us out of the way. John did her dirty work. We fell for it, and now Ed and Raymond are in jail."

"Right on," said Carly. "So you're saying you want to pretend to do exactly what John asked you to do. Buy the resort and keep it for yourselves."

"Exactly. John said that but my guess is he didn't mean it. It was just his bluff to keep us at the Tiki Hut. If he had said something that angered us, we might have got up and walked out of there. But he kept us there and now Ed and Raymond are the prime suspects in Denny's murder and Judith is in the clear."

Gabe pulled crackers out of the cupboard. "You really think Judith Otsby murdered Denny?" He opened the refrigerator and pulled out a wedge of Jarlsberg.

"I don't know who killed Denny," said Liv. "If it was that hockey player lawyer of hers or some other hired hand. But someone did her bidding and now Ed and Raymond are paying the price."

Gabe handed Carly a cracker with cheese and said, "But what's the goal of telling Judith we're going to buy and run the resort ourselves? I mean, what's the endgame?"

"The goal is to infuriate Judith. If we light a fire under Judith Otsby, then we can watch her underlings and see what happens."

They heard a thump against the front door. Ms. Ramirez barked and didn't stop barking. Gabe stepped toward the door and said, "Who is it?" There was no answer. Carly bent down and picked up Ms. Ramirez. The dog growled at the front door. "Who's there?" said Gabe.

No answer. He reached for the handle, took a breath, then opened the door just a crack. He saw no one, then looked down and said, "Oh, no."

CHAPTER 36

Liv and Carly joined Gabe at the door and saw a dead raccoon, the size of a Labrador retriever, lying at the foot of the cabin's front door, blood trickling from its mouth.

"I don't get it," said Carly. "A raccoon ran into your door and killed itself?"

"No," said Gabe. "Raccoons don't do that. Someone threw a dead raccoon against our door."

All three looked up from the dead animal and into the night, for what or who they did not know. The night offered nothing in response other than strings of lit pathways and cabin porch lights.

Liv shut the door and locked it. "Now do you believe me when I say this situation is untenable?"

"Well," said Carly, "at least we know Raymond Lussier isn't responsible for this. He's in jail."

"True," said Liv, "but that's all we know other than we're getting under someone's skin."

Gabe sighed. "I'll drag that thing into the woods. Let nature do its thing."

"No," said Carly. "Call the front desk. Let them deal with it. I don't want you anywhere near those woods."

Gabe and Liv had three swings at doing this the easy way. The first swing was at Mack's widow, Diana Ahlstrom. The next morning,

Liv called Diana from the cabin and put her on speakerphone. Gabe and Liv filled in Diana on everything they'd learned since arriving at Ahlstrom's and finished by saying that if anyone knew about their mother's affair, it was Mack.

"Which he must have," said Gabe, "because why else would he have told you that we had different fathers?"

"That makes sense," said Diana.

"We know of two people Mack might have told," said Liv. "One is Andrew because they were childhood friends. And the other is you, yeah? So did Mack ever mention anything about who our biological father is? Or was?"

Ms. Ramirez went to the front door and growled at the dead raccoon who was no longer there. Carly picked her up and carried her back to the couch.

"No," said Diana. "I would tell you if Mack had said anything more about your biological father. Because I would want to know if I were in your situation."

Liv was an expert on speakerphone. She said, *Now I'm going to press her* to Gabe and Carly, but only with her eyes. With her voice she said, "Did Mack have a personal or business relationship with any older men in Chicago? Did he have a mentor? Or a friendship that wasn't easily explained?"

"There was an older man in our building. He lived on our floor. After his wife died, Mack and I would sometimes run errands for him. And once, he had an eye appointment and had to get drops, so Mack went with him to make sure he could get home okay after having his eyes dilated."

Liv nodded *interesting* to Gabe and Carly but said, "Did the older man live in the building before you and Mack moved in?"

"Yes."

"What's his name? Maybe—"

"His name is Julius Madden," said Diana. "And he is not your father."

Liv shared a dubious look with Gabe and Carly but said, "And why do you say that?"

"Because he's Black and you're both blond-haired and blue-eyed," said Diana. "I'm sorry. This must be frustrating. If it makes you feel any better, I think you're right. I think Mack did know about your mother's affair. It explains so much of his behavior. And discovering it must have been a terribly traumatic event for him because he wouldn't even talk about it." There was a pause and then Diana added, "Whatever happens, promise me one thing."

"We'll try," said Gabe.

"Visit me. You visit me in Chicago and I'll visit you in Los Angeles and New York. You used to be a family of five. Now you're a family of two. Please put a stop to whatever pushed you all apart, and let's start pulling each other together. It's too late for Mack, but it's not too late for you. And as your sister-in-law, I would like to be a part of it."

It had been two days since Gabe and Liv knocked on Alan Cohen's big oak door on the north end of Steamboat Bay. He answered it this time the same way he had the first time—slowly. He wore khaki pants and a plaid wool shirt of browns and blues. He looked freshly showered and said, "I expected you two might be back. Please come in. Can I offer you coffee or juice?"

The siblings agreed to coffee. This time they passed through the living room and sat at an old farm table in the large kitchen looking out on the lake still topped with gray slush despite a cloudless blue sky.

"Have you decided to exercise your option to purchase the resort?" said Alan Cohen. He smiled with kind eyes. "Or do you still think I might be Mack's father?"

"No," said Gabe. "We don't think you're Mack's father."

"Well, that's good," said Alan Cohen. "Because if I were, you'd think me pretty awful. Never seeing him. Having no relationship whatsoever with him. Especially with your mother leaving you all way too soon."

"Actually . . . ," said Liv. "We're wondering if you're *our* father."

"What?" Alan Cohen's smile faded. "Why would you wonder that?"

"Because we were wrong about our mother's affair. Not that she had one, but the timing of it. It wasn't when Mack was born. It happened when each of us was born." Liv went on to explain the cognac bottle and perfume bottle and how they dated the letters to when they were conceived.

Alan Cohen stood from the kitchen table, walked to the refrigerator, and returned with a carton of milk. He sat and said, "I'm terribly sorry. I didn't offer you milk. Would you—"

"You're avoiding our question, yeah?" said Liv.

"Yes," said Alan Cohen, "I suppose I am." He looked at Liv and then at Gabe and added, "But not for the reason you think. I promise you, I am not your father. I had no relationship with your mother other than a friendly hello in passing."

"Then why the diversion with the milk?" said Gabe.

"Because I find it terribly sad that you're on this quest. I believe everything you've told me about the chest and its contents. And I'm sorry to say it hurts my heart. If your mother was so in love with the man who wrote those letters, why didn't she leave your father for him? It wasn't her marital vows—those she broke time and time again. And you could hardly say it was her sense of duty toward her children because the affair must have pulled her away from both of you and Mack. So why? Why didn't she leave your father for him? Why did she make that terrible mistake?"

"You think it was a mistake?" said Liv.

A loon landed on a spot of open water in Steamboat Bay. Gabe couldn't take his eyes off it. A moment later, the loon's mate popped up to the surface from below. Steamboat Bay was *their* bay. They'd spend the summer there and hopefully hatch and raise one or two chicks. Their echoey, whistle-like calls would accompany each sunrise and sunset. Gabe had forgotten how much he loved loons.

"You don't think your mother made a mistake?" said Alan Cohen. "Family is powerful. Powerful like the forces that bind an atom. That power can be beautiful when the bonding particles are rooted in love and honesty. But when they're rooted in lies and deceit and betrayal, a family's power can be devastating. It's why I never ventured into that institution. I didn't trust myself to not be distracted by the next shiny object. It is human nature, after all, to want what we don't have. When I was a younger man . . ." Alan Cohen opened the carton of milk and poured some into his coffee. ". . . This isn't about me. It's about you. And I'm sorry for what you're going through."

Liv said, "Why did you offer to back Gabe financially if he wanted to buy the resort?"

"Because," said Alan Cohen, "I love Ahlstrom's. I don't want to see it turn into Otsby's or a solar and wind farm."

Gabe kept his eyes on the loons as they paddled circles around each other in a sort of dance.

"I don't believe you," said Liv.

"Why not?"

"Because you don't know Gabe. You don't know him or his ability to run a resort and yet you're willing to gamble millions of dollars on him? That's a sign of something deeper than your love for the resort. You either loved our mother or you love us because you know we're your children."

"That's ridiculous!" Alan Cohen shouted. Gabe refocused his attention on what was happening inside the house. "I do love

Ahlstrom's! And not because of your mother or because of you. I love it because that place gave me my life. I know it's just a North-woods resort like hundreds of others, but not to me. I grew up in Chicago. I went to college in the city and worked for Marshall Field. I was off to a successful start by anyone's standards. Any-one's but mine. I was dying inside. Imploding. I was so deeply unhappy. I was born in the wrong place. I was born into the wrong life. And Ahlstrom's showed me where I belonged. I can't even remember why I vacationed there the first time. Maybe I saw a brochure. Maybe I heard about it from a friend. I honestly don't know. But when I first stepped onto the property I thought, *I'm home*. I continued working my way up the corporate ladder, but Ahlstrom's was my go-to vacation spot. Ahlstrom's recharged me. And it's where I dreamed of building this house. That's why I've offered to back you, Gabe. Not because I think you're a genius when it comes to resort management, but because I want that place to exist. And I'm no simpleton when it comes to business—I'm not throwing money away—believe you me that deal will be structured in a way that if you screw up, I'll still own it. And one way or another, I'll get it back on its feet."

The silence that filled the vacuum after Alan Cohen's outburst was painful. No one opened their mouth for half a minute until Liv said, "Bullshit. You've made it very clear in both of our visits that your alone time and freedom are important to you. If you acknowledge that we're your children, all that will be threatened."

"I'm telling you—"

"Look at this place," said Liv. "It's your fortress of solitude, right? On an existential level, we threaten that. I think you're so hell-bent on remaining isolated that you're lying to yourself. I was a kid when you were at our resort, but I wasn't naïve. I saw the way you looked at our mother. That look was not about isolation. That look was not about solitude. It was love. Or at least lust. You won't even admit that so how are we supposed to believe anything you say? Don't tell me what I saw isn't what I saw."

Alan Cohen looked from Liv to Gabe and back to Liv. "Get out," he said. "Get the hell out of my house."

Gabe looked out at the bay. The loons were gone.

· CHAPTER 37 ·

"You ungrateful little shits!" screamed Judith Otsby. "I offered you the deal of a lifetime!" She sucked a few deep breaths of oxygen into her nose and said, "All you had to do was sign a piece of paper. Don't you see what a curse that resort is for you? It took your mother. It took your father. Now your brother and uncle are dead. What's wrong with you Ahlstroms? Why do you insist on destroying yourselves? I can put a stop to that. Why don't you just collect your payout and go back to your cities and live your elitist lives?!"

They stood crowded around Judith's hospital bed that wasn't in a hospital—it was in the same main-floor bedroom where Liv and Gabe had last seen her. Andrew Otsby sat in a recliner, his expression worn, his tolerance of his mother beginning to look more like a veneer than something solid. And John stood ever-present with his cup of water and bendy straw.

"Your blood pressure, Judith," said John. "Please calm yourself."

"You're the problem with my blood pressure, John! Why can't you talk some sense into these Ahlstroms?! I mean, for Christ's sake, John, do something to earn your keep around here!"

Gabe and Liv looked at John to see if he'd respond, but the man who asked them to reject Judith's offer said nothing.

"Mother," said Andrew. "Dad's right. You need to calm down. Otherwise, you may never get out of that bed."

"Oh, real nice, Andy! Real nice. Why am I the only one who fights for this family?! Why am I the only one who cares? I hate to think what'll happen to everything Otsby when I'm gone. The way things are going, there will be a dozen resorts called Ahlstrom's and Otsby's will be a distant memory!"

"That's not going to happen, Mother. You're being a tad theatrical."

"I'm being theatrical?" said Judith. "How about them?!" She pointed a trembling finger at Liv and Gabe. "They're turning down free money! Free money for doing nothing! That's theater because it's based on no reality whatsoever!"

Judith's automatic blood pressure cuff began its python-like squeeze on her upper arm.

"It's our reality," said Gabe. "That resort's been in our family for generations. We're not going to just hand it over to you and walk away."

"You can and you will! And you're not handing it over. You're selling it for an astronomical profit! What the hell is wrong with you?" She fixed her gaze on Liv. "And you. You're a businesswoman. How can you run a successful business when you make pigheaded decisions like this?!"

The blood pressure cuff released its hold and sounded like a tire releasing its air.

"Goodbye, Judith," said Liv.

"Listen to me, you spoiled brats. You have crossed the wrong person. You do not want to make an enemy of Judith Otsby. Oh, you think that's a joke? You think it's funny?! You'll find out how funny it is. And you'll wish you'd never been born!"

"Hope you feel better soon, Judith," said Gabe.

Liv said, "It was, as always, a pleasure."

And with that, Gabe and Liv left the room. Andrew pitched himself forward out of the recliner the way people do—reluctantly—and caught up with them in the foyer. John didn't dare leave his fuming wife.

"I'm sorry," said Andrew. "I'm sorry she's so fixated on her idea of one resort with a bay in the middle of it. And if there's anything I can do to ease the situation, please let me know."

"There is one thing," said Liv. "It's not really about your mother, but something else has come up, and we thought you might be able to help us."

"Name it."

"You've mentioned you spent a lot of time at our house with Mack . . . I assume that was true even before Gabe and I were born, yeah?"

"Yes," said Andrew. "Especially then. Only then, really."

"This may sound strange, but we're wondering if you know anything about our mother having an affair."

Andrew caressed his clean-shaven chin and said, "I know this much: Mack suspected Bette was having an affair."

"Did Mack say why he had that suspicion?" said Gabe.

"Are you sure you want to hear this?" said Andrew. "It was a long time ago, and I don't know what good digging up the past can do at this point."

A pair of cardinals hopped outside the window along the branch of a birch tree. The bright red male and subdued red female, surrounded by white bark, looked like models. Gabe loved cardinals because they didn't migrate. They stuck out in winter like real Minnesotans.

"We're sure," said Liv. "Gabe and I want to know the truth. Bette's secret has been buried long enough."

Andrew motioned for them to follow him into the living room, where he sat in a wingback chair worthy of Robert E. Lee. Gabe and Liv sat opposite Andrew on a floral print couch with curved wooden legs and armrests.

"We were in the lunchroom at school," said Andrew. "I was sitting next to Mack and talking away, but his head was in another place. It was like he couldn't hear me. Like he was in a cloud. A dark cloud." Andrew took a moment to let the memory rise to the surface and added, "So I asked Mack what was up. He had the most profound look of disappointment on his face. And disgust. And then he told me that he thought your mother was in love with another man. What were we, twelve then? We didn't know what romantic love felt like, but we were old enough to know it existed. And I guess we were old enough to know what it looked like."

"Which was?" said Liv.

"Happiness. Your mom was just so damn happy. That's what Mack said, and I saw it, too, when I was over at the house. Your mother would disappear for hours at a time. She was happy when she left and she was happy when she returned. But the biggest thing I remember Mack talking about was that none of your mother's happiness was directed at your father. She was happy about something else. Or someone else. Mack was sure about that."

Judith shouted from the back bedroom, "Stop adjusting my bed, John! You're going to fold me in half like a Russian gymnast!"

Gabe waited to make sure Judith was finished berating her husband then said, "Did Mack know who the person was? The person who made our mother so happy?"

"No, but Mack wanted to know who it was. I remember once, I was over at your house, and your mom said she was going into town to run some errands. She asked Mack if there was anything he wanted from the supermarket and he told her whatever it was. She was about to leave but remembered she wanted to take a dress in for an alteration. When she went to get it, Mack hatched a plan. The two of us ran to the family pickup truck, jumped in the bed, and hid under some tarps. A few minutes later, your mom got in the cab and drove away. Mack hoped we were going to catch her in the act. In the act of what, we weren't exactly sure. But she did exactly what she said she was going to do. She drove into town, ran a few errands, and drove home. Mack tried a few more clandestine attempts to find out what she was up to, but as far as I know, he never learned anything more."

"So I assume you have no idea who the man was either," said Liv.

Andrew shook his head. "Not a clue."

Gabe checked in on the cardinals. They were still on their birch branch, and he wondered who was watching whom.

"We have reason to believe our mother met her lover in Ed's cabin while Ed was out on the pontoon boat fishing with our father and guests," said Liv, "usually between two and four o'clock in the afternoons. That would have been during the season. But it was the same time of day they went ice fishing in the winter. Did Mack know anything about that?"

Andrew Otsby settled in for a solid think and after a few moments said, "Not that I'm aware of. I think he would have told me if he'd found out anything." Andrew shifted his weight from one side to the other in the wingback chair. "Do you mind if I ask why all this is coming up now?"

"CNN!" yelled Judith from the back bedroom. "Blech! Give me that remote, John! Give it to me!"

Gabe said, "We're asking about this now because we just learned about Bette's affair. Shortly before Mack died, he told Diana that he had a different father than us. We assumed that meant he had a father who wasn't Bobby Ahlstrom. But based on some of our mother's things we've been going through, we think it's the other way around—that we have a different biological father. And based on what you've just told us about Mack's suspicion, it adds up. Our mother had an affair during the years Liv and I were born. So Mack could have known about the affair, even if he didn't know who it was with."

Andrew Otsby nodded and said, "One thing Mack did tell me—it drove him crazy that your father either didn't know about it or, if he did know, he didn't do anything about it. Mack looked down on Bobby for that. He felt ashamed that Bobby was either not paying attention or was too weak to stand up to Bette." Andrew shut his eyes. "It's so sad. Two people fell in love with each other at the wrong time and it tore your family apart. It's nothing short of tragic."

"Denny's killer is close," said Liv, driving the Tahoe back toward Ahlstrom's on Highway 371 and checking her mirrors to see if anyone was following. "And he probably killed Mack and has threatened us with both his letter and a dead raccoon."

"Maybe we should go to Chief Haaland and tell her everything we know," said Gabe.

"We have," said Liv.

Gabe checked the temperature on the dash. Forty-seven degrees. That's spring in Minnesota. It teases. It disappoints. Often it devastates. He said, "Chief Haaland doesn't know how aggressively Judith has been trying to buy Ahlstrom's. She doesn't know Tyler Luther threatened us. She doesn't know—"

Liv interrupted her brother. "Do you think Chief Haaland would do anything that risks pissing off Judith and her big donations to the Birchwood police? Do you think Haaland would question Judith without hard evidence?"

"No. No, she won't."

"Me either," said Liv. "So let's try to get some hard evidence."

Gabe watched a flock of wild turkeys peck their way along the shoulder and said, "We've tried, Liv. We've tried and we have nothing. And people are getting mad. Judith just screamed at us. Alan Cohen kicked us out of his house. Chief Haaland looked like she wanted to punch us outside of Ed's cabin. And all this animosity isn't exactly making me feel safer."

Liv found a parking spot in the Ahlstrom's lot. The Knitters of the Northern Plains had begun to check in—the lot was full of Subarus with bumper stickers that featured balls of yarn and quaint sayings like Knit Happens and Got Yarn? Liv and Gabe walked out of the parking lot and onto the paved path when Winona appeared and said, "Is it true? Tell me it's not true." She wore a fleece pullover under a down vest and an Ahlstrom's beanie. Her hands were in her vest pockets. She'd obviously been outside waiting for their return.

"Not sure what you're referring to," said Gabe.

"Are you exercising your option to buy the resort?" Her eyebrows narrowed and her brow scrunched. "Because that's what I hear. You're going to buy it and Gabe's going to run it and that's that."

"Who told you that?" said Liv.

"I have sources," said Winona.

"Okay," said Liv, "everything that's happening right now: your anger, your attitude, your cartoon character head of steam, yeah? It's only as valid as your sources. There's nothing worse than a smart person armed with stupid information."

A man wearing a Red Pines jumpsuit walked by with a leaf blower. The corporation had brought in replacements for the incarcerated Ed and Raymond.

"Are you telling me it's not true?" said Winona. "You're not buying the resort? Is that what you're saying? Tell me the truth. You owe me that much."

"We owe you nothing," said Gabe. "And you'll know the truth when you hear it from us, but you're not going to hear it now."

"Why not?" said Winona. She looked as if she were about to scream.

Gabe and Liv turned away from Winona and headed toward Cabin 14, hearing Winona's frustrated exhale behind them. When they stepped into Cabin 14, they found Carly sitting with a person they'd never seen before.

CHAPTER 38

"Gabe and Liv," said Carly. "This is Deena Petrocci. The lawyer you hired for Ed and Raymond."

Deena had shoulder-length gray hair and large lensed glasses with heavy black plastic frames. They said hellos and shook hands and Liv asked Deena about Ed and Raymond.

"They'll either be charged or released tomorrow morning," said Deena. "My guess is released. The police don't have enough evidence to arrest Ed much less get a conviction. Yes, his fingerprints are on the gun, but in a manner that suggests he never fired the gun. For instance, his fingerprint is not on the trigger."

"The police told you that?" said Gabe.

"Not directly," said Deena. "But I asked if they'd found Ed's fingerprint on the trigger and could see by their reactions that they hadn't. Both Ed and Raymond are comfortable. I explained the situation and that I thought they'd be out tomorrow. Raymond's criminal record makes his situation more precarious, but he's been a model citizen since leaving prison. I think he'll be released and not charged. And he's being very sweet with Ed. Kind of making a game out of it. Fortunately, they're the only two prisoners in the Birchwood jail at the moment, so it's pretty quiet there. Ed seems to be doing just fine."

"Thank you," said Liv. "That makes me feel better."

Deena Petrocci stood. "I'm staying here at the resort if you need anything else. Otherwise, I'll be back at the police station tomorrow morning. I'm sure I'll connect with you by mid-morning."

"Thanks," said Gabe. "We really appreciate all you're doing."

"My pleasure. Seriously. I love it up here. Spent most of my summers at my grandparents' cabin on Lake Winnibigoshish. If it were summer, you'd find me standing on the dock with a fishing rod. Talk to you tomorrow."

After Deena Petrocci left, Gabe and Liv told Carly about their eventful day, and in turn, Carly said, "I went through the chest again."

"And?" said Liv.

Gabe walked over to the fireplace as Carly said, "I didn't learn anything new. But the chest could help us find out who your biological father is, assuming the note on the door and dead raccoon mean he's local."

"But you said you didn't find anything new," said Gabe, opening the flue.

"Right," said Carly. "But your mother took such care to hide her lover's identity. And just for the record, I hate the word *lover*. I just don't know what else to call him. Anyway, she took such care to hide the guy's identity. And her genius in using Ed's cabin. The fact that it backs against a large woodland so whomever she met in there—"

"Her *lover*," said Liv.

"You know it. The woods allowed him to approach unseen. And there's the way she kept everything locked in this chest with two separate locks that required two separate keys. The fact that she asked Ed to keep the chest because no one ever goes into Ed's cabin other than Ed. And her lover took similar precautions. Typing his letters. Neither signing nor dating them. And like your mother never told you—it's such a big thing to keep from you. And it sounds like neither Mack nor your father knew who it was either. They might have suspected she was seeing someone, but Bette was able to hide the man's identity. An absolute miracle in a town this size."

Gabe paused making his teepee out of kindling to look over his shoulder to see that Carly had a tentative look in her eyes, which darted from Gabe to Liv and then back to Gabe. It was as if she was afraid to move from qualifying her idea to actually stating it.

"My point is this," she finally said. "The elaborate measures they took to hide their affair were necessary because of how news travels in a small town. If one person found out, everyone would find out. So maybe we can use that same dynamic to flush out your bio dad."

Liv folded her arms and leaned against the kitchen counter. "The dynamic of news traveling fast?"

"Yeah, man. We spread the word about what we know so far. The truth. Mack said you had different fathers. Your mother had an affair. The evidence in the chest dates the affair to the years you were both born. And after we tell the truth, we start bullshitting."

"Ah," said Liv. "You mean we start baiting a trap, yeah?"

"You got it," said Carly.

"I'm glad you two are so in sync," said Gabe, "but can someone please tell me what the hell you're talking about?"

CHAPTER 39

They called Winona and met her at the bar. Not in the bar. At the bar where employees, locals, and Knitters of the Northern Plains gathered for happy hour. It was all-you-can-eat pizza night and the pizzas were spread out on one side of the bar, illuminated and warmed by red heat lamps. Over a dozen Funsters sat in one corner of the room playing cribbage on six boards in a round-robin tournament sponsored by Miller Lite, or so it seemed.

"Background?" said Winona. "Why do I need background? Why not just tell me whether or not the resort is mine?"

"Because," said Liv, "we want you to understand why we've been so erratic."

"Your words, not mine," said Winona, holding up her hands to add *it's not my fault.*

Donna the Funster approached the bar with two empty pitchers and said, "Fill 'em up with regular, please. And check the oil while you're at it." Donna laughed at her joke, which you had to be sixty-five to get, and no one at the bar other than herself was.

The bartender took the pitchers as Gabe said, "Listen, Winona. What we're about to tell you is privileged information. We'd like you to promise to keep it to yourself."

"Of course," said Winona, who had no credibility whatsoever. She had lied by omission to Liv. She was currently lying by omission to Liv's husband, Cooper. "Your secret is safe with me."

Gabe took a deep breath to escalate the drama and said, "Bobby Ahlstrom is not our biological father."

The bartender put two full pitchers of beer on the counter, but Donna the Funster stayed right where she was.

"What?" said Winona. "What do you mean Bobby Ahlstrom's not your biological father."

Annabel Johnson approached from seemingly nowhere and said, "Excuse me. Sorry to interrupt. But wondering if you have any updated checkout plans for Cabin 14?"

"Hold on a sec," said Liv. Then she told Winona about Mack's claim that he had a different father than Liv and Gabe. But Gabe and Liv found a chest that contained love letters and other items and Carly was able to date the cognac and perfume bottles to the years Gabe and Liv were conceived.

"I can't believe it," said Winona. "Did my dad know?"

"You know . . . ," said Donna to the bartender. "I'd like to order some food as well. Not that pizza cooking under the lights over there. I'd like to see a menu."

Annabel Johnson waited patiently with no intention of interrupting.

"We don't think Denny knew," said Gabe. "Our mother and whoever the guy was were extraordinarily discreet." He explained how Bette and her lover had used Ed's cabin when Ed and Bobby and Mack were out fishing with the guests.

"And you have no idea who the man is?" said Winona.

"No," said Liv. "It's remarkable how careful they were. No one seems to know of their affair. If we didn't have the guy's love letters to our mother, we would have thought Mack was delusional."

The Funster read the menu as if she were trying to memorize it, and Annabel Johnson quietly ordered a Diet Coke.

"And how is you having a different father holding up your decision about buying the resort?" said Winona.

"Let's just say learning the identity of our biological father has taken priority. Everything's on hold until we accomplish that.

Including me dealing with Cooper. Just so you know, I haven't had a substantive conversation with him since our last little chat."

"But how are you going to find out who your bio dad is?" said Winona. "You just said your mother and the man were incredibly discreet. If no one knows—"

"No one does know," said Carly, "but as careful as they were, Bette and the man couldn't have foreseen how advanced and sophisticated DNA collection and analysis would become." Carly paused. She looked at Winona and then around the area as if to make sure no one was eavesdropping. In truth, she was doing just the opposite—making sure people were eavesdropping. Donna the Funster, Annabel Johnson, and the bartender all practically leaned toward her. Which was good because the next bit of information was the important part. It was also completely untrue. That's why they had to bait the hook, bait it with the fattest and juiciest of worms.

Carly continued, "There's this company in Europe that can find trace amounts of DNA, even in the oil of latent fingerprints. It's a super delicate process, but they think that since the contents of Bette's love chest were sealed for so long without contamination, that they can isolate the DNA of Gabe and Liv's biological father. Then they can compare that with the DNA in the databases of ancestry sites and we'll most likely learn at least what family their father came from."

"Why can't they just use your DNA?" said Winona. "I mean, half of your DNA is the same as your father's. Why do they need his?"

"Two reasons," lied Liv. "Our biological father's is undiluted. And if we use ours, we'll have to wait months for the results. But this company has expedited access through INTERPOL and other law enforcement agencies. It's expensive. But it's worth it." Liv lowered her voice. "After all, whoever the man turns out to be, might have had something to do with your father's murder."

"What?" said Winona.

"Shhhhh."

Winona whispered, "So how long will it take? When will you get the results?"

"The company flies into Minneapolis tomorrow morning," said Gabe. "They'll be here by afternoon. Then they'll collect samples from the chest, which we're storing in Ed's cabin because he's in jail and no one ever goes in there and that's the least likely place it'll be exposed to contamination. We should have results within a week. Normally, they wouldn't do this for someone not affiliated with a government agency, but one of Liv's artists dresses someone very high up in the executive branch." Gabe rolled his eyes. "Don't look at me like that, Liv. I'm not going to say who it is." He turned back toward Winona. "Anyway, that's what's going on."

Winona Ahlstrom was smart, sophisticated, an Ivy League–educated electrical engineer who was about to earn her MBA from Wharton. If Winona bought Gabe, Liv, and Carly's concocted story, anyone would. And it appeared Winona did.

"Wow," she said. "I hope you find out who it is. And I totally get why you're up in the air about the resort right now. Considering what you're going through, I can definitely wait a little longer."

The trio of liars repeated their story at three other bars while buying beer and wine, at a local bakery while buying elephant ears and cheese danishes, at two bait shops while buying Lindy Rigs and Rapalas, and at one church bake sale while buying bundt cake and something called Cookie Salad. Carly played the innocent hearing the story for the first time and asking the questions that led to Gabe and Liv telling her about the European DNA company that would extract samples from the chest in Ed's cabin tomorrow.

Getting back into the Tahoe, Gabe said, "I have one more idea on how we can spread the word. You know when someone accidentally calls you but doesn't know it?"

"You mean a butt dial?" said Carly.

"Yeah. Cooper accidentally called us the other day and we listened on his walk home. What if we faked one of those?"

"Faked a butt dial?" said Liv.

"Yeah. So we basically have the conversation we just staged for Winona and at the other places, but we do it as a phone call? You know, like a butt dial, but it's not an accident."

That's what they did on the drive back to Ahlstrom's. They recorded the conversation on all three of their phones, each located in a different spot in the Tahoe. They chose the version on Carly's phone, not for its quality but for its lack of quality. They wanted the recipients to be forced to listen carefully. Hopefully, they wouldn't answer the call but let it go to voicemail so they could listen multiple times. It had to sound real.

To test it, Liv walked down by the lake. Carly streamed the recording to a Bluetooth speaker in Cabin 14, and Gabe dialed Liv and put his phone on speaker. Liv answered her cell, listened, and texted her thoughts on how it sounded. They tried a variety of combinations, adjusting the recording's volume, speaker location, and the location of Gabe's phone until Liv said it sounded like the real deal.

They still had the key Winona had given them to the office basement. They used it to let themselves in under cover of darkness, then they took Denny's unopened security equipment to Ed's cabin. It was only a year old.

The trees were so dense around Ed's tiny abode that hiding cameras and Wi-Fi range extenders was easy, especially in the small, needled pines that fought for light under the maples and aspens. They ran power cords under the fallen leaves and needles, making them impossible to see. It was far more difficult to hide cameras inside the cabin—it was so small and sparse. But they managed to hide one in a propped-open tackle box and another in a tin of English toffee that they'd punched a hole in the side of.

When they returned to Cabin 14, they began at the top of the list and called the recipients one at a time.

Alan Cohen didn't answer. They played the recording on his voicemail. Same with Judith Otsby. Same with Renee.

Andrew Otsby answered and said, "Hello. Hello . . ." When the butt dial recording played, he did not hang up. John Otsby let the call go to voicemail. Tyler Luther answered the phone and said, "Hello? . . ." Chief of Police Julie Haaland let the call go to voicemail, as did Officer Schmidt.

They had spread the word. Liv, Gabe, and Carly had no way of knowing if those who let the call go to voicemail listened to the entire message, but those who answered—Andrew Otsby and Tyler Luther—listened to the entire thing before hanging up. Human beings are curious creatures.

They moved the chest to Ed's cabin and set it on his small table, unlocked and unguarded. Carly waited in Cabin 14 and watched an eight-camera split on a fifty-five-inch television. She recorded the live feed on a four-terabyte hard drive.

Carly, Gabe, and Liv didn't expect anyone to show up right away, but neither did they expect snow to fall heavy and wet in quarter-sized flakes. The weather had been so warm and they'd been so preoccupied, they never checked the forecast. When the snow began to fall, they had to make a decision.

Shortly after two A.M. one of the eight sections of the screen darkened with shadow. The snow still fell heavily, but the air temperature hovered just above freezing, and the ground had warmed so the snow didn't accumulate. Just a white blur of flakes above the wet forest floor. Flashes of lightning, the first of the season, lit the woods, and the trees cast tall shadows that looked like iron bars. Thunder rumbled overhead. The snow didn't impede the intruder's progress, but it did impede Carly's ability to identify who it was. As they'd hoped, word had spread. As they'd predicted, the individual approached from the back of the property, using the forest as cover. A minute after the figure passed through the frame of the rear camera, they appeared in the frame of the front camera. Still, the snow fell with such density and velocity that identifying the individual was impossible. That ended a few seconds later.

CHAPTER 40

Ed's tiny cabin was in complete darkness. The door was locked. It would have been suspicious to leave it unlocked considering how important the chest was—at least that's what Gabe and Liv had suggested while spreading their false rumor. They expected a window to be smashed. Instead, they heard the deadbolt turn. The intruder had a key. Or maybe it was more accurate to say, *still* had a key. The door squeaked on its hinges as it opened into the cabin, but no artificial light found its way in. The infrared camera picked up the person's image, but Gabe and Liv couldn't see it because they weren't looking at a screen. They sat in silence on Ed's bed. The intruder turned on a flashlight and shined it on the floor, moving the beam toward Ed's small table where the chest sat. Thunder rolled overhead.

Gabe felt Liv take his hand. This was it. The moment they'd hoped for. Planned for. Plotted for. They'd baited the trap and their prey had fallen for it. Ten days ago, they thought Bobby Ahlstrom was their biological father. Ten days ago, their brother Mack was alive. So was Denny. Now, with one flick of a light switch, they were about to learn the identity of their biological father and who killed Denny and possibly Mack. In one moment, their lives would change forever. But now that they were in the same room with *him*, Liv felt more nervous than excited. More anxious than curious. She held a remote switch in her free hand. They'd replaced the simple, naked lightbulbs in Ed's cabin with smart bulbs. More unused equipment from Denny's office basement.

Gabe felt nothing but doubt. The pursuit alone of this mystery man had helped get his life on track. He and Liv had worked together and in doing so, closed the distance in their oh-so-distant relationship. He and Carly cranked up their relationship from friends to romantic partners and Gabe felt quite sure they'd be life partners. So much good had come into Gabe's life in the past ten days. Learning this man's identity was sure to set the pendulum swinging the other way. Gabe fought competing urges. One was to jump up and bolt out of the cabin. The other was to reach for the knife he'd kept tucked into his boot since the night he and Liv went to Raymond Lussier's house. This man had killed Denny. He may have killed Mack. Why wouldn't he kill again?

The flashlight moved over the chest. Gloved hands flipped open the lid, reached in, and removed the bundle of letters. The gloves then returned the letters to the chest, shut it, and the person lifted the entire chest from the table.

Liv pushed the button on the remote. The overhead lights turned on. The intruder turned their head, and Gabe and Liv saw the last face they expected to see.

CHAPTER 41

He wore black jeans, a black beanie, black gloves, and a black down puffer. When he saw Gabe and Liv sitting on the bed, he shut his eyes. It was over. They knew. He exhaled something between fear and defeat. When he opened his eyes, John Otsby appeared resigned that he'd been lured into their trap.

"How did you know it was me?" he said.

"We didn't," said Gabe. "We spread the rumor all over town. We just hoped it would find the man we were looking for."

"Clever," said John Otsby. "Well, now you know."

"I don't understand," said Liv. "How can it be you?"

"I wasn't always an old man," said John Otsby. "I was younger than you are now." John smiled a sad smile and added, "It's a secret I've lived with for a long time. The loneliness of it has been unbearable." He looked around Ed's cabin. "This place has hardly changed. It's beautiful. The best moments of my life happened in this cabin."

Gabe said, "Will you tell us? Tell us everything? We're your children. We deserve to know."

"I don't think so. It's too late for that."

"Why?" said Liv. "How can it be too late for family?"

John Otsby smiled. "Yes—I used to think that, too. It's never too late for family. It's never too late to start anew. It's a lovely idea, isn't it? Let's hold on to that hope. But right now, I'm going to take this chest, destroy it, and we'll all go back to our lives."

"And pretend we don't know you're our father?" said Gabe. "How are we supposed to do that?"

"I'll tell you this," said John Otsby. "I never wanted you to come home. I never wanted you to know Bobby Ahlstrom wasn't your biological father. But it's meant a great deal to see you lately. It's a terrible thing for a parent not to know their own children."

"That was your choice," said Liv. "You're the one who's kept the secret, yeah? Not us. And you're not our parent. You're our biological father. Big difference."

Gabe and Liv remained seated on Ed's bed. John remained standing, holding the chest. Something in him appeared to give in, and he seemed resigned to having this conversation. He set the chest back down on the table.

"That's true," said John. "The word *parent* is wishful thinking on my part. But your mother wanted things otherwise. And as far as me keeping the secret, there have been practical matters to consider. If Judith found out about my affair with Bette, if she knew you two are the result of that affair, if she knew I begged Bette to leave Bobby and that the only reason Judith and I are still together is because Bette refused me, well, Judith would throw me out."

"So what?" said Gabe. "Wouldn't that set you free? Don't you want that?"

"I have endured Judith for over half a century. Married her when I was nineteen years old. Gave up my last name for her so she could continue to be an Otsby. Judith just keeping her last name wasn't good enough. I had to be an Otsby, too. So did Andrew. And I signed a prenuptial agreement before we married. If Judith and I divorce, the only assets I receive are those I've earned over the years. But Judith hasn't paid me a dime. She's insisted I don't work. I am not only her husband but her personal assistant, her caretaker, and her errand boy. But I am not her employee. I never receive a paycheck. Nothing is in my name. She's made sure of that. Without Judith, I have nothing. No home. No car. I don't have a credit card in my name. I don't even own the clothes I wear. She has a noose around my neck, and I know she'd use it if she learned about me and Bette."

"Andrew would support you," said Gabe.

"Yes, he would. But that's not freedom. That's just another version of the position I'm in now. Besides, Judith's very ill. She won't live much longer. I'm so close to being truly free for the first time in my adult life. I just have to wait a little longer."

"Your prenup wouldn't hold up in court," said Liv. "You'd be awarded millions. Over fifty years of marriage? Your sacrifice is undeniable."

John laughed. "And how long would that court case last? Months? With appeals, years?" He turned his body toward Liv and Gabe and leaned against the table. "Judith's dying. And you've experienced her mood lately. If she hears one whisper about my affair with Bette, Judith will tie up her assets in a legal knot that would take a decade to untangle. I'm seventy-one years old."

"If you want us to keep your secret," said Liv, "then tell us how it happened. You and Bette both had spouses and children. You worked at competing resorts. How did you and Bette fall in love with each other?"

John Otsby's shoulders dropped. His eyes pleaded for leniency then went to a faraway place and he said, "You promise that if I tell you, you'll tell no one I'm your father as long as Judith lives?"

"Yes," said Liv without hesitation, her eyes locked on John Otsby's.

"We promise," said Gabe. "We have no desire to see you suffer Judith's wrath." Lying didn't come easily to Gabe, but he felt no moral gray area in this situation.

John nodded and sighed. His face wore a wistful expression. He pulled out a chair from Ed's table and sat. "We were at a hospitality conference in Minneapolis. Judith didn't feel she could take the time so she sent me. Bobby did the same with Bette. Your mother and I were both from Birchwood. Bette and I knew each other, of course. Birchwood is a small town. All the towns around Leech Lake are. And Mack and Andy were best friends. I was a few years older than Bette so I didn't know her well, but neither of us was used to being away from home so we naturally gravitated toward one another. We ate dinner together. We had drinks in the bar together. We just talked. That was it. We talked and talked and talked about the resort business and our sons and our spouses and our lives in Birchwood.

"We clicked. I can't explain why. We just did. For three days and three nights. We spent almost all our time together, going to a few seminars and panels but mostly walking around the city. Visiting restaurants, the lakes, museums. We went to a play at the Guthrie Theater. On the last night, we sat in the hotel bar until it closed. I walked your mother up to her room, she invited me in, and still, we just talked. And when we were so tired that we couldn't keep our eyes open any longer, I said goodnight, and your mother walked me to the door.

"To this day I can't tell you who initiated it. I think neither of us did. We were like two magnets pulling at each other. That's how we first kissed. We stood at her hotel room door and kissed for five minutes. That's how long it felt anyway. I remember when we finally pulled away from each other, I felt so ashamed. I was a married man. Your mother was a married woman. We each had a child. We lived in a small town. We knew the same people. Went to the same church. I felt awful. Like the biggest heel in the world. A cheater. A liar. An immoral sinner. I said, 'I'm sorry. I'm so, so sorry.' Then I practically ran out of there."

A flash of lightning lit up the windows, and they heard a crack of thunder that rattled the plates stacked in Ed's kitchen cabinets.

"But it was too late. We'd fallen in love with each other. I know now that it happened because our marriages were loveless. We didn't know how loveless until we had something to compare them to." John shook his head and scratched the skin beneath his beard.

"Why didn't you leave Judith?" said Liv. "Why didn't our mother leave Bobby?"

"In the beginning," said John, "we had no intention of leaving our spouses. We tortured ourselves with denial. That night we kissed in the hotel room, that was the end of it. That's what we'd told each other. The next morning we were so embarrassed. Both of us. We hardly spoke to each other. It was over as far as we were concerned. We'd gotten out with just a kiss. It wasn't good what we did, but we'd stopped it in time to save our marriages and our families.

"When we returned home, we made it about a week before we started inventing excuses to run into each other. The church was assembling a committee to oversee the building of a new wing. We both volunteered. The Fourth of July celebration included a 10K. We both signed up for group training runs. And then the letters started. We were like spies in World War I. We used a sealed jar in the hollow of a tree trunk a few hundred yards behind Ed's cabin. I'd fish the point near there, push my johnboat into the cattails, and disappear. I tied up the boat and made my way to our tree. For a while there, we never missed a day. I lived for your mother's letters, and I believe she did for mine."

"They're beautiful letters," said Liv, half flattering John Otsby to keep him talking, and half meaning it.

John took the compliment. "Thank you. It's validating for someone else to see them. Especially you two." He smiled. "Then one day, we showed up to that tree at the same time. And whatever self-control we thought we had melted away. Bette and I were in love. We were in our thirties. Our attraction for each other was too powerful. We made love right there in the woods. That's when you were conceived, Liv."

Liv managed a smile, more out of courtesy than anything else. She wanted John to feel comfortable. Wanted him to think she was on his side.

John continued, "We weren't worried about getting caught that day because we were well behind Ed's cabin, and Bobby and Mack and Ed were fishing on the pontoon boat with resort guests. They went out every day unless the weather made it impossible. Pontoon time became our time. It was your mother's idea to use this cabin." John Otsby looked around the small space as if he felt Bette's presence. As if the sights and smells had brought her back to life. "But we didn't stop writing to each other. To see those letters again after all these years—it's like going back in time."

John's eyes glossed over. He tried to say more but couldn't. It looked as if he could barely breathe.

Liv said, "Did Bobby know?"

"That's a good question," said John. "I think Bobby must have known on some level. Not about me specifically—but that your mother was in love with someone else. Bette told me they were rarely intimate. Two or three times a year. She used to be the one who initiated that part of their life, but when she stopped, it almost disappeared. With so little frequency, it was easy to see the math didn't add up when she became pregnant with each of you. She confessed to me that each time she realized she was pregnant, she initiated an intimate encounter with Bobby. Just to create some sort of plausible deniability as to who the father was. But as far as I know, Bobby never confronted your mother about it. He was a good man, Bobby Ahlstrom. Worked hard. Kept his head down. Provided for his family. Treated Bette and his children with respect and kindness. Even you two, who he probably realized were not his—he never blamed you for coming into this world. And according to your mother, Bobby never even blamed her."

"Do you have the letters Bette wrote to you?" said Gabe.

"They exist, yes."

"May we see them?" said Liv.

"That's up to you," said John Otsby. "It depends on whether or not you can truly keep this secret until Judith dies. If you can, I promise to show you Bette's letters." John Otsby smiled with eyes of hope.

Liv returned his smile. It was time to go in for the kill. "Did anyone know about you and our mother? Did Mack?"

· CHAPTER 42 ·

John Otsby shut his eyes and said, "Mack saw us together once." He opened his eyes, reached into his jacket pocket, and removed a sterling silver flask. "Cognac?"

"Not for me," said Gabe.

"No, thank you," said Liv.

"It was our drink," said John. "Every time I came here for my hour or two of heaven with Bette, we drank cognac."

"You said Mack saw you once," said Liv.

"Yes. Bobby couldn't lead the pontoon fishing trip that day because he had driven down to Brainerd to pick up a new speedboat. So Mack captained the expedition—he was only thirteen or so. You were just a baby, Liv. Your mother used to bring you here to our trysts. She made a little bed for you and you'd sleep in that closet. That day, a thunderstorm blew in and they must have ended the fishing early. Ed always cleaned the fish after the pontoon trips at the little shack down by the boathouse. But he must have needed something—I don't know what—so Mack came up to the cabin to get it. He opened that door. Bette was on top of me and looking right at Mack when he stepped into the cabin. It was terribly awkward. Mack turned around and ran.

"That night, Bette tried to talk to him about it, but Mack refused. He was at that age when he still idolized his parents. Bette tried to explain that her relationship with Bobby had become more of a friendship than a marriage, although even that was stretching the truth. Bette and Bobby were friendly toward each other but their emotional relationship had gone the way of their physical relationship. They were co-parents and roommates and that was about it. Mack didn't understand. He was still a kid. He responded by withdrawing from Bette and Bobby and, unfortunately, the both of you. That day he walked in on us, I'm afraid it destroyed your family. And for that, I'm terribly sorry."

Gabe said, "Are you sure Mack saw that it was you?"

John Otsby shook his head. "Am I absolutely sure? Not one hundred percent. According to Bette, Mack never mentioned me by name. He hardly said anything in that one conversation they had after Mack walked in on us. But Mack and Andrew had a falling out right about then—they'd been best friends since kindergarten and then it was like they hardly knew each other. So Mack must have known it was me."

"Is that why it ended?" said Liv. "Because Mack knew?"

"Not at first," said John Otsby. "But that was the start of things going bad between me and Bette. We couldn't sustain the affair forever. We either had to leave our spouses or end the affair. I would have left Judith, but Bette wouldn't leave Bobby. In your mother's defense, you have to remember she wasn't born an Ahlstrom and I wasn't born an Otsby. Without our spouses, we'd be starting from scratch. Starting with nothing and with four kids to help support. No one in town would have hired us once the affair became public. Not after our great sin. A future together hardly looked bright."

Liv said, "I think it might have looked brighter than the future Bette chose."

"Maybe," said John. "In hindsight, it sure looks that way. Who knows what would have happened if Bette had lived? We never stopped being in love with each other. We just stopped seeing each other." John crossed one leg over the other and held his knee between intertwined fingers. "I want you to understand something: to Bette, it felt impossible to leave Bobby. You'll see in her letters, that is, if you can keep my secret, *our* secret, just a little longer."

"We can do that," said Gabe.

"Thank you," said John.

"Hold on," said Liv. "You don't speak for me, Gabe."

"Okay . . . ," said Gabe. "But you said—"

"It doesn't matter what I said. I don't know if I can keep John's secret."

"What are you talking about, Liv? You just promised him."

"Yeah, not to tell someone who lives around here," said Liv. "But I have to tell Cooper. He's my husband."

"Are you kidding?" said Gabe. "After what he did to you? Not telling you about Winona?" Gabe shouted. "He doesn't deserve to know anything!"

Gabe's voice reverberated around the tiny cabin.

Liv took a breath to remain calm then said, "Cooper's still my husband. And maybe if I'm honest with him then he'll start being more honest with me."

"That's ridiculous," said Gabe. "You're being an idiot right now."

"Fuck you!" said Liv. "And how can you keep John's secret after knowing what you know? I mean, what the hell is wrong with our family? Everyone tries to be so loyal to each other we end up living a life based on lies. Mom didn't tell Dad about John. Mack didn't tell Dad about Mom and John. Mom didn't tell us about her and John. John hasn't told anyone about his affair with Mom. And look what good it's done! We're a fucking mess! Why do you want to keep going down that path, Gabe?"

"Because if we can just keep our mouths shut until Judith dies," said Gabe, pointing his finger at Liv, "then we can finally have the honest, open relationship with John that we should have had all these years! Why can't you see that?"

"Bullshit," said Liv. "We can have that now."

"No," said John. "Please, Liv. Please wait. I promise Judith won't live much longer."

"How can you promise that?" said Liv.

John shut his eyes and shook his head. "She's very sick. Her heart is failing. You saw her."

"I can't believe this," said Liv. "And I can't believe *you*, Gabe. I thought Carly might have changed you. But apparently not. You're still running from the truth, yeah? Still intent on ruining anything good in your life. Same old Gabe."

"Don't!" Gabe's face reddened. "Don't ruin this! We have a father again! Our real father. Don't you dare get all high and mighty and principled about telling your lying husband or anyone else about John and Mom when all we have to do is wait a few more weeks after John has waited forty years. Don't wreck it and don't squash me like you did when we were kids. Give me a chance for happiness, Liv. Give me one fucking chance!"

Liv looked at Gabe and then to John and then back at Gabe and said, "You two deserve each other. Father and son, right? What a joke." She stood from the bed, went to the door, looked back at her brother, and said, "At least now I know where you get your cowardice from." Liv left the cabin and slammed the door behind her.

A long, dry silence filled the tiny cabin. John's chair squeaked on the pine floor. Neither man looked at the other. Liv and Gabe had had no idea who would walk into their trap but they did know their reputation. The Ahlstrom twins, who weren't really twins, never got along. Never wanted to return to Leech Lake. Never wanted anything to do with family. Everyone thought so. Everyone *knew* so. Everyone except for Liv and Gabe (and now Carly), who knew that they had found a way to get along. Found a way to love each other. But whoever walked into their trap did not know that. So the Irish twins could play good cop, bad cop to earn their father's trust. And because they didn't know who the man would be, it would take some improvisation.

The best improvisers know their stage partners well. Know their strengths, their weaknesses, their insecurities, their comfort areas, their go-to safe places. But no improviser knows another better than children who grew up under the same roof. All that vulnerability with no way to hide your true self at that tender age.

John finally turned his head toward Gabe, sighed, and said, "Why is Liv being like this?"

"Liv's Liv. I thought that maybe she'd changed. But she hasn't."

"Do you think she'll tell Judith?"

"She might. As payback."

"I don't understand," said John. "Payback for what?"

"For Judith trying to hurt Liv by telling her that Cooper was funding Winona."

"Wasn't Judith doing Liv a favor by telling her that?"

"I think so," said Gabe, standing up from the bed and pacing the small space. "But Liv might not see it that way. She's vengeful and holds personal grudges against anyone she thinks is against her." Gabe looked out the window into the black night.

"You have to stop her, Gabe. You have to convince her to keep her mouth shut."

Gabe turned around to face John. "I'll try."

"Trying's not good enough. You have to guarantee it." There was urgency in his voice. Urgency on the brink of panic.

"I can't guarantee it. Liv's going to do what she wants to do. She always has." He took a step toward John. "But let me ask you something: is it possible Judith already knows?"

"I don't understand," said John. "Why would you ask that?"

"I'm just wondering if Judith somehow learned of your and Bette's affair, and learned of it recently, would she really throw you out? I mean, without you, Judith has no one. You make her life function, at least what's left of her life. Maybe at this point, she's more concerned with her reputation. With her legacy. Maybe she doesn't want to leave this earth in scandal."

"What are you implying?"

"There were two people who could have known about you and Bette. One is Mack because he walked in on you. And the other is Denny because he and Bobby were close. And now both Mack and Denny are dead."

John's eyes narrowed. "You're accusing Judith of murder."

"Well," said Gabe. "The night before Denny died he basically threatened you by saying, 'You deserve everything that's coming to you.' That could have been Denny's way of telling Judith he was going to expose your affair. I know Judith didn't pull the trigger herself—she can barely walk. But she seems to have no shortage of sycophants working for her."

"Oh my," said John. He shook his head and shuddered. "Oh my . . ."

CHAPTER 43

"Judith is ruthless," said John, "but ruthless enough to commit murder? I don't know . . ." He rubbed his hands together, fist in palm, the act of a great contemplator. "And the police arrested Ed Lindimier for Denny's murder."

"Yeah, they did," said Gabe. "But Liv hired a lawyer for Ed. Brought up some big gun from Minneapolis. And the lawyer told us that Ed and Raymond will be released in the morning. The police can only detain them for thirty-six hours and they don't have enough evidence to make an arrest."

"Really?" said John. "I heard they found the murder weapon and Ed's prints are all over it."

"Apparently, the ballistics report confirmed that the police found the gun that killed Denny. They found it in Ed's cabin. But the fingerprints aren't in the right place. Ed just picked up the gun when he found it. Picked it up by the barrel. He never touched the trigger."

John shut his eyes for a few seconds, stood, and ran his fingers through his hair. "Ed probably wiped his prints off the trigger."

"I asked the lawyer about that possibility," said Gabe. "But she said Ed's other prints were not consistent with the way a person holds a gun. And if he wiped prints off the handle and trigger, he would have wiped them off the barrel, too."

"Oh boy," said John. "If that's true, maybe Judith is somehow involved . . ."

"Pause the video," said Liv.

They were no longer in Ed's cabin. They were in Cabin 14 watching what the cameras and microphones had recorded earlier. John had gone home and taken the chest with him. What John didn't know was that the chest was fake—they'd purchased one that looked close enough at an antiques store earlier that day. The contents were also near duplicates, including the bottles of cognac and perfume. The only genuine items in the fake chest were John's letters to Bette because those were impossible to duplicate accurately, at least with the tools they had in Birchwood, but they did photocopy John's letters to ensure they survived and pulled a few originals for their own keeping. And evidence.

The other thing John assumed was real was the argument between Gabe and Liv. But that, like the chest, was also fake. John thought Gabe was on his side. Gabe sat at the keyboard and mouse with Liv and Carly on either side of him. All three looked at the big screen.

Liv said, "Rewind it to the spot where you tell John that Ed's getting out of jail in the morning."

Gabe reversed the video. The scene moved backward in fast motion until Gabe stopped it and hit play. Again they watched:

". . . the fingerprints aren't in the right place. Ed just picked up the gun when he found it. He never touched the trigger."

John shut his eyes for a few seconds, stood, and ran his fingers through his hair. "Ed probably wiped his prints off the trigger."

"Pause, please," said Liv. "It's that moment right after you tell him. Can we watch that in slow motion?"

Gabe rewound the video. They watched the same section again, but in slow motion.

"Whoa, man," said Carly, "you can actually see his whole expression change. Just for a few frames, then he pulls it together to turn on Judith."

"John killed Denny," said Gabe. "And maybe Mack. Our bio dad is a murderer."

"Dude, he definitely killed Mack," said Carly.

"What makes you so sure?"

"It's his confidence that Judith will be dead in a couple of weeks. You can see it on the video. He says it a few times. *Just a few more weeks. If Liv can just wait a little longer . . .* That's what you say when you want something to happen. Or when you're making it happen. This is just a theory, but I think the method John used to kill Mack is the same method he's using to kill Judith."

"I'm not sure I'm following you," said Liv.

"I think," said Carly, "that somehow John switched their medications."

"How would she—"

"Mack was on an anti-diuretic, which helped his body hold water. If Judith is on the opposite of that, if she's on a diuretic, which helps her body release water, and John somehow switched their meds, it would expedite the effects of their diseases. Mack would become extra dehydrated, which would cause his sodium and potassium levels to spike, which can cause a seizure. And Judith is holding extra water, which her body can't get rid of—and that can't be good for the swelling around her ankles and wrists and who knows where else inside her body. Her heart? Her lungs?"

"How do you know all this?" said Gabe.

Carly shrugged. "I lived with a doctor for a few years in my twenties. It's all he talked about. That's why I had to cut him loose."

"I'll never mention anything medical," said Gabe.

"My knight in shining armor," said Carly.

They went online to research Carly's theory and learned it was more than plausible. Water retention can take many forms including a bloated stomach, swollen ankles and wrists, fatigue, and coughing. Water retention can mean big trouble for people with heart ailments.

"The question," said Liv, "is what do we do now?"

They stared at the frozen image of John Otsby, his eyes shut, his face caught in a brief moment of defeat.

"If we go to the police," said Gabe, "and show and tell them everything we've found and learned, they'll probably investigate John Otsby. And who knows how long that will take? And if the police arrest John, will Judith support him? Because if she will, or if Andrew will, then they'll do what you did for Ed, Liv. They'll hire the best lawyer money can buy and John may walk free."

"I agree," said Liv, "and if John knows or even suspects he's being investigated by the police, he may destroy Mom's letters, yeah? I so badly want to read those."

Gabe nodded then said, "Plus, by the time the police are finished investigating John, Judith will probably be dead."

"Murdered dead," said Carly. "And if we go to the lawyer, Deena Petrocci, she may be ethically or legally bound to share what she knows with the police. And then we have the same problem."

"Ugh," said Gabe.

"What?"

"Our bio dad is a murderer, and we're trying to save Judith Otsby's life. Judith Otsby. Yuck. How in the hell did this happen?"

Carly put her arm around Gabe and kissed him on the cheek.

"I think I know the next step," said Liv.

· CHAPTER 44 ·

The next morning started with two phone calls. The first was from Gabe to John Otsby. Gabe stood with Carly on Ahlstrom's beach, a steaming cup of coffee in one hand and his phone on speaker in the other. He stared across the bay at Otsby's resort, its buildings dwarfed by trees, its beach empty during shoulder season. Somewhere south of there was Judith's Southern mansion where John hid himself from his wife in order to speak freely.

"Liv's agreed to hold off for a few weeks," said Gabe. "She won't tell Cooper or anyone else about you and Bette."

"How did you convince her?" said John.

"I reminded her of your letters. How much you wanted to be our father. How you begged Bette to leave Bobby so we could be the family we were meant to be."

"And that did it?"

"Almost," said Gabe. "I also told her if she couldn't keep your secret for a few weeks then she'd lose me as a brother. I told her I'd never speak to her again. If that happened, she'd lose her last two living biological relatives, you *and* me. She sulked a bit but she eventually agreed."

"Thank you," said John. "And please thank Liv for me and tell her we'll be a family soon enough."

Carly shook her head in amazement or perhaps it was disgust.

Gabe grimaced to show his agreement and said, "I will. Liv will appreciate that. I also want to tell you that we're going to tell Judith we'll accept her offer if she puts it back on the table."

"Really?" said John. "Why did you change your mind?"

"It's our way to protect you."

"Protect me?" said John.

"Liv and I have decided to let Ahlstrom's go. It's just too painful of a place for us. But we don't want Winona to raze the resort for her power plant. Even though we can't enjoy Ahlstrom's, other people should."

"Yes, they should," said John.

"So we're going to take Judith's offer because she or Red Pines will continue running Ahlstrom's as a resort, and we'll walk away with two to three million dollars. We'll set that money aside for you in case Judith finds out about you and Bette and cuts you off. It's not a loan. You're not beholden to us in any way. It's just yours."

John didn't respond.

"John?" said Gabe. "Are you there?"

"Yes," said John. He was crying. "That's the kindest thing anyone has ever done for me. Thank you, Gabe. Thank you, son."

Carly gestured throwing up.

"You're welcome . . ." Gabe could not bring himself to say *Dad*. "We're not comfortable meeting with Judith directly. She's too ornery. So we'll ask Andrew to bring us the contract. We'll sign it in his presence, and he can bring it back to Judith and her lawyer."

"I think that's a good idea," said John. "And again, thank you. I will never forget this."

Gabe wanted to say, *I'm sure you won't*, but instead said, "It's our pleasure."

A few hours later, Andrew knocked on the door of Cabin 14 carrying a contract and Judith's lucky red Montblanc pen. Liv and Gabe had ordered a lunch spread from the dining hall, and the four of them—Liv, Gabe, Andrew, and Carly—sat down at the kitchen table to eat before taking care of business.

"I'm surprised you've had a change of heart," said Andrew.

"It's a lot of money," said Gabe. "Kind of stupid to walk away from it. Especially for me."

Andrew looked at the big TV and computer and external hard drives. He was about to say something when Liv said, "We requested you to be the go-between on this because we want to ask you something."

Andrew seemed fixated on all the tech in Cabin 14. "Ask me what?"

"Would you please tell us why you and Mack stopped being friends all those years ago?"

Andrew turned his head toward Liv and said, "When we were in middle school?"

"Yes."

Andrew turned back toward the TV and computer and peripherals and said, "Are you going to tell me what all this equipment is for?"

"Yes. After you tell us about you and Mack."

"Okay . . ." They sat down and filled their plates. Andrew said, "Mack was my best friend. We spent a lot of time together. Fishing and exploring. We ate lunch together at school. Hung out on weekends. We had sleepovers and stayed up late watching movies. Normal kid stuff. One Friday or Saturday night, I slept over here when your family lived above the office. I think you were a tiny baby then, Liv. I remember your dad telling us to keep it down so we didn't wake you.

"Mack had bunk beds in his room. He was on the top bunk and I was on the bottom, and we were just lying there in the dark talking. It was so quiet in the house, we barely spoke above a whisper. Those moments were magical because somehow they made the world feel big. You didn't have any visual reminders that you lived in a small town in the middle of northern Minnesota. In the dark and quiet, anything seemed possible. Your wildest dreams seemed in reach. I can't remember what we were talking about, but all of a sudden I felt the courage to say something I'd been dying to tell someone. I'd realized I was attracted to boys. It was the 1980s and most queer people were in the closet, especially kids. It wasn't like today when so much is out in the open. Kids today are so matter-of-fact about their identities and orientation. At least in the cities.

"Coming out was a huge deal back then. You know my mother—my parents weren't an option. And Mack wasn't only my best friend, he was kind of my only friend. Mack, I trusted. That's what gave me the courage—that and I had to tell someone. It was just too damn lonely living with that knowledge by myself. So lying on our bunks in that dark room I told Mack I was gay."

Andrew paused, as if expecting a question or comment, but neither Liv, Gabe, nor Carly said a word.

Andrew continued, "Mack didn't respond for a few seconds. I was so nervous I felt like I was going to throw up. But then he said, 'That's cool.' And I believe he meant it. Mack really was trying to be supportive."

"Then what went wrong?" said Liv.

"I didn't know back then but I know now because Mack and I talked about it when we reconnected. Mack told me he didn't want anything to change between us, but it did. Remember, we were only thirteen or so. That's an awkward enough age. Most kids are just becoming aware of their sexuality. Hormones are kicking in. Straight cis kids start to see the opposite sex differently. Mack had told me which girls he thought were pretty and who he wanted to ask to the school dance. He knew what attraction felt like. So when I told him I was gay, he naturally thought I might be attracted to him. He didn't know how to deal with that at that age, and so he just drifted away from me. He wasn't mean about it. But even his *that's cool* sounded distant. At least for Mack it did. He just didn't know how to handle finding out I was gay."

"That's what he told you?" said Gabe.

"Yes," said Andrew. "About a year ago when we reconnected. He was so apologetic about it. So remorseful. But I never held it against him. AIDS was rampant in the 1980s. Everyone was afraid. There was so much misinformation out there. Mack was always kind to me. He just all of a sudden got busy with other things. Soccer and girls and the swim team and working at the resort. Every afternoon in the summer he took guests out fishing on the pontoon boat. We'd talk about hanging out together but we hardly ever did. He still ate lunch with me at school. Every day until about tenth grade when I pretty much stuck with the band kids and Mack started dating his first girlfriend. But passing in the halls, he always smiled and said hello. I knew he wanted me to be happy—he just didn't know how to be a part of my happiness."

Liv took a sip of bubbly water and said, "So you and Mack drifting apart from each other had nothing to do with your father and our mother?"

Andrew looked confused. "What are you talking about?"

"Hate to dump this on you, but when Mack suspected Bette of having an affair, he was right. She was in love with your dad."

"No," said Andrew, letting out a little laugh. "That's impossible. My father would not cheat on my mother. You know Judith Otsby. He'd be taking his life in his hands."

"Maybe that's why they were so careful," said Gabe.

Carly explained how they used Ed's cabin to meet and how they exchanged letters in the hollow of a tree trunk. Then Liv reached into a large envelope and removed the original letters of John's that they'd pulled from the bundle. She handed them to Andrew, who read one and then another.

"It sure sounds like my father . . . ," said Andrew. "But they're typewritten and not signed. Why are you so sure?"

"Do you want to see him talk about it?" said Gabe.

"What do you mean?"

Gabe went to the TV, turned it toward the table, and hit play on the computer. Andrew watched the entire thing, from the figure of a person approaching the cabin to Liv turning on the lights to John admitting and explaining the affair and begging them to keep the secret. Andrew watched Liv and Gabe's fake fight and John agreeing that Judith might have killed Denny Ahlstrom.

When it was over, the color had drained from Andrew's face. He could barely get the words out. "My father is your father?"

"Yes," said Liv. "We're half-siblings. It's such a difficult thing to grasp, right? We've sure struggled with it—so we wanted you to hear it from John himself."

Andrew swallowed with difficulty and said, "And you think my mother killed Denny?"

"No," said Carly. "We don't think that."

"But what was all that talk about Ed and the fingerprints and my mother—"

"The Ed part is true," said Gabe. "He had nothing to do with Denny's death. The part about your mother was a lie to make your dad feel more comfortable."

"Why would my mother killing Denny Ahlstrom make my father feel comfortable?"

"Because he killed Denny Ahlstrom."

Andrew looked sick.

"And we believe he killed Mack. And we believe he's in the process of poisoning your mother."

CHAPTER 45

Andrew went to his parents' house and returned an hour later with a prescription pill bottle full of pills, then Liv, Gabe, Carly, and Andrew drove to the police station together. The Birchwood police station had not been redecorated since it was built in 1976 to commemorate the USA's bicentennial. They gathered in a conference room with navy blue sheet–paneled walls, a red and white checkerboard linoleum floor, and a table of navy Formica with Chief Haaland and Officer Schmidt seated at the head. There was a large TV on one wall, and flags of the United States and the state of Minnesota draped around oak poles.

"Let me get this straight," said Chief Haaland. "John Otsby murdered Denny Ahlstrom and Mack Ahlstrom to keep them quiet about his affair with Bette Ahlstrom." Her mouth contorted into a dubious grimace. "An affair that happened forty years ago?"

"Yes," said Liv.

"And you're absolutely positive about this affair?"

Gabe set his laptop on the conference table. "Can I hook this up to the big screen?"

"I got it," said Officer Schmidt, who fished an HDMI cable out of the table's center console and hooked it up to Gabe's laptop. Apparently, some things had been updated since 1976.

Gabe played the video of John confessing his affair with Bette all the way through to when John said, "I want you to understand something: to Bette, it felt impossible to leave Bobby. You'll see in her letters, that is, if you can keep my secret, *our* secret, just a little longer." Then Gabe paused the video.

"Okay," said Chief Haaland, "John admits to the affair. He's afraid if Judith finds out she'll cut him off. But why kill Denny? And why kill Mack?"

"John believes that Denny knew about the affair," said Liv. "The reason he believes that is Denny told Renee that Bobby deserved a better wife. Winona overheard him say it and she told us. And it's our guess that over the years, Denny and Winona have told a few other people. That's all it would take for word to spread."

Chief Haaland nodded. "You're right about that. Because the day Bobby Ahlstrom died, that's what Denny said to me. 'Bobby deserved a better wife.'"

"But Denny never said anything to John until the night before Denny died," said Liv, "when Denny yelled at John, *You deserve everything that's coming to you!* which implied that Denny would tell Judith about the affair to hurt Judith for buying Red Pines."

"Okay," said Chief Haaland. "I get that. John felt threatened by Denny's comment. But why would he kill Mack? And how?"

"John assumed Mack knew because Mack walked in on John and Bette in Ed's cabin."

"Yes," said Chief Haaland. "I saw John talk about that on the video. But that happened forty years ago. If Mack didn't say anything in the past forty years, why kill him now?"

Andrew took a deep breath and said, "The reason Mack didn't say anything in the past forty years is because Mack didn't know."

"What?" said Chief Haaland. "How could he not know? He walked in on them."

"Yes," said Carly. "Mack walked in on them but all he saw was his mother naked, which would shock any twelve-year-old boy. We're guessing he turned around so fast that he didn't see John.

But Bette assumed that Mack had identified John and that, we believe, is what she told John."

"But Mack didn't," said Andrew. "I'm sure of it. He would have told me. Or I would have noticed something strange in Mack's behavior. And if I'd known my father was having an affair with Bette Ahlstrom, my father would have picked up on something strange in my behavior. But I didn't know. I acted perfectly normal around my dad. In fact, I was extra friendly with him because of what I was going through in my personal life. My mother didn't feel safe to me then. Hell, she doesn't now. So based on my behavior, my father must have assumed I didn't know. And if Mack didn't tell me, his best friend, he wouldn't tell anyone. Then Mack and I drifted apart, and my father thought he was in the clear."

"Okay," said Chief Haaland, "that explains why John felt safe all those years ago. But why all of a sudden murder Mack now?"

"John killed Mack," said Gabe, "because Mack and Andrew rekindled their friendship. Remember, John assumed that Mack knew but didn't tell Andrew when they were adolescents. But now that they're adults, John must have thought it likely and felt threatened by Mack. And the how of it, that had us stumped, too. But Carly has a theory, and Andrew just proved it correct."

Chief Haaland and Officer Schmidt swiveled their eyes toward Andrew. He removed the pill bottle, twisted off the cap, and dumped its contents: white, disc-shaped pills. "This is desmopressin acetate," said Andrew. "It's an anti-diuretic. It helps the body retain water. It's what Mack took for his diabetes insipidus."

"And . . . ?" said Chief Haaland.

"And they're in this bottle labeled as Demadex, which is prescribed for my mother. The pills look identical. But they're not identical. Demadex is a diuretic used to treat swelling related to, among other things, heart disease. Desmopressin acetate, which is what these are, have the opposite effect."

"Your mother's been taking the wrong pills?" said Chief Haaland.

"Not just the wrong pills," said Andrew, "but the exact opposite of what she should be taking."

"And you're sure—"

"Positive," said Andrew. "Pills sometimes look the same but they're all inscribed with a code to identify them. But no one looks at the codes—they just look at the bottles. My father somehow switched Mack's and my mother's pills when they visited in Chicago, and poor Mack must have taken the wrong pill in the morning, then feeling it wasn't working, took another. And then another. And by the time he realized something was seriously wrong, his electrolytes were so out of whack he suffered a lethal seizure."

"And your mother's health problems?" said Chief Haaland.

"Are compounded by taking the wrong pills. I checked her vitals before I left the house and she's not in immediate danger. As soon as she stops taking these, she'll start to improve. That's why I confiscated the whole bottle."

Chief Haaland drummed her fingers on the red Formica table and looked from Andrew to Gabe to Carly to Liv and finally to Officer Schmidt. "Hunter," she said, "I think we'd better pay John Otsby a visit."

"And you'll release Ed and Raymond?" said Liv.

"Not yet," said Chief Haaland. "I don't want word of their innocence to reach John Otsby before we do."

· CHAPTER 46 ·

Raymond Lussier was right. The police do like low-hanging fruit, especially when it comes to murder suspects, which is why Chief Haaland felt extraordinarily grateful for Liv and Gabe's ground-work on John Otsby. She showed her gratitude by allowing them and Carly to observe her interrogate John via a live video feed in her office. Andrew declined her offer because he thought it would be emotionally devastating to watch and he needed to convince his mother to go to the hospital, which would be no easy feat.

"I don't understand why I'm here," said John. He sat on one side of a metal table in a small room. He had come in voluntarily. He was not handcuffed.

"We told you," said Chief Haaland, "we'd just like to ask you some questions."

"About?" said John.

"Where were you the night Denny Ahlstrom was murdered?"

"I was at home with Judith."

"Any other alibis than Judith?"

"The whole town, practically," said John. He looked calm. Confident. "They were there when Denny shouted us off his property."

"That's not what an alibi is," said Chief Haaland. She offered John a warm, kind smile. "Did anyone else see you at home? Andrew, maybe?"

"I was asleep when he returned from the bar. So no. Any other questions?"

"Yes," said Officer Schmidt. "Can you tell us why your finger-prints were found on a prescription pill bottle that belonged to Mack Ahlstrom?"

John Otsby's expression changed from calm and confident to the last thing Liv or Gabe expected. He looked interested. Intrigued. Almost enthusiastic. "What do you mean?" said John.

"The Chicago PD ran Mack Ahlstrom's prescription pills through their forensics lab," said Chief Haaland. "Your prints were found on the bottle, and even more interestingly, the bot-tle contained the wrong pills. The pills in Mack's bottle were for Demadex, not desmopressin acetate as the label stated. Can you explain that?"

John smiled. "The pharmacist must have made a mistake. And you know," added John, lowering his voice conspiratorially, "Mack's wife is a pharmacist."

"Yes. She is. But why were your fingerprints on the bottle? And why did some of those pills also have your fingerprints on them?"

Earlier that day, before Chief Haaland had called John Otsby and asked him to come into the station, she called Diana Ahlstrom in Chicago. Diana confirmed that Mack's prescription bottle con-tained the wrong pills, then she carefully bagged the bottle and walked it to her local police station. The forensics lab in Chicago had not yet called Chief Haaland with results. But as she told Gabe and Liv and Carly before the interrogation, John Otsby didn't need to know that.

John Otsby had no answer for Chief Haaland's question. He just sat up straight and smiled.

It was at this point that Liv leaned over to Gabe and said, "Look at his eyes. He's out of his mind. Totally batshit crazy."

"His smile is freaking me out," said Gabe.

"John," said Chief Haaland, "you look happy. Why is that?"

John shook his head. He began to cry. But his smile stayed put.

He was crying tears of joy. He opened his mouth to speak, and the words came out just above a whisper. "I'm free."

"Free? Free from what?"

"Not what," said John. "Who. I'm free from Judith."

"I see," said Chief Haaland. "And why are you all of a sudden free from Judith?"

"Because I killed Mack. And I killed Denny. And now you're going to lock me up."

"That's what you call freedom? Getting locked up?"

"Yes," said John. "I have been Judith's prisoner for over fifty years. Not behind bars. Not that kind of prisoner. No, being a prisoner of Judith is far worse. I thought I'd be free when she died, but now she won't die because you know about the pills. But that's okay because she can't get at me in jail. I won't have to deal with her anymore."

Liv and Carly and Gabe all looked at each other with expressions that ranged from *holy shit* to *OMG*.

"I understand you had an affair with Bette Ahlstrom forty years ago," said Chief Haaland.

"Yes. I loved Bette."

"And one day when you were making love in Ed's cabin, Mack walked in on you two. Is that why you killed Mack? Because you thought he'd tell Andrew?"

John Otsby nodded but his eyes were somewhere else. "Back when it happened, I hoped Mack would tell Andrew. And I really hoped he'd tell Bobby. Then Bette's marriage would fall apart and she'd be free to be with me. We could have lived our love in the open. But Mack didn't tell anyone. And Bette didn't leave Bobby. So I've been stuck with Judith. I have suffered, Chief Haaland. You don't know how much I have suffered. And now it's too late. Bette's dead. I'm old. Judith's not going to die. It's too late. It's just too late . . . Promise me you won't send me back home."

In Chief Haaland's office, Gabe said, "It's weird. He's crazy enough to kill but not so crazy that he can stand Judith."

Carly squeezed his hand, and Liv just shook her head.

Chief Haaland said, "So why did you kill Mack if you wanted to be found out? And why did you kill Denny?"

"I wanted to be found out forty years ago," said John. "But I didn't want to be found out now. Judith would ruin what's left of my life. Judith would ruin everything I've suffered for. So when Mack and Andrew became friends again, I thought Mack would tell Andrew about that day he burst into Ed's cabin. I always thought Bobby knew about Bette and me but put up with it. I assumed he told Denny. Denny had never said anything, but I thought he'd changed his mind about that because he hated Judith for buying Red Pines. So Mack and Denny had to die. They had to die so my suffering wouldn't be wasted."

"He's a total loon," said Liv. "He's out of his gourd."

"He's the loon of Leech Lake," said Carly.

"Let's hope it doesn't run in the family," said Gabe.

"No," said Carly. "That kind of crazy comes from being married to someone like Judith Otsby." She smiled. "Unless marrying a tyrant runs in your family." She raised her eyebrows.

Gabe laughed. But Liv shut her eyes and rubbed her temples. She, like John, had married badly.

Chief Haaland said, "I gather you switched Mack's and Judith's pills when visiting Chicago."

John nodded. "About six months ago, Mack and Diana invited us all to dinner at their condo. I said it was nice to see old friends from northern Minnesota reconnect after all these years. Of course, I didn't really think it was nice. I was concerned. And to make matters worse, Mack looked me dead in the eye and said that Andrew was his sibling as much as Liv and Gabe were. *A sibling as much as Liv and Gabe*, he said. And all while looking me right in the eye, as if to tell me that, yes, he knew and I'd better watch my step." John widened his eyes as if to say, *What do you think of that? I'm no dummy.*

In the observation room, Gabe said, "Do you think Mack knew it was John?"

"I don't think so," said Liv. "I think Mack was just saying Andrew was like a brother to him. But we'll never really know, will we?"

"And then," said John, "after dinner, I was in the bathroom and saw Mack's pill bottle on the vanity. I googled desmopressin acetate and learned it's an anti-diuretic and what it's for and also noticed the simple disk-shaped white pills looked exactly like some of Judith's pills. Then on another visit, I switched Mack's and Judith's pills. I didn't think it would work, but it did."

"Did you try any other ways to kill Mack before that?"

John smiled his oh-so-strange smile again and said, "I hired a man."

"What kind of man?" said Chief Haaland. "A hitman?"

"No," said John. "Just a man I met in a bar. Not a nice place. Rough characters. Which is what I was looking for. I went there several times when visiting. Late after Judith was asleep. Got to know a few fellas. One had served time for murder. Third time I saw him in there, I offered him fifty thousand dollars to make Mack's death look like an accident. I gave him twenty-five thousand upfront and promised him another twenty-five thousand when the job was done. The guy took the twenty-five thousand dollars but all he did was make a half-assed attempt to kill Mack by posing as a mugger. But then he lost his nerve and some do-gooder tackled him. I know this because I heard Mack tell Andrew the story. I looked for the man at the bar two other times to tell him to finish the job. But I never saw him again."

"And Denny?" said Chief Haaland. "How did you kill him?"

"I knew Denny went on his late-night patrols," said John. "He

bragged about it all the time. Said he was better than any security system he could buy and he knew because he'd bought some.
Bragged about he couldn't get to sleep if he didn't take one last
patrol of the resort carrying his trusty .22 pistol. So that night
after he threatened me and kicked us off the Ahlstrom's property, I intercepted Denny on the far side of the resort. He asked
what I was doing there. I told him I had an idea to keep Judith
out of Ahlstrom's. We walked down by the lake, I took the gun
off Denny and shot him in the forehead. I had no choice—he
was going to ruin my life. I'd stashed an inflatable raft down the
shore and used it to push myself and Denny over the thin ice to
the raffle car. I was just trying to create a diversion by strapping
Denny into the car. The fact that it fell through the ice was a
lucky coincidence."

"What do you mean?" said Chief Haaland. "You were trying to
create a diversion?"

"Maybe diversion isn't the right word. Maybe *spectacle*. Or *sen-
sation*. Because of the car and the thin ice. That's what I wanted
people to focus on. Then I rafted myself back to shore, deflated the
raft, and dragged it through the woods. I wiped my prints from
the gun and dropped it in front of Ed's cabin hoping he'd pick it
up. Then I continued to the back of the property where I'd stashed
my car in a copse of pines."

Chief Haaland turned from John to Officer Schmidt and said,
"Hunter, do you have any questions?"

"No," said Officer Schmidt, "I think we got what we need for
now."

"I have a question," said John.

"Yes?" said Chief Haaland.

"Can I please go to jail now? I'm ready to start my new life."

CHAPTER 47

John Otsby did not go to jail. After a mental health evaluation, a judge sent him to a psychiatric hospital. Liv and Gabe refused to visit John. Andrew was his only visitor and reported back that John seemed most happy there.

"He's psychotic," Andrew told Gabe and Liv. "Absolutely no remorse for killing two people and trying to kill a third. His wife."

Judith finally agreed to see a doctor, who straightened out her medications, and her health rapidly improved. Her mood did, too. She wasn't pleasant, but she talked incessantly about being the victim of John's deceit, and Judith found nothing more satisfying than feeling like a victim. According to Andrew, Judith also seemed unconcerned about Mack's and Denny's deaths, as if they were somehow weaker for dying and she was stronger for having lived. Judith implied that life, like business, is not for the fragile.

Minutes after Chief Haaland questioned John Otsby, Gabe and Liv wanted her to ask one more question. Where were the letters Bette had written to him? Chief Haaland asked, but John refused to answer, saying those letters were all he had left of Bette, and like their affair, he insisted they remain private.

"Maybe he'll change his mind," said Chief Haaland. "It doesn't seem to be very stable."

They all thanked each other for a job well done, then Liv and Gabe said their goodbyes.

"Hold on," said Chief Haaland. "You got room for two more in that Tahoe?"

"Little Liv! Little Gabe!" said Ed. Officer Schmidt led Ed, Raymond Lussier, and Deena Petrocci into Chief Haaland's office. "Me and Raymond played cops and robbers and we were the robbers so we had to sleep in jail. But now the game is over and we get to go home."

Liv looked at Raymond and mouthed, *Thank you.*

Raymond responded with the slightest of head nods.

Liv, Carly, Gabe, Ed, and Raymond ate dinner in the dining room. Elk burgers with wild rice hotdish on the side. When Liv asked for the check, the server said it had been taken care of by the gentleman at the bar. They looked over and saw Alan Cohen sitting alone with a glass of red wine. He raised it toward them and smiled.

That night, Carly watched the recording from Ed's cabin a dozen times looking for a clue as to where Bette's letters might be. The next morning she woke up with a hunch.

· CHAPTER 48 ·

It took the four of them nearly until noon to prove Carly's theory correct. The silver maple must have been two hundred years old, eighty feet tall, and six feet across at the base of its trunk. It looked very much alive, although dormant, despite the large hole in its trunk four feet off the ground. No one wanted to stick their hand inside—something could be hibernating or nesting in there—so they used a phone flashlight and a stick to explore.

Carly saw it first. Gabe reached in and pulled out a stainless steel tube about ten inches long and four inches in diameter and capped at both ends, the caps fastened tightly by a circumference of nuts and bolts.

They carried it back to Cabin 14, and Ed fetched his tool kit. A few minutes later, Liv pulled out a sheaf of letters. Unlike John's, they were handwritten, signed, and dated. Ed was anxious to get back to his spring cleanup work and left. Liv, Gabe, and Carly read Bette's letters one at a time and passed them back and forth. Cabin 14 was dead silent other than the sound of paper being folded and unfolded, furled and straightened.

"She was so in love," said Liv, who smiled through tears. "I can hear her voice again. It's so clear."

They read for two hours, and although both Gabe and Liv would reread the letters dozens of times over the course of their lives, it was Bette's last letter to John that explained so much.

Dearest John,

I have barely slept in the past week and my head's a mess. The beauty of our love has been met by a more powerful and opposite force, and that is the tragedy of having fallen in love at the wrong time, after we married others, and after we had children.

When you ask me to leave Bobby for you understand my refusal is not a choice. I can't do it. I want to but I'm unable. I would love to go away with you and leave Mack with Bobby. Mack would be okay without me. He might even be better off. He hates me, you know. He hasn't looked me in the eye since the day he walked in on us in Ed's cabin. He hates me and he hates the babies because he knows they're not Bobby's. He knows they were born from lies and moral failings.

I tell myself that I could muster the courage to leave if I simply admitted that I made a mistake sleeping with Bobby at seventeen years old, that I made a mistake accepting Bobby's offer to marry me, and that it's time to correct those mistakes and start anew. So why can't I do that? You know me. Tell me, John. Why can't I embrace our love and trust our love?

I know one thing. The way Mack looks at me with hate and disgust is the same way I see myself. I hate myself, John. It's poison the way I feel. When I look in the mirror the person I see disgusts me. So when I feel your love I ask why. Why does John love me? How can he love me when I am so unworthy?

Maybe it's Bobby's goodness I can't get past. He is a saint of a man. He doesn't love me like you do and he may not love me at all. I don't know if love or at least romantic love is in Bobby's nature. It's in his nature to work hard and be kind. It's in his nature to be polite. It's in his nature to be sweet. He is to me. Always. And he is to the kids, even the babies he knows are not his. And it's in his nature to look away. Bobby knows I'm in love with another man. He does not know it's you but he knows

I've found someone. He sees my distraction. He sees the distance in my eyes. He's taking it like a hero, just like when he stepped up to marry me thirteen years ago.

The saddest part of all this is it's taking me away from my children, especially the babies. Your babies. I see you in their eyes, John. Their smiles. Their little giggles. The way they turn their heads. I see you in them and it fills me with grief and, if I'm honest, terror. This love, our love, my love for Olivia and Gabriel, is ripping me up inside. Those children are a product of you and me. Our hearts may be broken but theirs are not. Not yet. And they don't deserve to be. Olivia and Gabriel are innocent, but I am failing them as a mother. I spend so little time with them. The only godsend is that they have each other. Like babes in the woods. And that they have Bobby. I know it must hurt you to read these words, but he is saving them. Saving them from my negligence. How do I leave a man like that? I can't. I have sealed my fate. Apparently, love does not conquer all.

I have one favor to ask. When we bump into each other as we no doubt will at events in town and the supermarket and church and the kids' school, please hold your head high. Take Judith's hand. Put your arm around Andy. Let me see you marching forward, living your life, loving your family. And please say hello as I will to you.

I believe our secret will be safe for a long time. Maybe forever. Let's hold that secret dear like an amulet hiding under our clothing and resting against our chests, protecting us from meaningless lives. May our love go the way of Moses, leading others to a promised land that we cannot enter ourselves. I can accept that fate. I hope you can, too.

I will love you always,
Bette

That afternoon, Gabe and Liv asked Ed if he'd bring a rowboat down to shore.

"Oh, sure," said Ed. His eyes sparkled. "The first boat of the season." He unlocked the boathouse and wheeled an aluminum rowboat, furnished with oars and personal flotation devices, down to the beach. Gabe sat at the oars. Liv sat in the bow. And Ed, wearing his knee-high Wellingtons, pushed the boat into the water.

"Don't fall in," said Ed. "The cold will get you."

The lake was open near the shore, but as Gabe propelled them toward the middle of the bay, the boat's metal hull scraped against chunks of floating ice. They passed the spot where the car and Denny had fallen through the ice. Both Liv and Gabe thought of their deceased uncle and each felt an aching sadness, but neither said a word.

A few minutes later, Liv said, "This looks like a good spot." Gabe stopped rowing, and the boat glided to a stop in the placid bay. He looked back at the resort. He hadn't seen it from the middle of the bay in nineteen years. He shook his head and said, "So much has changed."

Liv looked back at Ahlstrom's and then at Gabe. "But for the better, yeah?"

He knew she was not talking about the resort. He nodded and said, "Yeah. For the better." The siblings shared a smile as genuine as the Northwoods birch trees. "Shall we?"

Liv reached into her jacket pocket and removed the small urn of Mack's ashes Diana had given her in Chicago. Mack did the same with his urn and said, "Rest in peace, big brother." Together they dumped his ashes in Steamboat Bay. It was the last place Mack had been before running to Ed's cabin and bursting inside. It was the last place Mack had lived his life innocent and unencumbered, happy and full of wonderment.

· CHAPTER 49 ·

Liv waited until she returned to New York to confront Cooper about his clandestine financial shenanigans with Winona. His transgression was so egregious, so unforgivable, he didn't even try to make excuses. Liv asked him directly, "Are you hoping to sleep with her?"

Cooper half chuckled before saying, "No . . ."

It was Cooper's little laugh that gave him away. She asked how many other young women he was *investing in.* When Cooper tried to evade the question, Liv reminded him that the discovery process during their divorce proceedings would tell her everything she needed to know. Cooper admitted that Winona was not the first young woman he'd pursued, that he'd fallen out of love with Liv, and that yes, divorce was probably the best thing for both of them. And just like that, it was over. Liv never slept in the house on Bedford Street again.

As much as she blamed Cooper, Liv blamed herself for not seeing what was right in front of her. For years. Gabe was right. Her marriage was like their parents'. She had Bobby Ahlstrom's blindness and ignorant acceptance. And she had Bette Ahlstrom's self-sacrifice and self-denial. Learning of her parents' shortcomings and secrets was as eye-opening as turning on the light in Ed's cabin to reveal John Otsby. And it changed Liv's life in the most beautiful way.

She and Cooper sold the townhouse on Bedford Street and split the proceeds. Liv purchased a two-bedroom unit in a building on Christopher Street, moved in the few belongings she wanted, took a leave of absence from work, and bought a one-way ticket to Milan. She had plenty of money and no responsibility to anyone other than herself. After a week in Milan, she bought a first-class rail pass and took off with nothing but a backpack. Rolling through Europe, first western then eastern, Liv thanked Mack every day. It felt as if he'd sacrificed himself for her. She had gone to Chicago a damaged person. She had left Leech Lake on the road to recovery. Next year, she'd do the same in Africa.

Liv had exercised her right to purchase Ahlstrom's from Renee. With Gabe's permission, she had Alan Cohen draw up the purchase agreement in both their names. They hired Raymond Lussier to oversee the day-to-day operations with Ed serving as his assistant. Red Pines continued in their role, although Gabe and Liv rejected all of Judith's ideas. The only change they made was firing Annabel Johnson from Brainerd, whom they'd discovered was playing double agent, funneling information back and forth between Judith Otsby and Winona without the other knowing.

Six weeks after Carly's surprise visit to Leech Lake, she took a pregnancy test and passed with a blue plus sign. Gabe and Carly were so damn in love with each other that the unexpected news felt like nothing short of a blessing. Gabe's first call was to Liv, and with a new Ahlstrom on the way, the thought of living three time zones and three thousand miles apart felt impossible. Liv told Gabe and Carly the apartment on Christopher Street was theirs if they wanted it until she returned. They did not.

In June, Gabe and Carly returned to Ahlstrom's. And when Carly saw the trees leafed out, the foliage a shade of green she thought impossible, the lake blue like molten sapphires, she said, "I do." As in "I do want to live here. Can we give it a shot? See if I can at least make it through one Minnesota winter?" After all, Minnesota was only one thousand miles and one time zone away from Liv.

The reason Gabe and Carly had come back to Leech Lake in the first place was for real "I dos." Liv caught a flight from Vienna. Andrew came up from Chicago with Diana. Renee drove up from Minneapolis. Winona returned from Philadelphia. Carly's parents, siblings, and cousins, all twenty-nine of them, flew in from Southern California. Ed and Raymond tied the resort's four pontoon boats together to form a marital flotilla. And in the middle of Steamboat Bay, not far from where Liv and Gabe had spread Mack's ashes, Ed served as Gabe's best man, and Andrew, recently ordained by the Church of the Latter-Day Dude, performed the ceremony. Alan Cohen left his house and socialized the entire day. Raymond Lussier wore a tie. Chief Haaland wore a dress. And the golden retrievers and Ms. Ramirez wore flowers on their collars.

The next morning, Gabe said he'd give it a shot. He and Carly were, after all, both experienced in the hospitality business—that's what real bartenders do—and so why not? The ghosts that had haunted Gabe seemed to have been unchained. And why did LA deserve The Gabeson more than the residents of or vacationers in northern Minnesota?

Ed continued living in his cabin. Raymond moved into the old living space above the office. And Carly and Gabe moved into the house Denny and Renee had built when they first owned the resort, keeping Winona's room intact for when she visited. Renee didn't have the heart to move the golden retrievers to the city when they'd grown up on a lake with room to roam. Carly and Gabe took them, and Ms. Ramirez embraced her growing family, which, seven months later, grew more when Carly gave birth to a baby boy. They named him Mack. Mack with a K. It was January. And Carly learned to how to bundle a baby and herself for long winter walks, not pushing a stroller but towing a sled where pink-cheeked Little Mack sat strapped to a seat, observing leafless trees, green pines, red cardinals, and dogs hopping through the snow like rabbits.

Sixteen months later, Gabe and Carly still lived at and ran Ahlstrom's, and Raymond had earned the title of manager. Carly had a second child, a baby girl. And Aunt Liv visited often. Winona built her first rural wind and solar farm just outside Birchwood's city limits. It was a success in delivering cheaper, cleaner energy to Birchwood and nearby communities, and she took orders to build more plants all over the world. Winona had rejected Cooper's romantic inclinations, and he moved on to the next pretty face, but he made a fortune by investing in her. Winona moved to Florida so that she'd never have to face another Minnesota winter and never have to pay state income tax.

Liv and Gabe lost one half brother but gained another. Andrew visited Leech Lake several times a year. He was Uncle Andrew to the babies, and Andrew spoiled them rotten. Judith Otsby's health improved. She became more mobile but no less ornery, trying to buy out other resorts and overly influence local officials. Although she owned forty-nine percent of Ahlstrom's through Red Pines, she never realized her wish to rename it Otsby's West. She never realized her dream of ferrying resort guests back and forth across Steamboat Bay. Judith made threats, of course, but Gabe and Liv hired Alan Cohen to make sure Judith's influence stayed on her side of the bay.

Six summers after Mack and Denny died, Grandpa Ed and Uncle Raymond took Carly and the kids out on the pontoon boat to catch panfish. Liv and Gabe stood on the dock and watched the people they loved experience what they had known so well. Gabe's daughter, Maddy, was daring enough to cup the fish at the head, slide her palm down over its spiky dorsal fin, and remove the barbless hook. Then the kids took turns naming each fish before Maddy dropped it back into the water.

Liv said, "Your daughter is brave."

"She gets that from Carly," said Gabe.

"And your son is peeing off the pontoon boat."

"He gets that from me."

Maddy waved to her Aunt Liv. She waved back and then said to her brother, "I don't remember you peeing off the pontoon boat."

"That's because you were away at college."

"Oh," laughed Liv. "Late bloomer."

"Yeah," said Gabe. "It runs in the family." He looked at his sister. Liv's pale eyes shined in the afternoon sun. "But a bloom is worth waiting for."

ACKNOWLEDGMENTS

Sibling relationships take shape when we're barely old enough to walk, but the patterns and hierarchies become so ingrained that they're nearly impossible to change. That's the underlying premise of this book, murders aside, and I'd like to thank my own siblings, David and Ken, as we, on the verge of becoming old farts, still strive to improve upon the dynamics forged in the wayback of a Chevy station wagon.

I'd also like to thank my professional brother, Pat Hazell. In our midtwenties, Pat and I wrote a play called *Bunk Bed Brothers* that examines sibling dynamics in a more comedic setting. Our long discussions helped till the soil for this book.

Thank you northern half of my beloved Minnesota. For your lakes and woods and resorts. And for the good people and wildlife who live there year-round. How lucky I am to have you a few hours away.

And thank you to my agent, Jennifer Weltz, my editor, Kristin Sevick, and everyone at Forge. Collectively, this is our seventh book together and there will be at least one more. That's something in this era of *moving on and jumping ship and Hey, what's that shiny thing over there?*

As always, thank you to my wife, Michele, my first reader and favorite hang. And to our kids and their partners and our pets, who trek up to Leech Lake with us every winter for a week of eating, drinking, watching movies, playing games, talking about hiking but not doing much of it. It's my most favorite family time. And hey, I milked it for the setting for this book.

ABOUT THE AUTHOR

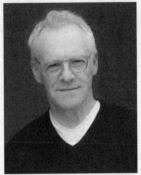

Leslie Parker

New York Times bestselling author MATT GOLDMAN (he/him) is a playwright and Emmy Award–winning television writer for *Seinfeld*, *Ellen*, and other shows. Goldman has been nominated for the Shamus and Nero Awards and was a Lariat Adult Fiction Reading List selection. He lives in Minnesota with his wife, pets, and whichever children happen to be around.